Between
You and Me

by

Lynn Turner

Between You and Me

Cover Art by *Kim Mendoza*

The Wild Rose Press, Inc.
PO Box 708
Adams Basin, NY 14410-0708
Visit us at www.thewildrosepress.com

Publishing History
First Champagne Rose Edition, 2017
Print ISBN 978-1-5092-1682-6
Digital ISBN 978-1-5092-1683-3

Published in the United States of America

Dedications

To Mrs. Shaw, who called me her "Little Writer"
until I believed it.

~*~

To my lovely beta readers, who called me "Author"
until I achieved it.

~*~

To Shay, for listening.

~*~

And to my family,
who catch me talking to walls
and never question my sanity.

"I believe there is nothing more serious,
   more fatal to the heart than longing,
   the hunger of one soul for another."

                                        ~VàZaki Nada

Chapter One

Love at first sight didn't happen for guys like Finn Kane.

Besides, the anomaly that sent his heart pounding like he'd just run from The Office lounge and out into the chill night air felt too violent to be love. He didn't know what the hell it was, but it was unsettling. The irony made him laugh. The raw, choking sound drew startled eyes as it left his throat. He watched a couple jaywalk across the street to get away from him.

Christ, they think I'm crazy. He laughed again. *I probably am.*

He needed to pull himself together, but the idea of running in his condition was so absurd that he couldn't help his hysterics. Stairs could be challenging on a good day, and the ones leading up from the speakeasy beneath Chicago's famous Aviary were steep and many.

Winter had come early to the Windy City. It was October, and already the cold seeped into his bones. He resisted the urge to rub away the warmth unfurling in his left leg.

It's all in your head.

God, he hadn't needed that pep talk in twenty years…the last time he let anyone see him limp. Pride wouldn't let him keep walking. Neither would his damn leg. He looked up to see a few more people quickly averting their eyes as he accepted defeat and flagged a cab.

"Just drive around," he gritted, easing his tall frame into the back seat.

Something in his tone stopped the cabbie from asking any questions. The meter started, and Finn scooted to the other side of the seat, his back to the door. He used both hands to lift the offending leg onto the seat.

All in your head, he repeated the mantra again.

No. All because of a woman he'd never laid eyes on until half an hour ago. But it hadn't been her beauty that first caught his attention. It had been her voice…

She owned him from the moment he first heard her speak. He couldn't see her yet, had no idea who she was, but he knew from her voice that she'd be beautiful. She could have been ordering a cocktail rather than entertaining some of the entrepreneurs lucky enough to make the guest list for the invitation-only event that night. It wouldn't have made a difference—not to the hairs of his neck and arms that stood on end, or to his skin. That…electricity.

Just from the sound her words made as they left her mouth.

He could only think of a handful of people with voices like that—who made it feel as if they'd touched listeners without being near them at all. Frank Sinatra and Whitney Houston when they sang; Sean Connery and Morgan Freeman with their omniscient tones; maybe Anthony Hopkins or the guy from the old Bell Atlantic commercials…Oprah.

But this voice was…more. Different. It commanded the small group that shielded her from his gaze but it *paralyzed* Finn. It was like her voice existed in a frequency to which he alone was attuned. He was squandering an opportunity, ignoring his own small group members who were buzzed from their cocktails and the prospect of success. He didn't blame them when they left him alone to go network with people who hadn't frozen into living statues. People capable of carrying on conversation.

It didn't matter though, because someone in the woman's small group shifted and he could finally see her. He felt self-satisfaction that lasted a single breath before his heart tried to break from its cage. Pulse beats in places he never paid attention to like his temples and wrists sped up like he was running rather than standing there. He was right. She *was* beautiful.

Her face was high-boned and delicate, with full, round lips and sultry brown eyes that looked black in the dim light of The Office lounge. She turned to look at him, and dark curls brushed her shoulders to fall behind her.

Sexy.

Hers weren't the only eyes on him, he realized through his haze. It took him a few seconds to come out of it. "It" felt like his entire body was waking from numbness. Tingling that started in his fingertips and shot to his toes. He was rooted to the floor. And sweaty. He hoped she wouldn't want to shake his hand.

Fuck. What did she say?

"I'm sorry," he said. "Could you repeat that?"

His voice sounded gruff and far away. He needed to get a grip. *Fast.*

She accommodated his idiocy with a smile. "I asked what brings you to Chicago, Mister…"

He cleared his throat and took a leaden step toward her. "Kane," he offered. "Doctor Finnegan Kane—Finn, please." He sounded like a maniac. And he still hadn't answered the damned question. He cleared his throat again. "I'm from Seattle. I work in biotechnology."

There. He'd strung two complete sentences together.

"Drugs?" someone asked.

"Devices," he answered.

His eyes were riveted to her face, but he could see the others in his periphery. They dispersed like waves when a pebble hits water. Right. Devices were risky investments. That's why he was here in the first place. He swallowed hard against his nerves.

Don't screw this up. You've done this a dozen times.

"So…" She came closer.

Oh God, so close…

"Was that some kind of party trick, or do you have something interesting to share with me?"

She stood two feet from him. He could smell her. Her unique scent took root in his brain and made his entire being vibrate with need. His blood pumped so hard it made his head swim, and the pitch he had been able to recite in his sleep was nowhere to be found in his suddenly pea-sized brain. He couldn't understand how she was so composed when he felt like he was drowning…how what he was experiencing could be one-sided.

Fuck's sake, you're blowing it.

"I'm developing neuroprosthetics," he blurted to shut out his thoughts. "Smart limbs that communicate seamlessly with the nerves and the brain."

That made four complete sentences. He was on a roll.

She leaned toward him with obvious interest, and he decided to just hold his breath against her assault on his senses. He *needed* this. He was forty-one with a twenty-year-old dream that he was *this* close to realizing. Two. Feet. Away.

"Robots?"

He took a breath to answer, and her scent hit him again. *Jesus.*

"There's no need to be nervous, Doctor Kane."

Her tone was light. Like she was teasing him. Trying to get him to relax.

"I won't blow the whistle on you for crashing this party."

Shit!

"Your name was handwritten on the list. Not typed," she said. "So who do you know?"

It was the second time she'd smiled. But she was much closer this time, and now those distracting lips twitched at the corners.

"My colleague's husband is Jamie Faulk," he said.

His tone had deepened, but she didn't seem to notice. Recognition lit her expression, and he was distracted by her skin. Golden brown. Like raw sienna.

"The chef! He knows his wines. I've never seen anyone create such spectacular pairings," she said, oblivious that she'd abandoned her professional tone. "He saved my life a few times."

Her humor was infectious and he chuckled. "Mine, too."

Tonight, for example. And just like that, some of his tension was relieved. Well, almost. The urge to touch her persisted; to bend his head and kiss her, to fit his hand in the dip of her waist where it arrowed down to the perfect spread of her hips…

But the ice had been broken.

"He made a couple of calls to get me in," he said.

"If Jamie Faulk thinks you deserve a foot in the door, let's make it worth his while, shall we?"

She outstretched her hand.

"Emanuela Monroe."

Emanuela Monroe. Neurons fired in his brain as he made the connection. Of Hurst Capital. Huge firm out of New York known for its eccentric CEO and cutting-edge investments. She'd made Principal last year at only thirty years old. *Why didn't I recognize her?* Because the photo of her on the firm's website didn't begin to capture her luminous skin, the depth of her eyes. He needed to stop feeling things…and thinking things like *luminous fucking skin.* This tiny, soul-sucking goddess was a force, and he needed to impress her.

Her small hand clasped his, the soft pads of her fingers grazing his palm. His thumb caressed her skin out of pure reflex, and his eyes shot to hers. They were wide open and shockingly dark—almost black, full of questions, shifting over his face, then down at their hands. He swallowed. His usual handshakes didn't last this long.

She gently removed her hand, probably suspecting he was going to hold it hostage forever. She managed to find her voice first, but she'd taken a step back. "I… Tell me about these…"

"Neuroprosthetics," he finished for her.

His voice sounded weak, not at all confident. He

assumed by the way she averted her eyes that he had a similar effect on her. She nodded, looking at his shirt collar...or maybe his neck. God, this was torture.

"They *are* a lot like robots," he said. "But they appear lifelike, and the remote control is the nervous system. I've designed a bi-directional brain—computer interface—that allows for two-way communication with the brain and nerves."

She looked at him then, as if he had three eyes.

"Two-way communication provides sensory feedback," he said. "Touch something hot and a message is instantly sent to your brain to snatch your hand away. With this feedback, my devices can anticipate what the brain wants to do next. They can carry out a series of commands that seem simple to a typical person."

"Like what?"

He eyed her cocktail glass, held at its stem by manicured fingers. "Well, if I were to take your glass, it would be a single, fluid motion. For someone with a bionic arm, it's four," he said, extending his arm toward her. "Raise arm..." His eyes met hers in a brief moment of hesitation, but she didn't flinch, so his hand went for the stem. "Aim..." The moment lasted seconds, but the whisper-light touch of their fingers as his wrapped around the stem seemed to slow down time. "Grasp." He pulled it from her fingers, his eyes never leaving her face. "Retract arm."

She smiled again. "I hope you like red."

"I'm more of a whiskey kinda guy."

They shared a laugh. A moment of release. She took back her glass.

"There." He motioned toward her. "See? It's

something we don't think about. We can feel the glass in our grasp, its temperature, how heavy it is…we don't need to see it to sense those things. My devices would imitate these sensations for the wearer."

"Ah, so it makes for less clumsy movement. More efficient."

"Exactly. I'm not sure any device will ever be as fluid as a natural limb, even if it's more powerful, but mine would greatly improve functionality and quality of life."

She observed him for a moment. It felt like she was looking *into* him, and the unnamable energy from their handshake resurfaced, thickening the air again. His left leg felt fatigued, and he couldn't help but shift his weight to his right. The effect she had on him was beginning to take its toll.

"What makes you the best person for this venture?" she asked at last. "It's risky, and visually lifelike prosthetics are already on the market. Insurance companies would see them as cosmetic. Are they worth it?"

The pulse in his temples picked up again. Her questions were reasonable, but she'd struck a nerve. His brain shrank back to pea-sized, and he acted impulsively. He bent to his left and lifted his pants leg until the hem caught halfway up his calf.

Emanuela frowned at first, but her brow smoothed seconds later. He gave her an ironic smile, sensing the exact moment she'd picked up on the flatness of color in his leg, the lack of pink tint to match the rest of his light sandy skin. There were no veins or identifying marks or hair. The barely-audible whirring sound it made when he rotated his foot drew her stunned eyes back to his.

He released his pants leg and straightened again. "To someone like me, it's worth everything."

Chapter Two

He kept catching her off guard.

After five years of unconventional approaches from hopeful entrepreneurs, Emanuela was intrigued that someone could still surprise her. A taxi driver once earned himself a kidnapping charge when he refused to let her out of his cab until she listened to his entire pitch. He'd put the safety lock on, prompting her to call 911. She'd quit her favorite café when another man ordered her usual double espresso and cardamom bun without a moment's hesitation, pitching to her on her way out. An inexperienced woman had even joined her yoga class and suffered mild injury just for the chance to speak with her.

So when something dark clouded Doctor Kane's eyes before he flashed his artificial leg, Emanuela forgot how to breathe. It was stunning, watching his pupils grow like that—compressing the blue of his eyes until they were dark gray.

Oh no, I've offended him.

"I'm sorry," they said at the same time.

"No, I am," he said. "I'm not usually so...intense."

Her head jerked to the side in disbelief. His earlier intensity had stripped her bare, turned her inside out, and made everything else around them drop from the edge of the world. She was still trying to ground herself...still trying not to feel naked beneath his gaze.

"You're not a very good liar," she said with a tentative smile.

Finn laughed outright. "No. I guess I'm not."

"I admire passion. And honesty." She took an uneven breath and forced herself to meet his eyes. They weren't getting anywhere trying to ignore the tension between them any longer. It had become a phantom third party, and she hated how it distracted her. "You make me…uncomfortable, Doctor Kane."

He looked horrified.

"It's okay," she said before he could stutter another apology. "Somehow I think you know exactly how I feel."

There. She'd called it out. So she could openly take in the curling ends of his dark hair, the slight bend in the bridge of his nose, and the wide mouth parting into an understanding smile that made her eyes flit back to his. They were sharp, intelligent eyes, and they'd narrowed with his smile.

Her admission seemed to make him relax. "I can answer your question now, Miss Monroe."

He shifted his weight and motioned toward two empty barstools. After declining another drink, she prompted him with a nod.

"I've been a below-knee amputee since I lost my leg in a car accident when I was sixteen," he said. "The word disabled was like a slur to me then. I would have rather died than be disabled. I thought I'd have to live in a wheelchair."

Emanuela was grateful not to have anything in her hands. They trembled from the edge in his deep voice. She wondered about the accident, but decided it best not to push. Not now, anyway. She leaned forward.

11

"Did you?"

"Hell no." He smirked. "I was a tenacious kid, pushed myself hard in physical therapy. Eventually I got strong enough for my first prosthetic."

"That was…"

"Ninety-two. Not too many options back then cosmetically. I had a pretty pronounced limp those first years, but I wasn't teased much. The thing that got to me the most—and still does sometimes," he looked away for a moment, "was the staring. I don't mind questions so much now, but strangers staring at me like I was some sort of freak motivated me to pursue this idea. I wanted to lose the stigma."

"You don't limp now. Is it because of the leg you showed me? Did you make that?"

His ears turned red. "*Ah,* unfortunately I did not, but that would have been a *great* excuse for exposing myself."

They laughed together, and her heart tapped a quick rhythm as she realized he was watching her. Studying her face. "What?" she asked before she could catch herself.

He shook his head. "Nothing. It's just nice to be able to laugh about it. Not take myself too seriously. I can usually tell when people are being polite out of pity."

"Does that happen a lot?"

"If it's obvious that I'm wearing a prosthetic. Or the rare occasion that I limp, which happens if I overexert myself, or if I'm under duress. But I'm used to wearing an artificial limb. This is the eighth one I've owned, and the most versatile. If I want to swim or do rigorous physical activity, I have to wear a leg specialized for those things. My smart limbs will withstand water and more pressure than standard prosthetics."

Her eyes trailed over his athletic form. "You're in great shape." *Oh my God.* She didn't mean to sound so…flirtatious. "I just meant…"

He chuckled again. "No, I get it. Truthfully, future prosthetics might surpass the abilities of mere mortals. Olympians have won gold wearing modern prosthetics."

"And yours? What will yours do, Doctor Kane?"

It was the moment of truth. She watched him inhale deeply before he plunged, his eyes looking right into hers.

"Make people feel whole again. Not because we're incomplete," he said with conviction. "Although it *is* a little about that, about the way society perceives us. When people see you differently, they often *treat* you differently too—" He collected himself and met her eyes again. "It gives us back complete control. Movement will be effortless. More natural. It will feel like having that limb grow back. And that's… It's…"

"Everything," she finished for him at a near-whisper.

He swallowed and nodded, bereft of words, and that was fine with her. The ones he'd spoken were enough to make her emotional, which wasn't good, because she was out of wine, and Finn…*Doctor Kane,* she chided herself…was imploring her soul with his eyes again.

"You've spent twenty years developing this idea." She crossed her legs and straightened her spine, deliberately adjusting her demeanor. "My only concern is that you might be a one-trick pony. Convince me you've got staying power."

Finn cleared his throat. "I know my market intimately, Miss Monroe. There are almost two hundred *thousand* amputations performed each year in the U.S. alone. Half of those amputees are anywhere from twenty-one to sixty-five years old." He held his hands in front of him, palms up, as if he thought she could read his sincerity in them before he spoke again. "Even if they have iron willpower, their limbs are only as capable as the technology available. My research background ensures that my devices will stay ahead of the curve, and challenge what it means to be 'disabled'."

Excellent answer. Her earlier enthusiasm welled up in her again, and she inhaled a deep breath to conceal her smile. He made her feel inspired for the first time in *months*...and emotionally spent.

She'd been aware of him to some extent from the second she'd seen his name on that guest list in barely legible scrawl. She'd admired his determination to find an "in." And then later she'd memorized his expressive face as he spoke, listened to his passion, witnessed the way he looked at her like she could save him from drowning... She wanted to bolt, or throw herself at him—neither of which would bode well for her reputation. She needed him to get the hell out of there. "Do you have a prototype?"

"Not yet. That's why I'm here tonight. I'll need funding to build a prototype, but my proposal is ready."

"Good. Send it. You'll hear from my office soon after."

She stood again, and he followed suit. She tried to

temper her expression, swallow the knot in her throat. They were back to that strange place again, frozen at the edge of the world where time and space seemed to blur. Her heart raced, wanting her to fight or flee, but only one option was logical.

She trained her eyes on his collar again, on the rapid pulse in his neck. He hesitated a moment, like he wanted to say something else and then caught himself. Instead, he stepped closer, and stretched out his hand. "Thank you, Miss Monroe."

She inhaled his soapy aroma and her throat went dry. Did he smell like this all the time, or was it courtesy soap? Why did it even matter? *Damn him!* She accepted his hand. *Damn him. Damn him. Damn him.* "I'll be in touch."

He squeezed her hand gently before he tore his eyes from hers, spun on his right heel, and left the lounge. It was subtle, but she noticed his stagger as he walked away…and she wondered if he too felt like he'd left part of him there with her.

Chapter Three

Eight Months Later

Emanuela rubbed her temples, pressing the speed dial for her assistant. "Hey, Lids, put the Do Not Disturb Sign up for me, will ya?"

"Sure thing! Anything special?"

The thick envelope on her desk, postmarked from Seattle, may as well have come with a neon sign...or a cardboard replica of Finnegan Kane, all sharp eyes and resonant voice, begging her to open it. The hairs at her nape stood on end, and her face went hot.

"I hope so." Emanuela removed her blazer, slipped off her shoes and moved to the soft leather couch in her office.

K, here goes. She tucked a pillow behind her back, slipped on her reading glasses, and dove in.

****

Lydia tapped at her door at six a.m. "Miss Monroe? A-are you okay?"

Emanuela stopped pacing and glanced down at her bare feet and disheveled clothes. She could imagine what a few hours of sleep on her office couch had done to her hair and makeup, and several paper coffee cups were strewn about the floor.

"Miss Monroe, you're going to wear down the carpet!"

Emanuela dismissed Lydia's warning with a wave. "I need a meeting with Philip first thing. Whatever he's got booked, move it around. He's gonna wanna see this."

"Of course. Should I stop by your apartment this morning?"

Emanuela gave Lydia a sheepish nod. "Thanks, Lids! I'm also gonna need a caffeine transfusion. Know where I can get one of those?"

"Clean clothes and a coffee, got it! And, Miss Monroe?"

"Hmmm?"

"Congratulations," Lydia said with a knowing smile.

Emanuela smiled and went to work typing up her summary. Philip liked his technical mumbo jumbo in layman's terms. Short, sweet, and to-the-point. It made for much shorter meetings and deliberations. She was finishing up when her office door opened softly.

"Sorry, Lids, almost do—Philip!"

She scrambled to get herself together, stuffing the tails of her blouse into her skirt.

"Sorry, Em. Lydia accosted me on the elevator just now telling me to clear my first appointment for you. So here I am." Philip strolled into the office, his hands in his pockets. He chuckled a moment later, and Emanuela looked down at her blouse. It was wrinkled, and sported evidence of the takeout she'd ordered during her office slumber party of one.

"I—sorry. Lydia is bringing me more clothes."

"It's fine." He took a seat on the far end of the couch near the door. "You're my best guy. You could walk around in sheets for all I care," he said with a grin.

She groaned, exhaling her tension away.

"So, I assume I've been summoned for some good news? What have you got?" he asked.

"Innovation. *Real* innovation. Do you remember that proposal I told you about—from the amputee developing smart limbs?"

"Of course. You were on the fence, weren't you? Something was missing."

"Yes, a prototype. I was sold on the idea, but it sounded like fantasy. I wanted to see something real... Well, he's done it, and the images are remarkable," she said, handing him her summary. "This Doctor Kane could effectively fast-track prosthetic medicine into the future. It could improve the quality of life for patients with missing limbs by giving them artificial ones that communicate with their bodies and carry out actions just like real limbs! It would also take away the stigma attached to walking around in the world wearing obviously artificial parts. I mean—Philip—look at this..."

She wet her fingers and flipped through the stack of papers again, finding the page she sought and handing it to him. "You can't even *tell*. That doesn't look like a prosthetic to me."

She straightened up, folding her arms and biting her bottom lip as she waited for his response.

"You're right," he said, barely glancing at the summary in his hands. "It's incredible. Things like this are only seen in science fiction."

Her eyes narrowed. "Oh my God, you've seen the proposal already! I can't believe I was up half the night reading everything I could find, assessing the competition—"

His lips twitched as he looked up at her. "There *is* none. I caught wind of other interested investors once word of a prototype got out, but no one's seen it yet, and Doctor Kane specifically asked for us. For you, Em."

"Makes sense." She trained her tone to sound casual. "He's comfortable with me."

"Well, he's had a rough go of it. The cost of development, safety certification and the various stages of testing nearly bankrupted him, and the project was axed by the time he came to us."

She cringed as one of the satirical headlines she'd read about it came to mind: *Perhaps Mankind Isn't Ready for Cyborgs Among Us.*

"I know. But it's in our lap now, and I want us to revive it," she said.

Philip stood and held her by her shoulders. "Your lap."

She lifted a questioning brow.

"You made first contact," he said. "So go to Seattle and convince Doctor Kane to sell the rights to his idea. After that, we get this thing into production and retire."

"*You* retire." She grinned. "I get your office. And a small island, maybe."

"That's my girl," he said with a gentle squeeze to her shoulders. He held her gaze for just a moment too long, enough to make her heartbeat pick up from the curious way he was looking at her. But someone cleared her throat before Emanuela could think anything of it, and the pair moved apart.

"Uh, I've got your clothes, Miss Monroe," said a red-faced Lydia.

"Thanks, Lydia," Emanuela said with a quick nod.

"Go get 'em," Philip said. "Itinerary will be on your desk this afternoon."

He turned to Lydia with a smile. "Miss Thompson."

Then he was gone.

****

As promised, everything she needed for travel was arranged. She was scheduled to fly out of JFK International early the next morning and arrive in Seattle before noon, local time.

Just in time for a one o'clock meeting with the good doctor, Emanuela thought as she finally crawled beneath her comforter at eleven p.m.

Her job could be unpredictable, but she loved it. Part of the reason, she admitted, was because of her easy working relationship with Philip. At forty, he was only eight years older than her, but because of his early and rapid success, he possessed wisdom and connections she hoped to attain someday.

She had shown up to his offices unannounced, a newly minted master's degree holder in business, and asked—no, *advised*—Philip to hire her. In answer to his simple, "Why?" she'd provided a file including every major deal that fell through since Philip began, listing each fatal error and what she would have done differently to ensure that those deals were successful. Emanuela smiled remembering the look on his face—a mixture of shock and amusement that, later, he'd told her was because she reminded him of himself.

Of course, she'd noticed his naturally tan skin, sexy dark hair, and charisma that seemed to generate somewhere behind his gentle brown eyes. She'd also noticed the way his easy smile lured many a woman to a short fling.

The attraction was there beneath the surface, but she would never act on it. She'd worked too hard to establish herself in an arena dominated by men, and she'd be damned if her success was accredited to an affair, however thrilling, with her ridiculously attractive employer.

"*Ugh*," she groaned. No one had touched her in over a year. And here, alone with her thoughts, there was no need to lie about why. A soft sigh left her lips as she sank into the pillows and let her hand drift down. Her body responded to the delicious memory of a faint five o'clock shadow, a deep voice full of passion, and expressive blue eyes…

****

"Allie stop laughing!" Emanuela snapped into her cell phone.

She was en route to the airport trying to stave off a panic attack, and her best friend of almost sixteen years was laughing her ass off.

"Stop, or I'll hang up," she warned.

"Sorry," Allie said, sounding not the least bit contrite. "But this break-down session is out of character for you."

"I *know*! Don't you think I know that? *Help* me!"

"Honestly, Em, just look hot."

"Come on, that's it? No last-ditch scheme to get me out of this?"

"That's it. Look hot and do your damn job." A second's pause… "Oh, and have *fun*!" she added.

"What? I'm *not* sleeping with him."

"Cut the crap, Emanuela. You've been smitten for *months!* I know what the guy smells like, and I've never even met him!"

"Allie—"

"He *breathed* on you, and the earth moved," she quipped, tossing her red hair over her shoulder. "You owe it to yourself—hell, to *me,* to see what else he's working with."

Emanuela giggled. "It's been almost a year though. He could be seeing someone."

"Then there shouldn't be a problem."

"You're right. I'm being ridiculous. This is *business.* I'm just gonna go out there, do my job, and come home," Emanuela said. "Thanks for the pep talk."

"Always a pleasure."

"Smart ass."

"Love you too, Em. Text me when you land."

"I will."

****

Emanuela took advantage of in-flight wifi for the first hour to read through and send emails. Philip popped up in her email chat:

—Hey Em! Just sending you off! This will be a cakewalk for you.—

Right. Classic Good Samaritan move. Just sweep in with a shiny check and profit a hundred times more than he would have from his own idea. She scratched an imaginary itch at her brow. Sure. Cakewalk. Except she'd met the guy and he seemed…incredible.

What the hell was wrong with her? She could do this in her sleep. It was nothing personal.

—Thanks, Boss!—

She clicked her laptop shut and settled in for the six-hour flight. *You're a bit of a mystery box, Finn. Can't wait to open it.*

Chapter Four

"Welcome to The Piano Lounge," a perky hostess greeted with a smile. "Do you have a reservation?"

"Yes." Emanuela nodded. "I'm with the Kane party for one o'clock."

"Oh, your party has already been seated. If you'll follow me, I'll take you to them."

"Thank you."

She tried not to let her nerves get to her as she followed the hostess through a well-designed maze of modern tables, plush chairs, and couches. The arrangement of furniture was obviously meant to make patrons feel at ease and, based on the hearty conversations coming from each table, it worked.

Okay, Em. Put your game face on. You've got this.

"And here we are!" Perky Hostess stated in her extra-nice customer service tone. "A waitress will be with you shortly to get your drink orders."

As the hostess stepped away to get back to her station, Emanuela's lips parted in awe. Doctor Kane and his party rose to greet her. He was as handsome as she remembered, but there was no trace of the naked vulnerability in his eyes that she'd noticed all those months ago.

She'd forgotten how tall he was. His wavy hair was longer, curling at the ends, with just a bit of salt and pepper running through the thick strands. His trousers hugged his toned thighs, and his shirt was rolled up a bit at the sleeves to reveal powerful arms. Her heart was in her throat as the face from her dreams stood before her. She swallowed it back down and snapped to attention.

"Doctor Kane," she said. She was impressed with how steady her voice sounded. A tremor ran through her arm at the déjà vu as her hand rose to meet his.

"Miss Monroe," he said with a brilliant smile. "Good to see you again. And Finn is fine. I only call myself a doctor on special occasions."

God, his voice…

"Likewise, Doctor Kane."

His smile widened. Fine wrinkles formed near his eyes, which seemed distinctly amused as they looked into hers. His grip was firm—and a bit too long. She resisted the urge to snatch her hand away as every nerve ending fired at the contact. His lips twitched.

He's enjoying *this!*

Finn turned to introduce his lawyer, Miles Hamilton. He was a well-dressed man, about her age with deep umber skin and a knack for detail, as she'd learned from the few emails they'd exchanged in preparation for today. She took his proffered hand with a nod. But there was another man whom she hadn't been expecting. He was the eldest of the three men, she guessed his age to be around mid-fifties. He was very pale, and his hair seemed like organized chaos, neatly combed on the sides and tousled at the front. His attire could be described the same way. It looked almost as though he'd napped in his clothes before he'd arrived.

"This is my friend and colleague, Dr. Faulk—" Finn said.

"Simon, please," said the older gentleman.

His smile reached his kind gray eyes as he motioned toward the empty seat. Emanuela shook his hand and sat down, snapping into game mode as she straightened her spine and addressed the trio.

"I'm happy to make your acquaintance, Doctor Faulk, but I must admit I'm a bit confused by your presence at this meeting. It was my understanding that this was to be confidential in nature, per Doctor Kane's wishes—"

Simon broke into hearty laughter. "You don't beat around the bush, Miss Monroe! I like that, don't you, Miles?"

Mr. Hamilton smiled. "We apologize for the last-minute addition, but I assure you, Doctor Faulk's presence here is relevant and necessary. I took the liberty of drawing up an offer on behalf of Doctors Kane and Faulk for your firm's consideration."

He reached into his briefcase, withdrew a laminated portfolio with blue ribbing, and handed it to Emanuela. She accepted the portfolio with her brows drawn. Her focus was singular at the moment, all business as she quickly read the cover page, *SimLife,* and flipped the packet open. The men gave her a moment to skim the first few pages, her eyes moving rapidly for a couple of minutes. The waitress came by to take drink orders but Emanuela was in the zone. For those one hundred twenty seconds, everything else around her was white noise. That was all she needed. Two minutes. Understanding dawned on her, and her brow relaxed.

Poker face, Emanuela.

She raised her head, making eye contact with Finn.

He stared back at her, the picture of confidence. "Doctor Kane, this looks like a business model for a startup."

"It is." His features were relaxed but there was a challenge in his tone.

She registered the new tension in the air. It seemed the other gentlemen were holding their breaths. Her eyes never left his. "Just so we're clear: you, together with Doctor Faulk, started a company with personal funds from Doctor Faulk, produced a safety-certified prototype, and are seeking additional funding from my firm to cover the cost of manufacturing in the near future. Is that correct?"

"It is," Finn said again, nodding once.

She questioned him with a lift of a brow.

He cleared his throat. "Right now, this field of research is very small. The only entity developing anything similar is the Department of Defense, and they're most concerned with military applications, of course."

"Of course."

"Because of the Department of Defense's own recent foray into this area of research, the certification we needed already exists."

Finn looked over at Simon and nodded.

He talks with his hands, Emanuela noted with an inward smile, still not giving anything away in her expression. He spoke about his work with such confidence, in a way that she could easily understand. And it was *hot.*

Simon took over. "The thing that makes our product unique, is the water and flame-resistant material we make the skin from." He looked at

Emanuela like a seasoned storyteller, pausing for dramatic effect before revealing the plot twist.

"Which is?" Emanuela leaned forward.

"Silicone!" he said, practically shouting.

Mr. Hamilton seemed to be trying to control a fit of laughter at Simon's hysterics.

Finn's arms were folded across his chest as he watched Simon's animated relay.

"We jam-pack the stretchy, soft material with tiny sensors that can pick up on things like heat, moisture, weight—things typical prosthetics can't discern," Simon said, on the edge of his seat from his efforts. "Then the prosthetic hand, for example, sends this information to the nerves of the patient's arm, which then send the information to the brain naturally."

Finn looked at Emanuela again, and she sensed that he was no longer trying to read her. He was trying to earn her faith. "We are confident that, once we've established our brand, we will have the reputation behind us to develop the technology further. Eventually, our devices may even be powered entirely by organic material."

She nodded. "May I see the literature? I'll need to read it myself, if you don't mind."

"Absolutely, I'll have a copy for you this evening."

****

The gentlemen occupied themselves with the menu to allow Emanuela a moment to absorb the wealth of new information they'd sprung on her. She sipped her drink and reviewed the business model again. She looked so elegant with her hair up, showing off the graceful curve of her neck. She examined the pages, her exquisite face twisted into a slight frown.

He'd been preparing himself for this moment for a few months now. When he first met her, he'd been trying to secure funding for his project for a few years, flying from state to state, meeting with investors, the private sector—even the military. But development in neuroprosthetics hadn't progressed enough to appeal to an industry that was interested in a bionic man or, at the very least, a bionic dog.

He'd nearly accepted military funding, but turned down a contract with the government because there were too many stipulations and too much involvement on their part in the direction of the research. Most medical venture capitalist firms invested in drugs, and weren't interested in "science fiction." Finn had just about given up when he came face-to-face with the CEO of Hurst Capital's right hand man. *Woman.* A devastatingly beautiful woman with the brightest liquid brown eyes he'd ever seen. He grinned inwardly. Those eyes now peered at him behind a blank expression.

"Just one question," she said. "Why the ruse? Why didn't you follow-up with a second proposal, detailing what you've just told me?"

"Forgive us for the deception," Finn said. "But we needed to keep everything under wraps to deflect any further attention. Even with a patented prototype, we're in a race to get our devices into production before other entities catch on. As you know, it's not always about who does it best, but who does it *first*. We'd like to be best *and* first."

"We were convinced we wouldn't get you to come all this way otherwise, Miss Monroe," Simon said. "I'm sure that once you've seen our prototype, you'll be as confident as we are."

His enthusiasm animated his entire face, relieving some of the tension in the air. A beat passed. Finn studied her, looking for any reaction at all. *There!* he thought. It was almost imperceptible, but he swore he saw a hint of a smile on her lips before a tiny jerk of her head turned her face away from him for a second.

"If you'll excuse me, gentlemen, it seems I have a phone call to make." She moved to stand and the rest of the party rose with her.

"Of course," Miles said, turning to Simon to say something in private.

Emanuela took that moment to look Finn square in his eyes. Her cool business mask disintegrated and she let him in. She leaned in so close that he could smell her hair, her skin. He swallowed as the sensory memory hit him like a freight train.

"Well played," she murmured.

Before she could pull away, he gripped her elbow. "Your move."

****

"Son of a bitch," Philip said, impressed. "I hadn't anticipated that he'd phone a friend."

"Neither of us did." Emanuela tried not to let her admiration show in her tone. "Obviously this new development changes things. Which way do you want to move?"

"Em, it's your deal to make or break. Go with your gut, and I'll back you up."

She had a feeling he'd say that. "My gut says we want in. It's risky, but the safety certification gives us a leg up. If we secure a deal, any future developments will go through us too."

"You know I'm all about taking risks!"

"No one knows that better than I do."

She heard him laugh as she glanced at her watch. "I'm in a working lunch right now so I hope to have a copy of an agreement we're all satisfied with by this time tomorrow," she said. "I'll get it to you when it's squared away."

"Sounds good. You know, I'm actually happy for the guy. He really turned things around for himself. I'm looking forward to meeting him soon. Relay that for me, will you?"

"Sure thing, Boss."

Pride welled up in her at his praise of Finn. *Where'd that come from?* She wasn't sure but she had to admit that she was looking forward to getting to know the brilliant Doctor Kane better herself.

****

When she returned, she discovered that Doctor Faulk, who informed her that his single other interest aside from materials science was all things culinary, had ordered for the table.

"I hope you don't mind, Miss Monroe," he said. "We ordered some variety in case there is anything you can't eat."

"Oh no, it's perfectly fine!" she said. "I can eat anything."

She glanced at Finn, who was watching her again with interest. She decided to ignore his perpetual stare for the time being as the quartet ate heavy hors d'oeuvres and worked together for the next hour and a half.

Miles and Emanuela were in their element discussing terms, conditions, and concerns. Now and then he conferred with Finn and Simon to make sure they were clear about something. They worked until they had enough for Miles to draw up a rough draft. Miles rose to leave, citing another appointment to get to.

They bid Miles farewell, and then Simon turned to Emanuela. "Miss Monroe! You are a revelation, my dear. I didn't know exactly what to expect when Finn told me about you, but you've exceeded my expectations." He gave her a warm hug.

She would've been taken aback if he'd been anyone else but, somehow, the gesture was endearing coming from him. They pulled apart enough to look each other in the face.

"It's my pleasure, Doctor Faulk. I get a lot of projects on any given day, but yours is truly inspiring."

They held each other by the arms as they spoke, but finally parted as Simon smiled down at her and tilted his head toward Finn. "We lucked out with this one!"

"We did," Finn said. "See you tomorrow, Sy."

****

Finn had been watching their exchange and something tightened in his chest at the sincerity in Emanuela's features. He could see how much she respected the older man and admired the work—*their* work. He couldn't wait for her to see what they'd been cooking up in person.

Finn and Emanuela suddenly found themselves alone. He couldn't pinpoint just when their bodies gravitated toward each other but there they were, just a foot apart, sizing each other up. She looked away first.

"Why don't we walk out together?" he asked.

The urge to slide his fingers into her hair to release

the pins that held it in place was about to get the best of him. She nodded and walked the few steps to her seat to gather her things.

Though he'd been watching her all afternoon, he hadn't had the freedom to take her in the way he'd wanted to since she arrived. He remembered the way her skin glowed in the dim light of the lounge, but the memory was nothing compared to how she looked in the light of day. *God, she's beautiful.*

"What?" she asked.

There was a hint of a challenge in her voice. He collected himself. *I can't tell you that I was heartbroken when I left you last time. I didn't know what it was...*

"You were amazing back there," he said, walking with her outside.

"I know," she teased. Her shaky voice belied her stoic demeanor.

"I mean it. Miles is good, but I could tell you made this challenging for him. He even enjoyed it, I think."

She looked away. "Doctor Kane—"

He groaned and took her by her elbow. "What am I gonna have to do to get you to call me Finn?"

Her mouth fell open and her eyes widened in shock. "I—don't think that's—"

He was watching her again. He was so attuned to her from having observed her every movement that afternoon that he immediately registered her flustered state, and knew exactly what she had been thinking.

"Stop looking at me," she said at last.

People maneuvered around them on the busy sidewalk.

"I can't," he said. "Have dinner with me."

"You're my client now. It would be inappropriate."

There was no conviction in her voice. She was softening toward him, and he was sure his soul was reaching out to her through his eyes.

"We'll be associates by this time tomorrow," he said. "If you say no to me now, I'll just ask you again then."

Her entire body relaxed visibly, as if her steely resolve had finally crumbled. "Fine."

"Fine?" He refused to contemplate her meaning. He hadn't realized until that moment how desperately he needed her to say yes.

She gave him a shy smile. "Ask me tomorrow."

Chapter Five

Finn inwardly cursed Emanuela's tailor. Her legs were covered today, he noticed with some disappointment, by black tapered trousers. The contrast of her crisp white shirt against her skin made her face look luminous, and her hair was up again, this time in a ponytail. She was covered from neck to toe, the picture of stylish modesty, but she was still effortlessly sexy.

This is going to be a long afternoon. He was unable to tear his eyes from her as she withdrew her attaché from the passenger's seat and made her way up the paved driveway to Simon's gorgeous, stark modern sixties home.

"Good morning," she said with a radiant smile.

"Miss Monroe!"

Simon made no effort to hide his pleasure at her visit. "Welcome to our little shop of horrors," he joked, waving a scrap of prosthetic hand.

"Jesus, Sy," Finn said. "She just got here, and you're about to scare her off."

He cast an apologetic look at Emanuela, but she had drawn her hand to her open mouth in mock terror at Simon's antics.

"It's okay, I'm quickly getting accustomed to this mad scientist," she said, allowing Simon to embrace her.

Finn swallowed, watching the exchange. Such an

innocent gesture but he knew if he were to hug her, that it would mean so much more. His smile was genuine but measured when she turned to greet him.

He wasn't sure whether to hug her or shake her hand…or to stare at her like a besotted fool. He felt magnetized to her—a blend of nervous excitement, anticipation, and sexual tension that had been building from the moment he knew she was coming. He had to touch her.

He offered his hand and she took it, but the feel of her soft skin made his stomach ache. The contact was so formal, and not nearly long enough.

"Glad you could come," he said in his deep timbre before reluctantly releasing her hand.

She peeled her eyes from his to look around the converted two-car garage. "Wow," she said, turning in place. "This is impressive."

The space was limited but well organized. There were bookshelves along the back wall containing texts, binders, and files. A large workbench strewn with an assortment of tools, scrap metal, and wire took up much of the space. A piece of machinery the size of a small refrigerator sat atop a small table against the wall to her left. Across from that, on the wall to the right, a cluster of monitors of varying sizes sat on a desk. A couple of the monitors were running complicated code; the largest of the bunch featured a three-dimensional graphic image of a prosthetic hand.

"You've discovered Command Central," Finn said. "This is where I design each prosthetic piece and run simulations to optimize their performance."

She nodded and leaned in to get a better look at the 3D image on the screen. The image reached for her, its long fingers wiggling into a wave.

"Whoa!" She jumped back, and Simon laughed.

Finn groaned. "Sy, that's two strikes already, and we haven't even started yet."

She turned in the direction of Finn's critical gaze and shook her head at the sight of Simon in some sort of sensor helmet, holding the very product she'd come to see. This was no scrap of metal. The prosthetic looked as lifelike as any living limb, and it was waving at her, wiggling its fingers just like the image on the screen.

"Okay, how are you doing that?" she asked, obviously sucked in by Simon's playful shenanigans.

Simon walked toward a small dinette set up in a corner of the space, elegantly set for two. There was a single rose in a slim vase in the center of the table, and two place settings, complete with toast, fresh fruit, and two glasses of ice water.

"Come have a look," he said with a big smile.

She set her attaché on Finn's desk and walked over to the table.

"That seat's for you." Simon nodded to the other chair and she sat down, ready for whatever was about to happen. "Do you see these snake-like patterns throughout the synthetic skin?" he said in his professorial tone.

She leaned in to take a look. "Uh-huh."

****

Finn had powered on the camera perched atop a tripod to record the exchange from the moment Emanuela had taken her seat. He leaned against the wall, his arms folded across his chest. She looked like an eager pupil with her wide eyes and her upper body leaning toward Simon in interest. He smiled to himself, watching the pair on the small screen.

"Those are sensors," Simon continued. "The sensors are arranged in this pattern so that the prosthetic hand isn't rigid, but moves fluidly, much like your hand, Miss Monroe."

"Ahhh," she said, understanding. "May I touch it?"

"Of course! You can even shake the hand." He eased it toward her so he didn't spook her. "Don't be gentle. Get in there and squeeze it nice and firm, the way you'd shake an adult's hand."

She raised her hand and grasped the prosthetic, wincing at the unusual sensation of the synthetic fingers gripping her hand right back.

"Whoa," she said again. "It feels…warm…and soft, like a real hand."

"Precisely! The softness is the silicone, and the temperature is controlled by those snake-like sensors that mimic the temperature of human skin. But that's just the tip of the iceberg."

She returned his infectious smile.

"There is still some time before dinner," he said. "Would you care for some refreshment?"

"I would," she said, playing along.

There were no utensils at her place setting. She looked up, and the prosthetic hand lifted a butter knife, holding the handle between its forefinger and thumb, using it to spread softened butter onto her toast.

"Amazing," she breathed, "but how—"

He tapped the strange helmet he wore, waggling his brows.

"Finn outfitted me with this wonderfully fantastical contraption for today's demonstration," he boasted.

"I did," Finn said, still filming. "A prosthetic hand can do more than a leg, so it makes for a more impressive prototype. Since I'm the only metahuman here," he joked, "this is the best way to demonstrate the way the prosthetic interacts with the nerves, and, by extension, the brain. The program you saw on the monitor behind me picks up each movement and translates it to a 3D image."

Emanuela's gaze practically caressed him. "It's remarkable. I'm excited to see more."

Finn was glad she'd turned around because the look she gave him before she returned her attention to Simon just about knocked him on his ass. *Dammit, Finn!* There had been nothing suggestive in her tone—but those *eyes*. The woman had a champion's poker face. She was all poise and professionalism. But her flirting made him want to snatch her to him and wreck that pristine picture, to kiss her stupid and mess up her hair. A muffled groan escaped him at the thought. Thankfully, the others in the room were immersed in conversation and missed his audible blunder.

Jesus. Keep it together!

The next half hour was mental agony. He was confident in the product itself. He hadn't been bluffing in their meeting yesterday. What he and Simon had accomplished was a big deal. Philip Hurst was her employer, yet Emanuela was the one they needed to impress. Although he didn't want to disappoint her or let Simon down, he was impatient to spend some time alone with her before she left Seattle. It was challenging enough to wait the entire morning without seeing her, or calling her feigning confusion about some point or other. He knew he needed to let her do her job, so he refrained from making a fool of himself.

He learned the limits of his patience that afternoon, forcing himself to stay collected and finish filming their demonstration for Hurst Capital. He brought the camera close to get a clear shot of the prosthetic grasping a cup of ice water, and Emanuela's look of amazement that the glass didn't shatter from the strength of the prosthetic, or slip from the condensation on the glass. For the humble but sweet finale, the prosthetic lifted the rose from its vase and offered it to Emanuela.

She clapped and looked into the camera with a smile. "I think we've got enough."

She sent Philip the footage for supporting material, and then made a conference call to Mr. Hamilton and Philip. They took a few minutes to confirm any new details in documentation before she put her phone on speaker so that Simon and Finn could hear the good news.

"Congratulations, gentlemen," Philip's voice rang loud and clear. "We're partners! Looking forward to working with you."

Finn, Simon and Mr. Hamilton exchanged congratulations, and Emanuela turned the speaker off to talk with Philip. Finn didn't mean to eavesdrop, but he was closing down a few programs and she was very close to his desk, wrapping up her conversation with her boss.

"Good work. You must have been up pretty late recalculating logistics," Philip said.

"I was, but I think you'll see that it was worth it."

"I'm sure I will. We'll celebrate when you get back! And Em…"

"Hmm?"

"You're my best guy."

"Thanks, Boss. See you Monday."

Finn wondered at the familiarity he detected in the tone of the conversation. It was obvious Emanuela had earned the trust and respect of her employer. Nonetheless, he couldn't shake the feeling that there might be something else between them. Though he tried not to let it bother him, he longed to get her all to himself, and hearing Philip's endearment for her wasn't helping matters. She was just an arm's length away from him, and he was about to take that moment to ask her out again, but Simon got to them first. He stifled a groan.

Simon turned to Emanuela. "How about that, huh? I think this is cause for celebration! I'm meeting my husband for dinner later if you'd care to join us. Finn, you can come too." He grinned.

The pained look on Finn's face must have given him away, because her eyes grew glassy and black before she tore them away and offered Simon a polite smile. "That's very kind of you, Doctor Faulk—"

"Call me Simon, Emanuela, if I may? You've seen my home and played with my toys so I'd like to think that we're friends now."

"Simon," she said. "I have to take a rain check. I've already made plans for this evening. I'm a huge fan of your husband though, and I look forward to meeting Jamie soon." This time she reached for Simon first, anticipating that he would give her one of his hugs.

"Until then, Emanuela," he said with a final squeeze to her slim shoulders. "Finn?"

"I have some things to attend to myself, Sy," Finn declined in a gruff voice.

Emanuela's eyes met his briefly before they looked away again.

"All right, I'll see you Monday!" Simon said, oblivious to the undercurrent between the pair.

The men shared an exuberant handshake-turned-hug, a gesture that drove it home that they had done it. They'd accomplished what they had set out to do in the face of constant rejection, and they would remember this day for years to come. The magnitude of the moment wasn't lost on Finn, but he felt like he had been waiting no less than an eternity for the chance to be near Emanuela again in a way that would seem inappropriate to the rest of their group.

****

The door leading from the garage into the house had just clicked shut when Emanuela felt Finn's presence behind her. Heat spread through her body. It started somewhere in her gut and sped its way to her throat, snatching the air from her lungs. She was frozen in place, waiting for him to make his move. Her skin tingled in anticipation, goosebumps rising on her arms. She tried to keep her breathing steady and even. The moment lasted seconds, maybe, but her mind took her back to Chicago eight months ago, back to the lounge where they were locked in the staring contest of a lifetime. That same charged air hummed between them. The same scent from his body permeated her senses and something inside her rejoiced to learn that it wasn't courtesy soap. It was him.

Then, finally, he touched her.

They sighed in unison, his arms encircling her, his big hands spanning her abdomen before locking her into a long embrace. Her body relaxed, her head falling back to rest against his shoulder. She felt him turn his face into her hair, heard him breathe her in like a drag from a cigarette. His deep, shuddering breath caressed her ear, making her shiver.

She felt so secure in his arms, fitting his embrace like they were carved together. He hadn't even spoken yet, and she felt her business veneer being stripped away. There was no need to pretend any longer that she didn't want this, that she hadn't been waiting for "tomorrow" to come when he'd ask her again. "Ask me," she whispered.

He loosened his hold, but before she could whimper in disappointment, his hands were at her waist, turning her to face him. He raised her chin with two of his fingers, his eyes locked on hers. "Have dinner with me, Emanuela."

His voice was so deep and rich, she felt like a wind instrument being filled with a soulful note. Every word resonated throughout her entire body and she found herself shivering again.

"I'd love to." Her eyes fell to his lips. They had tensed in expectation of her answer and she wanted to kiss them until they were soft and pliant again. He seemed to read her thoughts and moved his face closer to hers when the front door slammed shut and startled them from their embrace.

Before he let her go, he asked, "Where are you staying?"

"The Edgewater. Do you know it?" She didn't want to move away but did so anyway. She wasn't ready to advertise…whatever this was…just yet.

"I do," he said, returning her attaché and walking her out to her car.

They waved at Simon as he drove by and Finn held her arms in his hands.

"Pick you up at six." He reached around her to open the door.

She nodded and, on impulse, tilted her head to brush a soft kiss against his jaw. She pulled back, her eyes drinking their leisurely fill of him. His jeans, crewneck tee, and curling waves gave him a boyish charm, but his size and stance showed he was all strength and charisma. She felt her face warm at the amusement in his eyes at her obvious appraisal.

"See you at six, Doctor Kane," she said, teasing him with the formality. She slid into the seat with a devilish smile.

He leaned in until they were face to face. "I'm prepared to work for it, Emanuela."

A furious blush rushed to her cheeks, and he grinned in smug satisfaction as he shut her door.

Chapter Six

Emanuela stood in her hotel room in nothing but her underwear, critically examining the garments hanging in her temporary closet. She hadn't a *clue* what to wear. Nothing she'd packed for the short trip felt right for a date with Finn. She supposed she could transform one of her business dresses into suitable night attire with the right shoes and hair. *I don't want "suitable."* She tossed another perfectly decent sheath dress onto the bed in frustration.

She wasn't meeting friends for drinks after hours. She was having dinner with a gorgeous, exceptionally clever man who looked at her like she'd hung the moon. No, she didn't want "decent" at all. She wanted to knock his socks off, and she wasn't going to do that in any of her modest, albeit immaculate work frocks. The alarm clock on the nightstand said quarter to four. She bit her lower lip in thought. Deciding she was cutting it close but was sure she could manage, she rang the concierge for a cab.

****

Finn was beside himself as he finished a close shave and smoothed back his hair. There was no question of a deep attraction between him and Emanuela. It was both subtle and strong; an undercurrent in every interaction that rose to the surface and overflowed with a look or a touch. They'd had a taste of it months ago, and all they'd done was shake hands for Christ's sake.

He splashed cold water on his face as if the shock to his skin would shut down his thoughts. A handshake had almost killed him, and he shuddered to think of what a kiss might do...in the best way. But he felt more than physical attraction to her. The way she'd looked at him when he'd first met her, like she could somehow see to the heart of him, had made him uncomfortable at the time. He'd made his hasty exit that night and spent weeks trying to forget her. But it'd been no use. She was burned into his brain. He'd grown to accept it.

And now she wanted to get to know him. For the first time in as long as he could remember, there was restored vigor in his stride. He donned his jacket and navigated his modest silver Mercedes downtown to Emanuela's waterfront hotel.

****

Thirty minutes later

Finn rounded the fountain and pulled his car to the front of The Edgewater. He started dialing Emanuela's room, when movement near the entrance caught his eye. Seconds later, his heart slammed into his chest just once, and then stop beating altogether.

Whatever he'd told himself before he left that evening about taking his time to get to know her...about the way they shared a connection that was more than merely physical, about exploring the new emotional awakening in his heart...was forgotten the instant he laid eyes on her.

Jesus. His jaw went slack.

She made her way toward him, looking like liquid gold. Her stilettos blended with her skin, making her well-formed legs look impossibly long. Her dress started at that tantalizing place on a woman's thigh somewhere between demure and sinful, and hugged her everywhere it touched.

The deep champagne hue of the silken fabric glimmered with each fluid movement of her hips. Every one of her soft curves was masterfully displayed. Finn's eyes swept from her hips, up her slender waist, to the magnificent expanse of creamy, golden brown skin exposed by the top of the dress.

That was his favorite part, where the dress curved into the shape of a heart at her chest and wrapped around her arms, leaving her shoulders deliciously bare. He drank in the tousled ebony waves that fell just past her shoulders. Soft bronze shimmered along her cheekbones and her big, molten brown eyes seemed even brighter, set off by shimmers of gold on her smoky lids. Her lips looked soft and inviting, glazed in honey tones and parted in an alluring smile.

She was dead sexy and Finn was in a world of trouble.

****

Emanuela almost stumbled at his reaction to her. To a stranger, his expression might have appeared hostile or pained, but she knew it was the way she affected him. She slowed her stride as she approached, her heart beating much too fast. She felt every pulse beat, watching him push off with his right foot to get out of the car and come around to meet her.

A calm breeze carried his clean, masculine scent to her nostrils, making her breath hitch. She wanted to smooth her palms over the visible contours of his chest beneath his thin black sweater. He stopped in front of her and she stared into his eyes, his gray sports jacket making them appear more gray than blue. The way he looked at her made her want to fidget. She managed to control herself enough to get out a breathless, "Hi."

"Hi," he greeted her, his voice deep and measured. "You look…" He couldn't seem to find adequate words in his stupefied state, but his eyes traveled down her body again and worked their way back up, his words hanging in the thick air between them.

She sucked in an audible breath at his visual caress, flushing at the knowing smile on his handsome face. He reached out to take her coat and drape it across her shoulders, his hands gliding along her arms before releasing her again.

"Shall we?" he asked, opening her door.

"Thank you." She got in and reached for her seatbelt.

His eyes met hers again. "Let me."

Though she was perfectly capable of fastening her own seatbelt, she had no intention of stopping him. She was playing with fire and she knew it, but in that moment she felt every bit the fire goddess. It made her feel powerful and wanted. He reached across her and fastened her seatbelt, stopping on his way out of the car to press a gentle kiss to her cheek before closing her door.

"So, where are you taking me, Doctor Kane?"

Finn grinned. "There's a place about ten minutes from here that serves some of Washington's best wine. The cabernet is amazing. I remember you like red."

She was thrilled he remembered such a detail, but the memory of how that night ended stripped her of basic vocabulary. She felt his eyes on her, as if he could read her thoughts, and the electric energy returned.

"The restaurant is called Canlis and it's named after the family who started it," he said. "It's been around since the fifties and the backdrop is incredible. I figured since I don't have time to show you the city, I could at least pick a place with a great view."

"I have a thing for those."

"One of the original owner's sons lives in Scotland and cultivates one of the rarest single malt whiskey collections in the country. In case you've acquired a taste for it."

"Not a chance. Now I know the real reason you chose this place."

Their banter lasted the short drive to the restaurant. Parking was valet only, and Emanuela was surprised when the attendant provided no ticket to claim the car.

"They never get it wrong," Finn said with a smile.

****

The restaurant was the picture of rustic modern elegance, with stone accents, soft lighting and broad windows with stunning views of Lake Union and the Cascade Mountains beyond. The atmosphere was downright romantic, and Finn couldn't believe his luck that she was here with him.

He guided her through the lobby where a warm fire burned and light strains from the grand piano filled the room. After climbing a short, curved and dimly lit set of stairs, they were welcomed into an intimate room featuring just a few tables, set some distance apart for privacy in front of floor-to-ceiling windows.

"Wow," she said. "This is lovely."

"As you are." The pretty blush returned to her face.

He stepped behind her to help remove her coat and

was rewarded with a full view of her elegant back. He let his fingers brush the smooth skin he'd uncovered. He relieved her of her coat, his eyes falling to the enticing dip where her back met her rounded hips. His hand was drawn to that place, guiding her to her seat. He felt her tiny tremor at his touch and wanted nothing more than to explore her responses to his touch on every part of her.

It's still early, he reminded himself. He sat just inches away from her and accepted the wine list from their server.

The sun had just begun to set when their drinks arrived, and the two shared an easy rapport. He discovered she hated running, his favorite workout of all, but she enjoyed Pilates and yoga. He told her of his passion for the outdoors, and that he owned a boat out on Whidbey Island.

"I love the water," she was saying as their server presented a trio of amuse bouche.

"Compliments of the chef," he said. After detailing the ingredients and a courteous, "Enjoy," they were left alone again.

"Wow." She admired the beautiful arrangement of miniature hors d'oeuvres. "I don't remember which is which, but everything looks delicious."

"Here." Finn chose a tiny savory tart with a single sprig of thyme as garnish. "I think this is the mushroom one."

She made no move to take the morsel. Instead, she leaned toward him and parted her lips. He was happy to oblige, watching her take the entire bite into her mouth, closing her eyes on an, "Mmmmm."

It was the most erotic thing he'd ever seen.

"Oh my God," she said, licking her lower lip. "I'm sorry you didn't get to taste that one!"

"Oh, I'm fine. It was worth it just to watch you eat it."

Her throaty laugh forced her head back, and she gave him a playful smack on his shoulder. "No really. You got the short end on this one. Sooo good!"

She was so beautiful when she laughed. He marveled at how animated she was, and the million different expressions she made when she talked about her interests or something she didn't like. They chatted contentedly until the sunset demanded their undivided attention. They watched in comfortable silence, sipping their drinks until the beautiful scenery before them transformed into a cloak of midnight blue. The window became a mirror then, and they could see a few of the other patrons dining in their finery. Finn caught her gaze when it returned to their table.

"Do you want to know something?" she asked after a moment.

I want to know everything. "What's that?"

"I had no idea where we were going tonight. I didn't have anything to wear but my work clothes and I was worried that I'd be underdressed."

He eyed her in disbelief. He couldn't imagine that anyone as stylish as Emanuela would have nothing to wear.

"I had a couple of hours to find something...appropriate...and I—" She looked away.

He instantly understood. "You wore that for me."

The color that warmed her face again confirmed his assertion, and he felt the invisible restraints that kept him from touching her slipping away. She could have chosen any dress to match the understated elegance he'd become accustomed to, but she hadn't. The knowledge that she'd worn *that* dress, the sexy tousled hair and bedroom eyes just for him brought back the same feelings he had when he first laid eyes on her.

He reached for her chair, pulling it closer to him. She gasped in surprise, and he resisted the urge to pull her into his lap. His hand cupped her chin, his thumb brushing her bottom lip.

"Emanuela," he said, his voice suddenly deeper, waiting for her to meet his eyes.

She looked up at him, and he lowered his face to hers. He took his time, sampling the wine from her lips in soft brushes. Her lips were softer than he could have imagined. Sweeter. The more he tasted, the stronger his thirst became. Her tongue flicked his lower lip and he moaned, sweeping his tongue into her mouth, drinking her up. His lips trailed her chin, the smooth curve of her throat, drawing from her an uneven sigh. They were lost in sensation, unconscious of their surroundings until a low, deliberate clinking sound dragged them apart.

He smirked. Her cheeks flamed. They straightened in their seats to allow their server to set their first courses on the table. He detailed the dishes before them, then left them alone again.

They grilled each other about favorites, firsts and failures—about beloved pets, best friends and stupid mistakes they made in college. Through it all, Finn couldn't keep his lips off Emanuela, bending to press a kiss to a shoulder here, a wrist there. She didn't seem to mind.

They were no less than stuffed before they

departed, both high on the newness of whatever this was they were feeling and not wanting the night to end. He helped her back into her coat, turning her to face him so he could do up her buttons. It was the most innocent act, but felt so intimate. He looked at her the entire time, his quick fingers pulling each button through its hole. She gave him a beguiling smile in response, and he reached for her hand.

It was only nine o'clock, and it was clear and tame for a spring Seattle night. They made the short drive back to Emanuela's hotel, both quietly anxious at the thought that their time together was coming to an end. They felt keenly aware of their physical connection. It hadn't wavered the entire evening, even when they were engrossed in each other's conversation and with the incredible food.

Finn circled the parking lot and turned into a space, not ready to drop her off yet. "I can't thank you enough for everything you've done. I'll always be grateful to you for giving Sy and I our start."

She rewarded him with another smile. "I wish I could take credit, but you two threw me for a loop. I expected to come here and make you an offer you couldn't refuse." She winced at her horrible impression, and then sobered. "You surprised me, which is hard to do in my line of work."

He nodded in appreciation for what she said, but he needed to get something off his chest before he lost the moment. He reached for her hand, releasing the tension he felt on a sigh. She brought his hand to her mouth for a kiss.

He looked into her eyes. "I had such an amazing time with you tonight, that all of the events of the last two days matter little to me if you go back to New York and out of my life again."

He couldn't help the depth of emotion that colored his voice, but she didn't look away, which was encouraging. He didn't know what to call his feelings for her, but it would hurt if she behaved with another the way she'd been with him tonight. He sensed that she felt the same, watching her part her lips and then shut them again, swallowing hard. Her lack of words didn't matter though, because he could see every emotion she wrestled in the warm brown depths of her eyes. He drew in a single ragged breath before he crushed her to him for a kiss.

Gone were the soft, tentative kisses they shared earlier. Any trepidation was forgotten and replaced by hunger. He cursed, trying to get her seatbelt unfastened, but she had already managed to slide her hands under his lightweight sweater. He jerked at the touch of her cool, soft hands on his skin, her fingers running through the mat of curls on his chest.

She was relentless, feasting on his lips, jaw, cheeks, and neck. He groaned at her open mouth on his ear, her hot tongue flicking his lobe before sucking it into her mouth. He pulled her hands away, leaning back to look at her. A feverish flush of color highlighted her cheekbones, her breathing fractured.

He freed her of her seatbelt, making short work of her coat, bending his head to the lovely display at her neckline. He licked the valley between her breasts, grazing her nipples through her dress with his teeth. She moaned, arching her back, pushing her soft flesh into him.

He raised his head, seeing her look of absolute

awe. His dark eyes dragged over her form possessively before he hauled her onto his hard thighs and molded her breasts with his hands.

"You're so beautiful," he said, against her lips.

He made love to her mouth, his restrained passion from earlier now free. Nothing mattered but the urgent, desperate plea from their bodies to be submerged in each other. His hand skimmed her thigh beneath the hem of her dress and he tore his mouth from hers with a stifled growl. "Emanuela."

His voice was hoarse with the effort to control his lust. He halted their movements, holding her by her waist and waiting for her to come through her sensual haze. She looked at him again and gasped, and he knew the hardened expression he wore when he first saw her that evening had returned.

"Take me to your room," he said.

She shuddered against him, his big hands gripping her waist and removing her from his lap. After taking a moment to collect herself, she opened the door and climbed out. The cool night air did nothing to calm their heated bodies. He rounded the rear of the car to join her, taking her hand in his and silently making the short journey to her hotel room.

Chapter Seven

Only a heartbeat passed, just enough time to flick on the light in the foyer so a soft glow flooded the room before she was in his arms again. Finn's hands moved inside of her coat, skimming her waist, seizing her hips to press her lower body to his as he kissed her. Her soft moans joined his, creating an electric hum between them.

"Wait." He pulled away.

She made an anguished sound, opening her eyes with obvious reluctance.

God, he *wanted* her. But he also wanted to show her that whatever he felt went beyond the need to satisfy a sexual craving. He didn't know *what* it was, how to convey it—and she'd already slipped a trim thigh between his legs to rub him through his pants.

He groaned, stepping back to escape her sinful attack, tugging her along with him to the bed. He sat at its edge, pulling her between his thighs. He read the emotions in her eyes. Excitement. Anticipation. Doubt.

"C'mere," he said.

He drew her to him and just held her, one arm behind her back and the other beneath her hips, pressing his face to her chest. He dragged her scent into his lungs for a minute, feeling her trembling warmth like live wire in his arms.

She felt *so* good. Like coming home.

Her hands tangled in his hair, unconsciously teasing the curls at his nape. Even that slight touch made him moan, and he moved his neck to rub against her soft fingers. Their deep breaths slowed in synchrony, and he loosened his hold without releasing her. He lifted his head to look up at her moonlit face.

"This is insane," he said.

"I know." She stared back at him.

"I would have given my other leg for this."

She giggled. "For a hug?"

"Mmhmm." He tightened his hands on her waist. "I think anything else might kill me."

Honesty darkened the humor in his tone, and she shivered despite the warmth in the room. She dropped her hands to move her palms up his thighs, and the need to get closer to her grew stronger, pounding a rhythm into his ears.

"Before I kill you," she teased, looking down at his left leg, "I need to know that it won't hurt. Are you...is that okay?"

His soft laugh drew her eyes back to his. "That's not where it hurts."

She lifted her hand to give him a playful smack, but he caught it, bringing it to his chest.

"Here," he said. "Put me out of my misery."

****

She lifted her hands to his face, letting her thumbs brush his ears and he groaned. He leaned in and she closed her eyes. His lips were firm, his tongue bold as it filled her mouth, the sweet taste of him laced with whiskey. His hands were everywhere at once, kneading her breasts, stroking her waist, gripping her ass. The pads of his fingers created a delicious ache, and she broke their kiss to cry out. He pushed the hem of her dress up the satin skin of her thighs and the scent of her wafted into his nostrils. The fabric bunched at her waist, and her naked flesh was revealed to his hungry gaze.

"You smell so good, Emanuela."

His hot breath tickled her and she shivered, the pulse within her sending another rush of moisture at the rich timbre of his voice.

"You were naked under here all evening," he said.

"Panty lines."

Her wetness had seeped to her thighs, and he bent his head to taste her for the first time, humming his satisfaction. She whimpered in anticipation, her legs trembling as he licked his way up her thighs. Her hands gripped his hair and she pressed closer.

He growled, snatching her to him by her hips, burying his face between her thighs. His tongue plunged deep, curling up, his nose rubbing her clit in small circles.

"*Mmmmmm.*" She bit down on the soft fullness of her lower lip.

He continued to stroke her with his tongue, lifting a smooth leg over his shoulder and planting a hand on her thigh. She hissed each time she inhaled, releasing her breaths on ragged sighs. Pressure mounted inside of her and she couldn't speak. He sucked her clit into his mouth, applying more pressure with his tongue. She tensed around him for several seconds before she convulsed, holding him prisoner by his hair. Her keening cries ripped from her throat, and he continued to lick her until her movements slowed against his mouth.

"*Oh my God.*" She slumped against him.

His laugh came then, but hoarse with need for her. "I'm hurt. All that effort and you still don't remember my name."

"It's okay." She steadied herself. "You can try again."

****

He groaned, eager to accept the challenge. His hands glided over her hips, upward along her waist and across her exquisite shoulders to the zipper. He pulled it down, licking his lips at each inch of her glorious, naked back revealed to him.

His open mouth moved along her skin and she sighed, shimmying to allow her dress to fall to the floor. His languid gaze touched her everywhere, his mouth agape at the sight of her naked in front of him. His hands roamed her body for a moment, traveling over her breasts and the smooth plane of her stomach. She bent to help him out of his pants, kissing his thigh above the prosthetic before tugging them off.

"You're incredible," he said.

His fingers delved into her hair and raked her scalp, and she moaned long and deep. He gently tilted her head back and covered her mouth with his, stealing her breath as their tongues met and met again. Minutes passed before he released her, both of them panting and breathless. He bent and lifted her by her hips with ease, her legs wrapping around his waist.

"*Ungh, Emanuela.*" He trembled at the feel of her soft hand wrapping around him and guiding him into her warmth. "You're so beautiful. You're gonna get sick of me telling you that."

"Doubt it," she said, wiggling a little for good

measure.

Her teasing earned her a solid smack on the ass and she yelped. Finn grinned and sat down again with her in his lap. He whispered in her ear and she complied eagerly, swirling her hips in a slow rhythm. His hands roamed over her, the slow burn at this angle torturing him with pleasure. He caught her wild little animal sounds with his tongue, swallowing them down until they needed to break for air again. He looked at her dewy face, heard her fractured breathing and knew that she was close.

What if I just… He bent his head to take a pebbled nipple into his mouth and bit her.

"Fu-Finn!"

"Jesus." A new surge of wetness coated him. His excitement tripled at his discovery and his voice dripped sex. "You like that, baby?"

"Yes!"

He waited until she got back into her rhythm, clinging to his shoulders, before he assaulted her again. He bit her over and over; attentive to her breasts, her waist, her neck. The exquisite pain threw her off her rhythm once more and she clenched around him, releasing a sound like nothing he'd ever heard before as she rode him in earnest. Her need broke something in him and he thrust hard and deep. Slick flesh slapped together until release crippled her and she stilled, her rapid contractions pulling him deeper until white flashed before his eyes.

His release washed over him in waves and he growled into her neck, his sharp teeth piercing her shoulder. She sighed his name again, weak and trembling. He grinned at her, watching her try to catch her breath.

"What?"

He traced along the bruise he left on her shoulder with his finger, his grin growing to an all-out leer. "If all I had to do was bite you to get you to call me Finn, I'd have done it sooner."

****

They took turns using the bathroom, Finn first, so he could remove his leg and get comfortable while Emanuela showered. She wasn't withdrawn or shy when she emerged, which was encouraging. The sight of his artificial limb propped against the nightstand didn't seem to startle her, and he'd settled beneath the sheets to avoid any awkwardness. She slipped in and snuggled against his side. He angled his body toward her, propping his head on one hand and tracing her cheek with the other.

"You're so...proper," he said. "Watching you come apart is so sexy."

Her face flushed. "I like watching you too. I like how you say my name. The whole thing, *EMANYOU-ELL-A!*"

"You wound me."

Her honeyed laugh sent a jolt through him. An ache filled the space in his heart, the one left vulnerable after so many months of uncertainty where he felt like she'd gotten away from him. He had felt something similar every time Simon hugged her and he couldn't, and every time she called him "Doctor Kane" in that reserved, businesslike way. The sound of her merriment rang in his ears and he wished he had more time with her to hear it again and again.

"What are you thinking about?" she asked,

fingering the curls at his forehead.

He narrowed his eyes. He wasn't sure he understood what he was thinking himself, especially if she was anywhere *near* him. Whatever faculties he possessed were paralyzed in her presence and his thoughts got muddled. He decided he would try.

"You slay me," he said. "I don't know what this is, but it feels right. It's like I've known you for years. But it feels new and exciting too." He shook his head. "I'm sorry. None of this is making any sense."

"No, I get it." She blinked, thinking for a moment. "It's surreal, isn't it? We hardly know each other apart from—" Her eyes trailed along his chest and she looked away as her face heated again. "But I already feel so comfortable with you."

"Don't I make you uncomfortable, Miss Monroe?"

She gasped, and he knew that she was remembering the night they met. "I... Maybe that wasn't the best word for it." She stared at his mouth. "Upset. You upset me, I think. Shook me up. Nothing about you was predictable, and I'm *good* at anticipating things."

He nodded. "You upset me too. You ruined my social life, by the way. Turns out the brooding type isn't attractive in men of a certain age."

"Good. I wasn't having any fun either, you know. It was impossible to explain to a guy that he couldn't measure up to something I didn't even understand."

He looked down at her and the sweet pain filled his chest again. She was so strong, so powerful despite her small size. Her confidence and command of her profession made her even more attractive to him, and now she was allowing him to see past her bravado to something more vulnerable.

He raised his fingers to trace the fine features of her face, along the faintly smudged makeup around her eyes, a delicate cheekbone, and her still-tender lips. Stopping there, he gently pressed down and they parted, her tongue flicking the tip of his finger.

"Jesus," he said in reverent baritone, feeling her shiver in response. "What have we wrought?"

He curled an arm around her waist to pull her to him and angled his head to ply her mouth with long, lazy kisses. He heard her sigh and felt her turn so that her body was aligned with his. Her free hand moved to his nape and held his head to hers. He intended to use this moment to show her what he could not put into words. Talk was forsaken and all there was to do was feel.

He wanted her saturated in him, to make her feel like the most treasured woman in the world. The intensity of his feelings overwhelmed him, and he sensed the air between them change. This slow exploration of each other's bodies bonded them together stronger than before. Just like he could read her most intricate feelings in her eyes, he was reaching out to her with touch.

Her body responded, every part pressing to get closer. They took their time figuring each other out, tuning until they collided in perfect rhythm. She clutched at him and he wrapped his arms around her, not wanting to let go. But the reality was that they *would* have to let go. After one incredible night together, she was getting on a flight that would put three thousand miles between them and he wanted her to remember—remember this, remember him.

****

The full April moon streamed through the sliding balcony door of Emanuela's hotel room, bathing the room in soft, blue light. She peppered Finn's neck and shoulders with kisses before separating their bodies.

"I just need a few minutes." She pressed a kiss to his lips before rolling out of bed.

He took advantage of the moment to himself, listening to the shower running. He put on his boxers and maneuvered himself to sit at the edge of the bed. Next, he pulled the prosthetic liner over his stump with care and smoothed it up over his knee. He did the same with the sock, and then reached for the leg.

It was a minor inconvenience to take it off and put it on again, but hopping around the hotel room would be uncomfortable, and he didn't want to just spring his stump on Emanuela. He sat in the armchair of the small sitting area and tried to make sense of what just happened.

The chemistry between them was something he'd never experienced before, not with this intensity. His stomach muscles contracted. He could still feel Emanuela's thighs gripping his waist.

Yeah, no problem in that department. For whatever reason, he and Emanuela shared a connection that felt spiritual. His instincts told him that she felt it too. He felt it when they made love, the same way he read her tangled emotions in the parking lot hours before. He didn't know how or why, but whatever it was, he wanted in. The distance was sure to be a challenge, and he needed to know up front if she could handle being with someone like him.

She returned with her hair pulled into a high bun

on top of her head, her face clean of makeup, and she'd wrapped a towel around her still-damp form.

So beautiful.

"Hey you," she said with an impish smile.

"Hey yourself." He strode to her, leaning to peck her cheek.

Her eyes fell to his bare chest and her face turned pink.

"I'll take my turn now so you can get dressed without me staring." He grinned, grabbed his clothes and strolled to the bathroom.

****

Emanuela dried off, slathering on body butter before slipping into fresh panties and an oversized T-shirt. She hadn't packed formal loungewear or sweats. She hadn't expected to share the hotel room with anyone.

Not really. Perhaps she had hoped... But there had been no logical reason to suggest that this would happen. None *of this is logical. I mean, what* was *that?*

She hadn't been in a serious relationship in two years. Not since Greg proposed, and the screaming realization hit her that he wasn't whom she wanted. She stayed with him because, at thirty, she had been "about that age." He was a good guy, handsome, driven, and loved her. She appreciated the great things about him and felt flattered by his affection, but that's all it was for her. A fantasy.

She grimaced. She still felt shame at the way she led him on. They worked and mingled in some of the same circles so it was awkward that first year after their breakup. They could speak to each other now, and she was relieved. She wanted him to be happy. That thought brought her back to the present.

Is this what it's supposed to feel like?

She had written off swarming stomachs and perspiring palms as unrealistic expectations borne of too many chick flicks. None of her relationships had felt that way. The sex may have been good, even great, but nothing like what she just experienced with Finn.

The familiar current ran through her body at the memory of his mouth on her heated skin. She sighed. *What now?* She bit her lip and stared out at the moon reflecting off the water. She would ask him to stay the night. After that, she wasn't certain. For now, she wasn't ready for him to leave her yet.

****

Finn joined her, wearing his pants and the thin, short-sleeved sweater he wore to dinner. "Coffee?"

She was sipping some, black, from a paper cup. She shrugged. "I'm awake." He sat next to her on the leather loveseat, lifting her legs and pulling them across his lap. "I think I just learned the secret to the success of the formidable Emanuela Monroe."

"Oh you think so, huh?" She fingered a wet curl that fell over his brow.

"Maybe."

He was having a hard time getting his thoughts together. He was so resolute in the shower. He wanted to lay himself bare so that she knew what she was getting before he asked if he could call her after tonight. The memory of other women who seemed open to the idea of dating him and later changed their minds nipped at his confidence. He looked into her eyes, which were curious at his somber mood.

"Earlier, you said you couldn't explain something

you didn't understand…" He hesitated, looking down at her legs and stroking them softly. "What did you mean by that?"

"After all this time, I'm still not sure," she said, the struggle to find the right words evident in her voice. "Whatever I saw in you, I wanted to be close to it." She shrugged. "I just wanted to be close to you, for however long."

All the emotions from that night washed over him and the onslaught churned his stomach. "It was the same for me. But at the same time, I wanted to get far the hell away from you." He watched her face for any sign of hurt, but to his relief, she just nodded.

"I know." She frowned. "It was so strange. Almost made me sick."

He drew in a sharp breath, noticing her stiffen in response.

"What?" she asked.

"That's exactly how it was for me. It's how I'm feeling right now."

She nodded again. "We were both a little off. But your pitch was one of the more memorable ones I've had."

"Don't remind me. I don't think I've ever botched it like that before."

"*Excuse me?*" She smacked his chest. "Maybe I should rescind that offer."

He chuckled. He knew she was wide open, and he wanted her to trust him. It was his turn to be exposed. He tapped his leg. "This is the best one I've had so far, except I can't deep sea dive with it."

She reached for his hand. "How many do you have?"

"Just one. But I'm waiting for the military to finish developing those bionic legs so I can lift cars with my foot."

Her slim fingers traced his bigger ones. "You don't have to do that, you know. Self-deprecate. You've already seen me naked."

His eyes raked over her, his pulse jumping at her words. "You have no idea how much I'd like to see that again," he said, sensing her shiver. "But first I want you to see me too. The real me." He looked down at their hands. "Only if you're comfortable."

"I want to see. I just didn't know how to ask. Or if I *should* ask." She smiled. "I didn't want to offend you."

"You haven't asked me to spank you with it, so this is already an improvement from my last date."

Emanuela gasped. "*No...*"

He laughed at her horrified expression. "'Fraid so." He gently removed her legs from his lap and stood in front of her. "And *that* was an improvement from the date before that."

"Oh my God." She snickered. "That's awful."

"Well, *some* kinky stuff is fun."

"*Ugh.*" She narrowed her eyes. "Just drop your pants already!"

He grinned and turned away to do just that, bending to tug them off before coming back to sit beside her. Without further ceremony, he pushed on the front of the leg and a tiny motor whirred. "It's vacuum sealed," he said. "The button is hidden beneath this sleeve."

He pulled down the flesh-colored skin covering his knee and the prosthetic leg. Then, he removed the prosthesis and propped it against the end table, glancing at Emanuela.

"What's that?" she asked.

"It's a sock. Just makes it more comfortable. Tighter fit."

"How does it feel to take it off? Is it like taking your shoes off at the end of the day?"

"Wow." He smiled wide. "That's not half bad... It's more like taking off a snug pair of jeans. Just by the way it feels."

She nodded and he removed the sock, then peeled off the liner to leave his stump bare.

He watched her a moment, letting her take it in. Her eyes widened. Much of his leg was intact, halfway to his shin. It was smooth and conical, with a long pink scar at the tip of the stump.

"Some assembly required," he said.

She made a sound that was half-gasp, half-laugh. "I'm sorry."

"Don't be. I was shocked the first time I saw it too."

Her lips parted and closed again, darkness clouding her eyes. Finn could read everything in her face, and he silently agreed with the conflict he saw there. Part of him wanted to share the details about what happened, but another part of him wanted to preserve a moment that was new and exciting and full of promise. *Another time. If she gives me a chance.*

He lifted his stump, extending it in front of him. "Sometimes people are surprised I can move it. I can do just about anything, but walking tends to require two feet."

She laughed. "I don't doubt that you can do

whatever you put your mind to." She scooted in closer. "If not, we may have never even met."

"It's true." He snaked an arm around her waist. "And when I heard from your office, I knew my fate was in your capable hands, and part of me couldn't wait to see you again."

Her eyes turned the deepest shade of brown he'd seen from her yet. "Which part?" she whispered.

He groaned at the suggestive way she was looking at him and dragged her across his lap. "All of me," he said, against her lips. "Every part."

Chapter Eight

One Week Later

"They're ready for you, Miss Monroe," Lydia said, sticking her head into Emanuela's office. "Is there anything else you need?"

"Nope, thanks, Lids!"

Emanuela drained her coffee cup before collecting the materials she needed for the meeting. She jumped right back into the thick of things after she returned to New York. It wasn't difficult keeping busy. There was still the matter of finding a manufacturer for Finn's and Simon's smart limbs, and creating a demand among medical appliance companies, hospitals and the like before the innovative technology hit the market. Philip met her in the hallway.

"Morning, Em. Wow." He glanced at the stack of papers in her arms. "What's all that?"

"Supporting materials for Brian."

Philip chuckled, shaking his head and matching her stride.

"I don't intend to sit in the conference room all day, so I took the liberty of printing everything he'll interrupt me to ask for ahead of time," she said.

He allowed her to precede him into the conference room. "Your foresight is very much appreciated."

"Good morning," she said, distributing handouts to

the six other people in the room. She approached Brian's seat, and his eyes grew wide at the more significant stack she handed him, shooting her a dubious glare.

"I know how much you hate to be unprepared," she said, with saccharine civility before moving to take her own seat.

Philip reclined in his chair beside her, resting his elbow on the table and nodding the okay for her to start the meeting.

"This won't take long," she said. "There are some significant changes taking place this time around, and I'm prepared to answer any questions you might have moving forward."

Before anyone else could reply, Brian chimed in. "I don't see why we need to sabotage the business practices that have been working for us for years. We've had partnerships with Chinese manufacturing companies for over a decade," he said, as though Emanuela was oblivious to the company's history and needed a refresher course.

She fought the urge to roll her eyes. "We've enjoyed an amicable business relationship with Chinese manufacturers over the years; however, as the first item in your packet shows, the changing economic climate here in the States demands that we reevaluate where we send our business." She surveyed the room to gauge the reactions of the others. Deciding they were with her, she moved on. "I understand this change will incur higher costs on our end, but we have a pretty impressive list of new manufacturers, both here and in Mexico, who can compete with the quality and efficiency of Chinese manufacturing companies. The cost of—"

"What's the difference between going with the manufacturers in China we've *already* built relationships with and shipping everything off to Mexico?" Brian asked.

If you'd let me finish my thought, you'd have your answer, asshole. A migraine was coming on, and she willed it away. "The cost of transport and warehousing will be significantly lower with more localized manufacturers." *Prick.* He took a breath to speak again and she snapped, "You'll find NAFTA regulations in the second item," without looking at him.

She didn't need to look to know Philip's grin was there, and some of her irritation faded. "Not only will nearshoring our business improve relations between us and consumers, but if we can establish production sharing between us and Mexico, even Canada, we're likely to see a boost in economic activity between the regions."

"Which makes us all a little more money," Philip said. "I like where this is going, Em."

Emanuela smiled. Her attention to detail was second nature to her, to lift every edge and turn every leaf. She was Philip's biggest asset in the firm and everyone sitting there knew it, including Brian, who clearly couldn't resist speaking up again.

"It makes the laborers more money, too," he said, somehow making the statement sound perverse. "We're paying to transport them to and from facilities, regulatory costs, materials, labor—the list goes on and on."

Emanuela's patience unraveled. "It shines a spotlight on us as a leader in ethical business practices, as highlighted in item *three* in your packet. Ethics concern most of us in this room. I would hope it's pretty high on your list of priorities too."

The atmosphere in the room shifted uncomfortably, and Emanuela caught Philip's look of concern. Mercifully, he took over. "I'm sure we can all agree that change is necessary and good, but also comes with its own unique set of challenges. We need to work closely over the next few weeks to make sure we transition smoothly. In order for us to do that, we need to communicate effectively and often. Whatever concerns we have, we hash it out here. Understood?"

The meeting carried on for the further space of an hour before everyone felt confident enough to execute their individual tasks with limited supervision. Emanuela moved to get up from the table, and Philip gently grabbed her arm. "Is everything okay, Em?"

"Yeah." She looked at him with a strained smile. "Why do you ask?"

"What *was* that?"

She rubbed her temples and released an exasperated sigh. "I'm sorry. I don't know why I went berserk." She was accustomed to Brian's passive aggressiveness and would typically have a laugh at his expense or just ignore him. He was an asshole, but he was a valued member of the team and, as head of the financial division, his input mattered.

"Oh, Richards deserved every bit of the lashing you gave him," Philip said of Brian dismissively. "He's an ass. But it's not like you to let it get to you, so what gives? Do you need some time off? You've certainly earned it." He rubbed her wrist with his thumb.

Emanuela became hyper aware of his touch on her

skin, and eased her arm from his grasp. "I'm fine. I think I just need to eat. You pay me well but the food here leaves much to be desired." She threw a pointed look at what was left of the assortment of danishes and donuts on the table.

Philip laughed. "Come on! Those are good! Catered, not store-bought."

His look of feigned insult made her giggle, improving her mood. She gathered her things and walked through the door he held for her.

"They're delicious," she said, "but maybe some fruit would be good? Or something with *some* degree of nutritional value at all?"

They stopped in front of Philip's office, since his was closest to the conference room.

"Are you asking me to feed you?" he asked.

"I—" She was oddly nervous.

They had always shared an easy camaraderie and had lunch together often enough that his question shouldn't have seemed out of the ordinary. This felt different. He looked at her like he was seeing her for the first time, and she could sense that this wouldn't be one of their typical lunch excursions to him.

She couldn't process what her intuition was picking up *and* formulate a careful response on the spot, so she opted for something he would accept without suspicion that she was blowing him off. "I'd love to, but I think I'm gonna work through lunch today. I have some momentum going and I really want to finalize our top three manufacturing options today."

He nodded. "Best. Guy."

He winked and retreated to his office. She sighed and headed back to hers. She felt anxious. Tense. It was the third day in a row she'd felt this way.

Emanuela approached Lydia's desk. "Miss Whitney called during your meeting," Lydia said. "Also, there was a sign-for. I left it on your desk for you."

"Thank you." Emanuela grabbed a mint from the candy dish on Lydia's desk. "Hey, Lids?"

"Yes, Miss Monroe?"

"I feel a headache coming on so unless it's something big—"

"Do not disturb." Lydia nodded once.

Emanuela smiled warmly at her assistant and shut herself into her office. Kicking off her heels, she trudged to the desk and sat down. The package Lydia signed for was small, a perfect cube of a plain white box. The sender was a well-known printing company. She frowned. A successful business would have no reason to send free gifts. Grabbing the envelope opener on her desk, she slit the tape and opened the box. Nestled between packaging foam was a white coffee mug filled with an assortment of chocolate truffles. *Cute*. She lifted the mug from the box. Printed in black typewriter font against the stark white of the mug, was:

I'm jealous of the morning sun
who gets to be the first to see you
or the coffee cup
who gets to kiss your sleepy lips awake.

It was cheesy, but something about it was so personal that her heart trilled in her chest. There was no one she would expect such a gift from except— She emptied the box, looking for a note, a receipt-anything that would tell her who sent it, but there was none. She unwrapped one of the truffles and popped it into her mouth as she picked up the phone and speed dialed Allie.

"We're still on for lunch tomorrow, right?" Allie asked, sounding winded.

"We are." Emanuela's brows knit together. "Where *are* you right now?"

"*Ugh!* One of my weddings has been pushed up and I'm scrambling like mad to finish everything for back-to-back receptions this weekend! I just picked up the last of the supplies I need for the displays," Allie said, now completely out of breath.

She was the proud owner of Sugar, a premier wedding cakery in Lower Manhattan. They met in business school, and Emanuela was surprised to discover that Allie wanted to own a bakery. A few other students enjoyed jokes at her expense, thinking her ambitions weren't lofty enough. Now, her business was in high demand, especially during the spring and summer months, and hopeful couples needed to book well in advance if they wanted one of her gorgeous cakes.

"You're a magician, Allie," Emanuela said. "You've managed well under much more hectic circumstances."

"I know," she said, distracted.

"Glad I could help."

"Thanks, Em. I'll see you tomorrow."

Emanuela sighed and selected another chocolate. She was paying attention this time when she peeled off the thin foil wrapper. Then she saw it. There, printed on the inside in bold white letters, were three simple words:

I miss you

Her head jerked to the side a bit, then she opened another, and another, and another. Every single one contained the same three words. Her mouth spread into a wide, blissful grin, and she reached for her cell.

****

Finn's email notifications had been pinging away since seven-thirty that morning. It was hard to keep up with all of the messages in this particular encrypted account, but he managed to put a significant dent in it over the past few days and he was feeling pretty good about it. He was about to sign off for the day and then stopped, recognizing a familiar digital signature attached to a message. He hurried to open it, entering his private key and waiting for the message to finish decrypting.

Hello, Doctor.

I pray this message finds you well and in good health. We are so thankful to you for the supplies you sent. Maddie has grown a great deal and the prosthetic arm you sent last year is still functioning very well. The younger children here believe she is a superhero.

Simon Peter has not been faring as well. The meningococcal virus was diagnosed too late and the infection has spread to his leg. I'm afraid we will have to amputate. I am writing to urgently request a prosthetic leg for the boy.

Greatest discretion will be practiced, as always.

Your grateful friend,

Dr. Albaedo

"Dammit."

Finn designed each and every prosthetic limb, printed them from a 3D printer he bought with three thousand dollars of his own money, and shipped them abroad to patients in need. To doctors, nurses, missionaries and others, he was simply "Doctor." All correspondence between him and his colleagues abroad was encrypted to maintain anonymity and protect the small charitable movement he created.

He was elated to hear about Maddie's recovery. She was a precocious twelve-year-old who dreamed of becoming a nurse. Her arm had been crushed beneath the rubble of her collapsed apartment building during the devastating earthquake in Haiti in 2010. Her family could not afford the extensive surgery needed to save her mangled limb. She was now fitted with the second prosthetic arm Finn designed and would receive another in four more years after she outgrew that one too.

He removed a photo of the small Haitian boy from his wallet. Simon Peter was seven years old. Like many in his impoverished area, he didn't have access to sufficient health care. As it was, his family had traveled more than four hours from their shantytown on foot to reach Dr. Albaedo's clinic and, by then, his condition was severe.

Such a shame. He was pulling for the boy. He glanced at his watch. Simon was teaching all morning and wouldn't return until the afternoon, so he powered on the large monitor on his desk and, using the unique program he created to customize prosthetics for small children, got to work on Simon Peter's new leg.

He had been at it for two hours when his cell phone vibrated so hard it almost slid from his desk. He considered ignoring it, but he saw Emanuela's name on the screen and quickly answered. "Hey you."

"Hey."

There was a singsong quality to her voice, although

it was hushed.

"You're calling me from work." He smiled. "I didn't expect to hear from you until later."

"Oh, I could call back if now isn't a good time."

"Now's good. Now's *great*. How are you?"

"Honestly, I was having kind of a rough morning until this mysterious box showed up on my desk."

"Oh?"

"Yes, it's quite the intrigue. The sender left no note or any way to identify him. I think I'm being courted by The Phantom."

Finn laughed and leaned back in his chair. "You don't say! And what was in this mystery box?"

"The one thing, apparently, that I haven't bought for myself yet." She grinned. "There *was* a coffee mug with the sweetest, although corny, message printed on it and some delicious chocolates. Now there's just the mug."

"Corny? I'll have you know that I commissioned the finest poets in all of mass market printerdom to forge such a masterpiece, and you mock me for it."

Emanuela laughed outright, unable to keep up the charade. "I love it! I needed one. I think my assistant might personally thank you, so look out for that."

"Noted," Finn said, happy to hear her voice. "You said you were having a bad day. Wanna tell me about it?"

"No. At least not now. It's nothing I can't handle. I've been told I'm moody today and I think it's because…"

He frowned at her hesitation. "Emanuela?"

"I miss you too."

Though she spoke at a near-whisper, he still heard.

He was thrilled at the confession. The feeling that he was becoming much more emotionally invested than she was plagued him ever since he overheard Philip address her with such gentle familiarity back in Simon's garage. Finn was certain she felt the same pull toward him that he felt toward her, but thought perhaps she had something going with her boss, however insignificant, before he met her again. Hearing the sincerity in her voice restored his confidence that they were in this together. A wave of longing rose and fell through his body, starting in his arms and legs and flowing straight to his heart.

"That's—oddly, comforting to hear," he said. She sighed, and his arms itched to hold her. He crossed them over his chest and tried to lighten the mood. "You're not going to stand me up tonight, are you?" he asked. "Emanuela," he prodded gently after a long moment of silence.

"No, I won't stand you up."

Her voice sounded small, and he understood. This instant, she was the one most affected. Last night, it was he. They alternated this way each night of the last week, trapped in an emotional maelstrom that had them giddy at the start of every conversation and pining for each other at the end. Neither of them wanted to be flung out of the whirlpool that snared them, so around and around they went.

"Good." He made a valiant effort to sound upbeat when this was eating him. "I'll see you then, Emanuela."

****

The call ended, leaving Emanuela almost in tears. She hadn't realized the magnitude of her growing affection for Finn until the plane that carried her back to New York began its descent. She was usually very relaxed during landing, accustomed to the feeling similar to being on a roller coaster where her stomach dropped and she felt a little lightheaded. This time had been different. She hadn't wanted to look out the window at the night sky or the city lights. She couldn't. She had felt nauseous, sitting ramrod straight with her head back, her palms gripping the armrests and her eyes sealed shut against the dizziness that overtook her.

The plane taxied to the gate, and she made a concerted effort just to stand. It was then that she came to terms with a very real sense of loss. Finn hadn't gone anywhere. He was right where she left him, with three thousand miles of land and trees, water and mountain ranges between them. Part of her was still with him, the absent chunk bigger than she could have imagined.

Chapter Nine

"You wore *that* to work?" Finn cocked his head in disbelief.

Emanuela pressed the start button on her coffeemaker and turned around to lean against her kitchen counter. She had a slight frown on her face, eyeing him on her laptop screen. "What's wrong with what I'm wearing?"

He inhaled an audible breath, surveyed her form, and let it go slowly, pursing his lips. Her hair was up, her bangs side-swept and tucked behind diamond-studded ears. She wore a white, sleeveless dress that was tailored like a glove, with a thin black belt around her narrow waist. The high neckline drew attention to her defined collarbone and the graceful curve of her neck. He cursed under his breath.

"Nothing. You look beautiful."

She giggled. "You're *jealous.*"

Finn knew he was being stupid, but Emanuela was a beautiful woman and if she was walking around dressed like that every day, he was sure men were taking notice. They were able to be near her, maybe brushing her arm or catching her scent as she walked past.

"Of course I am," he said. "You could just wear something uglier."

Her laughter echoed in her kitchen. She brought

her coffee cup to the bar counter and sat down to be face-to-face with him. "Not a chance." She grinned at him over the rim of the cup. "Besides, I'm sure there's no shortage of women parading themselves in front of you every day. Maybe I'm the one who should be jealous."

Though she was teasing, he caught the pang of insecurity in her voice. They were still getting to know each other. They'd hardly spent two days in the same *state*, much less quality time alone together, so he would understand if their bond wasn't strong enough to hold her to him. He would understand but it would still hurt.

"Yes, countless women are throwing themselves at me as I toil away in Simon's garage," he said.

"You know what I mean."

He did know. Women often sent admiring glances his way or sat too close to him during his commute from Whidbey Island to Simon's house in the city. Still, he wasn't spending extended amounts of time collaborating on projects or having lunch with them. *Or giving them cute little nicknames*, which reminded him of something.

"So," he said, hoping he sounded interested and not like he was prying. "What's it like working for a guy like Philip Hurst? It's hard to box him in. His investments are all over the map."

"I understand. He's very smart and actually quite selective about the projects we take on. It's just that his choices have run the gamut, so people equate his unwillingness to limit himself to a single area to him being fickle. He doesn't throw money at things just for the sake of making good on his investment. He picks things he really believes in." She smiled. "And so do I."

Finn examined her expression, the way her eyes radiated warmth whenever she spoke of her employer. He knew the story of how she got her start. He'd lost count of how many times he read her bio on the firm's website.

"The two of you must be very close." He studied her face. "I imagine you're his most valued employee."

"We're friends. Working for him feels more like working *with* him and he doesn't hover. I enjoy that. But," she said, affecting a neutral expression, "all this talk of work isn't really doing much for this tension I've had all day."

His hair stood on end at her tone. *"Really?"*

"Really." She took another deliberate sip of her coffee.

He cocked his head to the side a bit, wondering what she was on about. "What did you have in mind?"

She took another sip, but tentative this time, like she was gathering her wits about her before she lost her nerve. "Music is very therapeutic. It can do wonders for stress. And since you aren't a fan of my outfit, I thought it'd be nice to put on something relaxing and get out of these restricting clothes."

It took a moment for her words to fully register in his brain. His brows shot skyward and his jaw went slack. "Can we—can you *do* that? With the computer and everything?"

"Mmhmm." She grinned and put down her cup. "Come on, I'll show you."

He sucked in a breath, watching her gather her laptop and adapter and walk backward, making sure that he could see her surroundings as she went. Her condo had the same understated elegance that she did. The open floor plan made it easy for him to see the wall of eight-foot windows in her living room, and the dusky skyline beyond. Her walls were stark white, set off by the vivid colors of her impressionist paintings.

"Nice place," he said, quite smoothly considering his rapid pulse.

"Thanks."

What he could see of her bedroom matched the elegance of the rest of the condo. The lighting was softer though, the walls awash in soft lavender with the same eight-foot windows along one wall. Emanuela set the laptop down on her bed, sitting the perfect distance from the screen so Finn could see her remove her jewelry. Her movements were slow and deliberate. She removed first one earring, then the other, and then her watch, placing each in a silver dish on her nightstand. Finally, she took off the dainty ring, pausing to flash a mischievous grin Finn's way before sliding it off her finger and adding it to the dish with the others.

He was riveted, his eyes traveling the length of her. She giggled with nerves, and he thought he must look like a lion ready to pounce. Without a word, she got up, positioning the laptop to allow him an unobstructed view, and took her time turning around so that he could get an eye full of her back. She tossed a smoldering gaze over her shoulder, then strutted to her stereo, gliding the tips of her toes along the floor with each step. It had its intended effect, and Finn cursed softly.

She hit a button and the mordantly seductive sound of horn, strings and brush against drum saturated the room as Nina Simone's "I Put A Spell On You" began to play. She milked the intro for everything it was worth, sashaying closer to the camera with one graceful stride on each second count, her hips swaying with each step. She removed her hairpins and, with a couple turns of her head and a tousle with her fingers, the soft, scented mass tumbled to her shoulders.

Finn was enthralled. Emanuela was positively feline, in fluid motion with the seductive strains of jazz pouring from her speakers. Her fingertips trailed upward along the sides of her body and ended in her lush curls. She flipped her hair and twisted, giving him a view of her side before she removed her belt in one svelte move, tossing it to the floor. She reached for her zipper—one quick tug to tease and then she pulled it down, the parting fabric revealing the smooth brown skin of her waist, inch by provocative inch.

With her chin still down, she raised her eyes and held his gaze for a few seconds. The image of her triggered his taste buds and he licked his lips. Nina's expressive contralto and climactic scat blended with the stringed instruments, intensifying the effect of Emanuela's strip tease on his senses. She exposed one, then the other of her silken shoulders, peeling her dress down to her waist.

She was driving him insane. Finn sat hostage to the sweetest visual stimulation he'd ever known, his hand unconsciously moving to his lap. His eyes and brain were full of her and the performance she was putting on just for him. She grabbed the fabric of her dress in her hands, sliding it up and down her hips a couple of times and then pushing it down, bending at her waist.

"Oh my God," he groaned, drinking in the sight of her most intimate places covered in almost sheer black lace.

She stood up slowly, her back arched, and stepped out of her dress before turning around. His eyes dropped to her legs and rose at a lazy pace, taking in her calves, her plump little ass, the dimples above it, and the ample skin leading up to her shoulders. She made sure his eyes met hers before unhooking her bra and shrugging out of it. With a roll of her hips she faced him again, holding her bra in place with one arm.

He made eye contact with her, and his heart stopped its furious thudding. She moved her arm, a sinful smirk gracing her lips, and allowed the pretty scrap of lace to fall to the floor. His mouth was open, nearly drooling, his eyes caressing her topless form.

It had only been a minute or so, evident by the way the music grew in intensity, Nina's vocals elevating to a sexy dual with an invigorated saxophone. Two minutes felt stretched to ten, like they were in a stunning trance the entire time. Emanuela drew closer and lifted her laptop to carry it into the bathroom, her taut tummy and the underside of her breasts filling Finn's screen. She set her laptop on the vanity and sat down to be face-to-face with him. Another song began to play softly in the background.

"Emanuela," Finn said, his voice strained with need for her, "I don't think I can handle more of you like—that—and not be able to..." He gave her an apologetic smile.

She blushed. "I know. I thought we could help each other—here."

She looked at him with wide, questioning eyes, and Finn groaned. He *definitely* caught her meaning. "You *do* miss me. Show me."

****

The look Finn gave her sent a jolt of desire that went straight to her clit. She sighed and let her hand fall to slide beneath the elastic edge of her lace panties.

"Show me how much you miss me," he said, rubbing himself.

His gruff voice sent another shiver down her spine. She moaned as her fingers glided through the trim curls of her mound and her swollen folds to brush her slick, taut clit. She couldn't believe she was doing this. She never thought she'd have the nerve, and even now she fought to keep her eyes open because the intensity in his eyes made her feel like she'd combust.

She couldn't look away. He was so beautiful and virally male, stroking himself and watching her come apart in front of him. He talked her through it, and she responded superbly to his voice, growing warmer with every word.

"Just imagine what we're going to do the next time we see each other," he said. "Show me how good it makes you feel."

The carnal image of him behind her flooded her memory and she shuddered. She continued to slide her fingers against her clit, applying more pressure, her body trembling and tiny spasms shaking her thighs.

"Good, beautiful." His voice sounded gruff and strained. "I'm thinking about how incredible it feels to be inside you and how soft your lips are on my ear."

"*Unh*," she cried.

He loved the special attention she gave his ears, and the memory of the husky sounds he made when her teeth grazed his lobes made her moan again. She couldn't wait. She missed his touch too much for this to be a slow burn, and the sound of him pumping himself faster sent her that much closer. She tensed and her eyes slid shut against the first wave of ecstasy. Her clit swelled against her rapid fingers and then sharp pleasure pushed her chest forward, her back arching as she hummed her release. She heard him growl low in his throat and pried her eyes open to watch, the final tremors leaving her body.

His eyes were on her too, and moments after she crumbled before him, his brow creased and he gritted his teeth. His body jerked forward and he shuddered over and over before his face relaxed again. They grinned at each other and Finn moved to clean himself up.

"Wow." She reached for her robe. "That was a revelation."

"Amazing. I didn't know we were this comfortable with each other yet."

"I've never done this before—not like this. But I trust you."

"I trust you too."

They were like teenagers in that moment, gaping at each other and delighting in their growing feelings.

"I like that dress, by the way," she said with an indignant pout. "It's getting warmer here and white is one of my favorite colors to wear in hot weather."

He chuckled. "I liked it too. I *didn't* like that it looked so damn good on you, and I can't see what you wear every day."

"The only reason you saw it today is because I had to stay late at work so I could make a conference call to one of our manufacturers in China. Their offices don't open until seven their time, so I stayed until seven tonight and didn't get home until after eight."

"Oh, I hadn't realized. You must be exhausted."

"I am but this was worth it," she said, waggling her brows.

They shared a laugh, just one among many over the next hour before Emanuela prepared for bed. She was finally unable to stifle her yawns any longer, and Finn chided her softly. "Go to sleep, Emanuela. We can talk more tomorrow."

She loved how he said her full name. People close to her called her "Em," but something about the way he said it, with a reverence in his deep tone, made her feel so beautiful.

"Goodnight, Finn."

"Goodnight." She fell asleep with a smile on her face.

****

"What's with the stupid grin?" Allie eyed Emanuela as the latter completed her order to the waiter.

"What? I don't have a stupid grin." Emanuela's smile grew wider.

"Okay, *see? There! That* stupid grin. What gives?"

The beautiful redhead's expression turned to one of absolute determination, a look Emanuela knew very well. *Shit,* Emanuela thought. "Nothing," she said, smoothly. "I've just been having a really good day."

She could temper her expression very well too, something Allie knew well enough to see that Emanuela was lying through her pretty white teeth.

"Uh-huh," Allie said. "Fine, don't tell me. But fix your face. You look goofy—and *beautiful.* What *is* that?" She indicated Emanuela's belted seafoam wrap dress with a swirl of her salad fork.

Emanuela dug into her salad, famished at the midday hour. She was a bit late for their lunch date. She had to make some last-minute changes to the non-disclosure agreement she drew up for the new manufacturers they contracted for Finn and Simon's smart limbs. She arrived at their favorite restaurant in SOHO a little after two.

"Donna Karan," she said, devouring another forkful.

"You should gift that to me for my birthday," Allie said, completely serious. "Green looks amazing on my complexion."

Emanuela threw her a disbelieving look. "No way. You make enough to buy a million of these. I'm keeping this one."

Allie shrugged, then reached for a pretty pale blue box and set it in the center of the table. "Here, I brought your favorite canelés."

"Yes!" Emanuela reached for the box with childlike giddiness.

Lifting the lid, she peered inside and smiled at the six beautiful French pastries, their glistening, caramelized crusts beckoning her to try one. They smelled even better than they looked.

Allie shook her head with a laugh. "You do that every time, and every time it's the same."

"I never know with you. I could open that box one day and lose some fingers."

"Not my style." Allie checked out Emanuela's plate with hungry eyes. "Oohh, that looks divine!"

It *did* look divine. The nori-crusted tuna had just the right amount of sear on the outside, and was presented on a bed of garlic rice and broccolini.

Emanuela's stomach grumbled and she grimaced at Allie. "Here," she said, half-heartedly. "Have some."

Allie grinned and cut a bite of Emanuela's tuna to taste. "*Oh* yeah," she said in an obscene tone. "That's good!"

She reached for another bite and Emanuela smacked her hand away.

"Hey, if this is what you wanted you should've ordered it. Hands off!" She wrinkled her nose at Allie for dramatic effect.

"Oh, you *are* in a peculiar mood today." Allie's eyes gleamed as they studied Emanuela. She continued to stare at her as she took a bite of salmon. "That kind of nauseating happiness can only mean one thing. But unless he's Superman, he's still a million miles away. So who's got you all—*that?*" She swirled her fork at Emanuela again.

Emanuela had always shared everything with Allie. After all, she told her about Finn the night she met him and they'd spent an hour talking about him in great detail through scandalized giggles. It was easier to talk about when it was just a phenomenon. When it wasn't tangible. Allie knew she'd gone out with Finn, but Emanuela wasn't ready to share the reason for her newfound giddiness just yet. In truth, she didn't know what the hell to call it herself. In the space of a week, he went from an intriguing stranger in a lounge, to surprising new client, and now? Her heartbeat sped up. He was someone she'd grown to care about very much.

Allie was scowling at her.

"What? I told you I've been having a really good day. I even had time for my run this morning," Emanuela said.

That worked.

"Em, it's not safe for you to go running around Central Park so early in the morning all by yourself. You should use the key I gave you. It's much safer in Gramercy."

Emanuela sighed, sensing where this conversation was headed. Two years ago, she'd moved into her twelfth-floor condominium on the Upper West Side. At two million dollars, bottom of the market, the place was a steal and it was the only way she could afford it at the time. And she *loved* it. The "West 90s" area wasn't as affluent as Allie's Gramercy Park residence but Emanuela didn't mind at all. It was lively but not loud, and still maintained a feeling of community that made her feel at home. She had access to theaters, art galleries and two nearby parks for recreation, and her morning commute to the financial district was less than thirty minutes whether she drove or took the train.

"I do use it," she said. "And it's beautiful but it's so *boring* in there sometimes. Half the fun of going for a jog is the people watching and smells and sounds. I could pass out *dead* in Gramercy Park and no one would find me until the maintenance people came around the next day."

Allie groaned. "Stop being dramatic. Use the key."

Emanuela stuck out her tongue at her worrywart of a best friend before changing the subject. "Are you excited for NOLA? I am. I think a change of scenery will be good for us about now."

"Oh God, I thought I'd told you…"

It was Emanuela's turn to groan. "You can't come."

Allie's face fell. "I tried to make it work! You

know I did, but I'm completely booked! *Over* booked, really. I need every available day for prep. I really was looking forward to our trip this year."

"No, I know. I get it," Emanuela said, hiding her disappointment with a small smile. "I guess we're getting too busy for these spur-of-the-moment trips, huh? Our lives are so unpredictable now."

"Wait." Allie's face lit back up again.

"Allie?" Emanuela knew that look. She could practically see the gears moving in her friend's brain.

"*My* life might be unpredictable right now but yours isn't. I mean, not consistently anyway." Allie waved off her own rambling in annoyance. "But *you* can still go!"

"No. Allie—" Emanuela shook her head. "This was supposed to be the two of us! It won't be any fun hitting the jazz festival and getting drunk all by my lonesome."

"But that's what I'm trying to tell you! You don't have to go alone. Take the good doctor with you instead! Oh my God, it's *perfect!*"

"I don't know—"

"It *IS*. Just imagine how much fun you'd have if you had a whole weekend to yourselves. No work, just good food, wine, and a big strong man to *hammer* out all your dents," she said, getting more carried away with every word.

Emanuela winced at her description. Only Allie could phrase innocent words in a way that sounded crasser than direct sexual references, but she had to admit that the idea sounded *so* good. "I do like the idea but it's such short notice."

"It's *three* weeks away! Besides, who cares? He's unemployed!"

Emanuela glared.

"He *is*, Em. Gainfully so, but still. It's not like he needs to put in for time off."

She's right! Emanuela thought, daring to hope.

"No need to reimburse me for the ticket, it's on the house," Allie said. "You need to get laid. Let this be my gift to you."

"Gee, thanks." Emanuela grimaced again.

"You're welcome, hon. I gotta run. I've got a tasting in thirty minutes." Allie gathered her things to leave. "Try not to get blue balls til then, okay? They've got apps for that." She winked wickedly before pecking Emanuela's cheek and taking off.

Emanuela shook her head, and the same grin she'd worn on her way in spread across her face. *They've got apps for that.* Boy, did she know it.

Chapter Ten

"Have I done something to offend you?"

Emanuela looked up from her notes to see Brian standing over her wearing a pained expression. "No more than usual."

He gave her a rare smile. "I expected you to go over my head in the final decision-making process but you didn't. I thought maybe you foisted the decision on me to see if I'd trip up."

The rest of the team started trickling into the firm's boardroom. The tech specialist was setting up the equipment to ensure that everyone in the room would be visible to Finn and Simon during the call. The large space was outfitted with high-backed, deep brown leather chairs, a large oak conference table, full-service mini bar, a fireplace, and a stunning view of the city's skyline.

"We might not be bosom buddies but I respect your expertise," she said. "Anyway, I couldn't have gone over your head even if I'd wanted to. Philip's call, but I liked your strategy and he agreed. You'll have the floor when the time comes."

Brian's surprise was obvious. "I—thank you, Emanuela."

She nodded just as Philip's strident voice preceded him into the boardroom. "Today's the big day! Signing day!"

He strolled in with three suited guests. Emanuela stood to greet them. She shook the hand of the petite woman whose plant would be responsible for the final assembly of the smart limbs. "Mrs. Martinez, I hope your trip here was pleasant."

"Thank you, Miss Monroe," Mrs. Martinez said. "It was comfortable. The additional information you provided was very easy to understand."

Emanuela was thrilled to learn that their firm would be signing on to work with a female head of manufacturing. It was a rare occurrence in her line of work to meet such a woman, and it was refreshing. She took personal care of any concerns the Tijuana plant leader had in preparation for their meeting.

"My pleasure." Emanuela smiled as Mrs. Martinez moved to take her seat. Then she greeted the heads of the manufacturing companies who would be making the smart limb parts. "Mr. Oliver, Mr. Vargas, pleasure to finally meet you both in person."

Introductions were made around the room, and light refreshments served before the four LCD screens in the center of the table—one facing each direction to accommodate everyone seated—lit up. The sound of an outgoing call echoed throughout the room. Emanuela's nerves fired in anticipation of seeing Finn in a matter of moments. She straightened her already impeccable clothes and smoothed her hair. Philip took his usual place next to her, handing her a coffee. The speakers crackled a second later, signaling that the call had gone through.

****

Finn's eyes narrowed, watching Philip Hurst give Emanuela her coffee before sitting much too close to

97

her, in his opinion. The armrests of the man's chair practically *stuck* to hers. He managed not to curse aloud, channeling his annoyance into a fidget by adjusting his tie.

"Good morning!" Philip said, much too cheerful for such an early hour.

Well, not for him, Finn thought. What was wrong with him? Of course the man was excited. They all were. This was a big day. He needed to get his head in the game. Thankfully, whatever contraption some benevolent geek at Hurst Capital had put together for the occasion panned the room, allowing him and Simon to become acquainted with everyone else in attendance. The sight of them all in their professional suits of armor gathered around the expensive-looking table just made it feel all the more momentous. He took a deep breath and Simon squeezed his shoulder, seeming to share the same sentiment.

"Good morning," Finn greeted everyone.

"Morning!" Simon boomed.

Emanuela's clear, assertive voice filled the room. To Finn, it seemed to reach through his speakers and caress his ears.

"To start, I'll quickly introduce our new manufacturing team and then we can take on any last questions or concerns you may have," she said, smiling into the camera.

The screen split. The larger part of the screen showed the entire room and its occupants, and the smaller one in the lower right-hand corner featured only Emanuela.

"Wow!" Simon said.

Finn lifted a single brow. He had to admit, their

geek was talented. Even in this medium, Emanuela took his breath away. Her hair was up again. It occurred to him that she might wear it that way to appear more put-together. In control. No matter, since it just drew attention to her beautiful face. She was talking. He should listen. These introductions were just a formality, of course. Everyone knew very well who the others were in attendance. They wouldn't be worth their salt if they didn't. Once the top choices for manufacturers were selected, Finn and Simon became familiar with each of them. The final decision rested with the firm, per their agreement in Seattle two weeks ago, and seeing who made the final cut impressed the pair. The camera panned again.

"Doctor Finnegan Kane and Doctor Simon Faulk," she began. "This is Gordon Oliver."

A man about Finn's age and stature appeared on the smaller screen.

"He heads PlaceMATS, a leading manufacturer of materials in Santa Clara, California. He'll be in charge of producing the artificial skin and sensors for your smart limbs."

The man nodded and Finn and Simon mirrored his greeting, and the camera panned again.

"Here is Anthony Vargas of SymBionic in Conroe, Texas, one of the biggest suppliers of robotic parts Stateside. He'll be producing all moving parts for the limbs."

Anthony was a round, balding man of medium build. He looked pissed, but it turned out to be his resting face. Finn held back a chuckle, nodding his greeting, and Simon nearly choked next to him. Finn kicked his comrade underneath the table and the camera panned again.

"Rounding out the team," Emanuela said, "is Alexandra Martinez. Her plant based in Tijuana, Mexico will assemble the components into the final products. The safe and climate-controlled storage facility is also located there."

Finn and Simon nodded in welcome at the soft visage of the bronzed, middle-aged woman who appeared on the smaller screen.

"Well done," Philip said.

For the life of him Finn couldn't figure out what the big deal was. Emanuela was amazing, that much was clear, but she had simply introduced a few people. That didn't merit high praise and a pat on her shoulder. He scowled and decided it was as good a time as any to say something-anything-to draw Philip's attention elsewhere.

"Will there be difficulty getting our products certified Made in the USA since they're to be assembled in Mexico?" he asked. "I know the label doesn't ensure quality, but that's the way things are perceived by the nation at large."

"You can take this one, Em," Philip said.

Fuck's sake. He's coddling her! Finn folded his arms across his chest.

She seemed confused for a second before she caught herself. "Thank you. I'm going to redirect to Mr. Brian Richards—"

"Just Brian," he said, interrupting in his typical manner.

Finn's jaw tightened to stop himself from smirking. *Ah, Brian the asshole.*

"Brian." Emanuela humored him. "As the head of

our financial division, he's best equipped to explain the marketing side of things. Federal Trade Commission rules can be tricky, but we've managed to come up with an approach that will guarantee the best quality of materials and construction possible," she explained. "Brian? All yours."

The camera panned again and Finn almost laughed out loud. Brian looked *exactly* the way he thought he would. That is, nothing stood out about him. He had an average build, average features and appeared to be average height. There was nothing gripping about his voice. *No wonder he's got a chip on his shoulder.* The man lacked charisma. Even now, he was talking and Finn wasn't paying attention.

"So," Brian said, "by contracting the production of individual parts for your products to well-known and respected companies here in the U.S., customers from industry to patients will be confident that what they're getting is safe and effective. Partnering with Mrs. Martinez to assemble the products saves money and creates job growth in the border region between Tijuana and San Diego..."

Brian was still talking but Finn's attention was on Emanuela's tense face. *What's that about?* She cast an apologetic look at Mrs. Martinez, who smiled back but gave Emanuela a quick nod to acknowledge her wordless apology. Whatever it was that Brian had said must've been quite the blunder. Finn looked at Philip to gauge his reaction but either he hadn't noticed or his poker face was better than Emanuela's. Finn tuned back in.

"Although the smart limbs will be assembled in Mexico, their individual parts will be made in the U.S., so they will fully comply with FTC standards. Storage is on-site and transport is much more cost-effective from Mexico into the United States than from overseas."

Emanuela looked into the LCD monitor nearest her, her warm smile reaching her eyes. Finn read her sympathetic expression and softened his features in response. This was a tedious task, and he knew she was working hard to make it seamless for his benefit. The manufacturers had to be flown in to sign non-disclosure agreements in person, in front of the firm's business lawyer and a notary. Finn hated to admit it, but he was grateful that Philip had been adamant about including him and Simon in the process. Full disclosure all the way through.

At that moment, Finn couldn't have repeated what Brian said if he was asked because Philip's hand was on Emanuela's arm and her attention was diverted. The gesture wouldn't have put him on edge if Philip's hand hadn't remained on her arm the entire time he spoke…and she wasn't leaning into him.

What the hell?

Finn watched her nod and search for something briefly, her brow creased in mild consternation. Then Philip handed her something. *What is that?* Finn wondered, and then he recognized the small object. *A pen?*

He grunted because he couldn't curse. Simon cut his eyes at him in question and Finn shook his head dismissively. *This is taking* forever. *Just get on with it.*

Emanuela scribbled some notes and then excused herself during Brian's too-long speech. Finn made a mental note to ask Simon for his annotated version later.

"If there are no further questions," Philip said at last, "we'll get the signing underway." He surveyed the room and the monitors to confirm that no one had anything to add. Satisfied, he addressed the pair on the screens. "I'd offer you gentlemen some refreshment if you were here." He smiled. "It'll just be a moment." He turned his earnest attention to Mrs. Martinez in a private conversation to the side.

Finn had already disengaged. The others were talking amongst themselves, so Simon turned to his friend with avid curiosity. "How long has *that* been a thing?" he asked, too low for anyone but Finn to hear.

"What do you mean?"

"Don't give me a hard time. You were in a good mood this morning, then all of a sudden you got antsy, you couldn't keep still, and you've still got that constipated look on your face. I can multitask, you know. Your fidgeting and your attitude got worse every time a certain lovely lady showed up on our screen."

Finn didn't say anything. He bit his lip in agitation and shifted in his seat.

"What I couldn't seem to figure out during this little show," Simon said, undaunted, "is *why*? I can't imagine she's done anything in the short time we've known her to cause you any upset. And then I realized it isn't her. It's you."

Finn cut his eyes at his friend, his expression flat.

"That was jealousy on your face, plain as day," Simon said.

Before Finn could respond, Emanuela returned with a slight, gray-haired woman who carried a clipboard and file. "Okay," Emanuela said. "What do you say we go ahead and make it official?"

Cheers erupted around the table and Finn was caught up in the moment right along with everyone else. A year ago, this was a fading dream. Finn had hoped to get this far, and here it was, happening right before his eyes. He felt many things in that moment; grateful, relieved, vindicated. But he couldn't shake the feeling that something was missing. He thought he would feel *content*. Where was that emotion? Watching Emanuela shake hands and congratulate her colleagues brought the feeling of longing back that he seemed unable to escape at just the thought of her. He ran his fingers through his hair and sighed.

"Maybe it wasn't just jealousy," Simon said, squeezing Finn's shoulder again.

He didn't push any further and Finn offered him a small smile of gratitude.

"I'm so sorry." Emanuela was speaking to them now.

A few of the others stayed behind, finishing their refreshments and talking in hushed tones. Philip was speaking with all three manufacturers near the mini bar.

"I know this isn't how you'd prefer to spend your morning. Thanks for being patient with us and the formality of it all," she said with a smile.

"No, thank *you*, Emanuela!" said Simon. "This has been a very informative and rewarding process. It's intriguing to see all of the moving parts of this machine working together."

Finn would have agreed in any other instant but he wasn't feeling like himself, so he attempted a halfhearted smile. Emanuela's smile seemed to falter in response, but Philip and the new manufacturing team drew their attention away to offer congratulations and farewells before they took their leave, and then it was just the three of them again.

"I need to wrap a few things up here, but feel free to call me if anything comes up," Emanuela said.

"It was so good to see you again, Emanuela!"

"It was *great* to see you, Simon."

"Take care."

Emanuela smiled after him and then focused her uneasy gaze on Finn. "I can call in a few hours, after I've finished up here."

"I'd like that," he said. "I'll talk to you soon."

****

"Are you okay, Finn?"

Emanuela was having an unappetizing lunch in her office. It was the first chance she'd had all day to talk to him alone. She sensed that something was up after the meeting, but she was forced to put this conversation on hold for a pile of paperwork a mile high and what amounted to a scolding from her boss.

"Quite honestly, I'm not sure how to answer that."

Dread crept into her throat, but she tried not to let it become evident in her voice. "I—can you just tell me what's wrong?"

Ordinarily, she would be up for the challenge of using her exceptional powers of perception to figure it out. Deep down, she knew the root of his anxiety because she felt it herself, but right now her heart was beating too loud and her head hurt too much so he would have to word it as best he could.

"Please," she said.

He sighed. "What was that, between you and Philip?"

"Oh, you saw that?"

"It was kind of hard not to."

She bristled a little at his tone. "I thought it would be…I don't know…a show of good faith, to defer your question to Brian. I laid into him at our last meeting and I don't usually do that, although he tends to deserve it…" She was rambling "Your question, ideally, would have been better answered by him instead of me. I overstepped by letting Brian take your question after Philip delegated to me and he embarrassed us as well as Mrs. Martinez."

"I don't think I understand—"

"Brian is great at what he does," she said. "But he doesn't have the best bedside manner. It was totally inappropriate for him to mention that we'd be saving money by contracting with Mrs. Martinez' company. It implied that we wanted to work with her merely as a means to an end and not for the quality of the services she can provide. Had I simply answered the question like Philip intended, this wouldn't have happened. We've apologized, of course, and our partnership with her still stands, but it's just not a great foot to start off on."

"Emanuela. God, I'm so sorry," he said. "I feel like a complete ass. I noticed an awkward moment between you and Mrs. Martinez but I confess I wasn't paying much attention to what Brian was saying."

"You were watching me."

"I was. And Philip."

She sucked in a breath. "Finn—"

"I don't want to text you. I don't want to call you—"

"*Finn!* I know the past two weeks have

been…difficult. The time apart is wearing on me, too. How are other couples able to navigate long distance relationships when we can't even survive thirteen days?"

"Emanuela…"

"Because we aren't a couple and this isn't a relationship." She scoffed. "You're about to break up with me and we aren't even together."

"*Emanuela,* I don't want to do those things because I want to *see* you. I want to hug you and kiss you and hold your hand—things *normal* people do when they're dating."

She sobbed. He'd almost given her a heart attack.

"See?" he said with an exasperated sigh. "Right now—*right now* I should be holding you."

A burst of laughter ripped through Emanuela's body. Even to her own ears, it sounded broken. Beautifully broken. Like wind chimes in a storm.

"Emanuela?"

"Come to New Orleans with me."

"What?"

"I'd planned to go with Allie, but she's booked from now until eternity, so I'm asking you. Come with me. I was going to ask you anyway but now just seemed like a good time to bring it up."

"When?"

"Two weeks from now. It's only a weekend, but it's the whole weekend. It's more than we've had altogether so far and I'm really…I miss you."

It was quiet for what felt like an eternity, and she was sure Finn was trying to think of any obligations that would keep him from seeing her.

"Okay," he said at last.

"Okay?" She knew what Okay meant but she needed to hear it again so she could play it over and over in her head, so that it was real.

"Nothing could keep me away."

Chapter Eleven

Finn spotted her before she saw him. She was off to the side, out of the way of the crowd of passengers swarming the baggage claim conveyor belts. Emanuela leaned against a white pillar, glowing and beautiful in her yellow sundress with her hair down in soft waves, the way he liked it. Her eyes were searching. She'd arrived the night before. He'd texted her when he landed fifteen minutes ago and now he smiled. She was looking for him. He was halfway down the escalator when her eyes finally found him.

Time is such a peculiar thing, the only constant in life, the only thing that can be trusted as fact. It's when something happened and for how long. Right now, time betrayed its constancy. For a moment, the loud hum of chatter, busy footsteps moving about, wheeled suitcases rolling across the floor, and periodic announcements over the PA system blended into meaningless white noise. Even the pace of his own heartbeat wasn't certain. It seemed to move faster, pounding in his chest during the crowded escalator's slow descent. It stopped altogether by the time he reached the bottom. For how long, he couldn't be sure. Damn time. It wasn't until his feet touched solid ground again, gravity planting him to smooth, polished linoleum that time picked back up.

He stood before her moments later, sensing her hesitation. She drew her bottom lip into her mouth as if contemplating how she should greet him. It was a long, nearly unbearable month apart. Though they had shared many intimate moments over the last four weeks, exchanged countless "I miss yous," and imagined this exact moment countless more, insecurity and doubt had needled at them both, because whatever this new thing was remained undefined. All of that melted away for Finn, who dropped his garment bag to the floor, his eyes never leaving Emanuela's, and reached for her.

His strong arms circled her waist and hauled her to him in a bear hug, her feet leaving the floor. Her arms rose to his shoulders and she buried her face in his neck, breathing him in. He did the same, turning his face into her hair and taking a long, slow drag.

"You smell so good," he mumbled against her neck.

He felt her smile. "You too," she murmured, not moving her face from the cozy nook in the curve of his shoulder. He wasn't sure how long he held her when her body relaxed against him, allowing him to hold her up. He smiled against her neck and then pecked his way to her ear.

"Hey you," he whispered, pulling away enough to look into her flushed face.

"Hey back."

Her tone was in that place just above a whisper that Finn knew took over whenever she was overcome with emotion. The clamor of their surroundings came back to them in full force and they reluctantly pulled apart. He hoisted his bag over his shoulder with one hand and reached for her hand with the other.

"How was your flight?" she asked, leading them toward the taxi depot.

"Long. But worth it." He looked pointedly at her and watched the pretty blush paint her cheeks again.

The crowds rolling into the Crescent City for the Jazz and Heritage Festival made it difficult to hail a cab on the fly. The exasperated looks on the faces in the long line said it all.

"This is madness," he said.

She just smiled and led him past the throng to the end of the line of taxies on the curb. A 1981 vintage marathon yellow checkered cab sat proudly at the back. Its curved corners and smooth lines stood out among the more modern taxis with their boxy shapes and big windows.

"Wow," Finn said. "This is amazing."

"I 'preciate dat," the driver said humbly, putting Finn's garment bag in the trunk and moving to open the back door.

Finn waited for Emanuela to slide in and scoot to the other side before ducking into the refurbished beauty himself.

"This is Morris," she said as the driver took his seat. "This cab's been in his family for almost forty years now. We've got him for the whole weekend."

"Miss Monroe is real generous," Morris said in his lilting drawl.

Emanuela smiled at him in the rearview mirror. "Well, you came very highly recommended."

"Nice to meet you, Morris," Finn said warmly.

He glanced at Emanuela and decided she was sitting too far away. "C'mere," he said, curving his arm around her waist and pulling her to him.

They were hip to hip, his long thigh against hers, and they sighed contentedly. He kissed the top of her head and she leaned into him. They were starting to relax into their easy company, any initial uncertainty after so much time apart replaced by the need to be close to each other.

Finn caught Morris's smiling glance in the rearview mirror, and then Morris navigated toward the 10 South. Traffic wasn't too bad during the half hour ride from the airport to the French Quarter, the "Voo ka-RAY," Morris called it. He entertained them with stories of drunken Mardi Gras passengers, and even weddings he was hired for to escort eccentric couples to the airport on their way to their honeymoon adventures.

Morris charmed them with his unique intonation, expertly steering the sleek little cab until the streets looked very exotic indeed. Finn took in the view from his window with awe, feeling Emanuela's gentle squeeze on his knee. There were people *everywhere*. An eclectic crowd filled each sidewalk beneath stunning displays of ornate balconies dripping with colorful bouquets. Morris carefully advanced through the busy streets until he turned onto Royal Street. It was as though every street leading up to it was merely to prepare for the visual impact of its bohemian elegance.

"Wow," Finn said again.

"I think this is one of the most gorgeous things I've ever seen and this isn't even my first time seeing it," Emanuela said.

He looked at her without a word, mirroring her expression, and her cheeks flushed.

At last, they stopped in front of The Cornstalk Fence Hotel, a magnificent, two-story Victorian house on Royal. It was tucked between two larger inns, resplendent with their charming balconies and centered in the heart of the French Quarter. Its wrought-iron fence boasted intricate carvings of slender cornstalks and wrapped all the way around a quaint little courtyard. It looked every bit the historic monument it was purported to be. White steps led to a small porch, and four white pillars held up the second floor balcony. Finn helped Emanuela out onto the sidewalk, and Morris retrieved Finn's bags.

"You call me when you need another ride, Miss Monroe." Morris tipped his well-worn cap.

"I will. Thanks again, Morris!" she said, returning his smile.

The moment Morris pulled off, the air between them changed. Finn's spine tingled at the knowledge that they had the entire weekend together. His pure joy at seeing her again transformed into the familiar intense longing that simmered beneath the surface whenever he was near her. They stood on the sidewalk, staring at each other.

"Emanuela," he said with a knowing smile.

She snapped out of her trance and walked through the beautiful front gate, narrowly missing bumping into it in her flustered state. He followed her with a wide grin on his face. The charge between them was always there, even thousands of miles apart, but it was strongest with no other immediate distractions—when it was just the two of them.

He followed her through the small courtyard, past the French fountain and intimate seating area toward the entrance. He was sure he'd have plenty of other opportunities to appreciate the landscape, but right now his eyes were locked on her legs. Her calves were exquisitely defined as she walked, the sound of her strappy brown wedges knocking against the pavement. She led him up the steps and into the house, the light fabric of her sundress stopping at the perfect place, giving him a peek of her toned thighs.

****

The interior of the little boutique hotel was stunning. It was fourteen feet from floor to ceiling, with gold leaf trimming and crystal chandeliers that seemed to blossom from their hanging chains. The deep burgundy floors and soft lighting created quite a romantic atmosphere, and suddenly the place Emanuela and Allie had originally considered "cute" seemed very suggestive.

She cleared her throat and led them past gilded mirrors and antique furnishings on either side. Vintage portraits in their elaborate frames shared golden yellow papered walls with sconces overflowing with greenery. The distance from the foyer to the beautiful stairwell with its fancy balusters, detailed moldings and painted cherubs overhead had seemed insignificant to her when she first arrived. Now it seemed to take an eternity.

Her back felt heated from the steady gaze she knew Finn held on her and she swallowed, somehow managing to make it up the flight of stairs without tripping over herself. Turning once at the landing and again at the top of the stairs, she opened her mouth for the first time since greeting the concierge.

"I'm sorry about the stairs," she said, her voice raspier than she intended.

"These are okay," he said of the short steps.

She looked back at him and smiled. "It's just down the hall."

He nodded and continued to follow her down a

similar long hallway that was even more dimly lit than the one downstairs until they arrived at their room. "Room 112," it said on the door. One other room shared the end of the hall with them, directly across, with an exit to a shared balcony between them. Her hands were shaking, but she miraculously got the door open and walked through without incident. If the ambiance seemed suggestive, then the room was positively *sexy.*

The Victorian French décor was romantic by design. Although the heavier golden curtains of the room's two larger windows were drawn, the harsh light of day was filtered into the room through translucent white draperies. The other sources of light came from a stained glass window in the tiny nook in a corner of the room opposite the door, a small crystal chandelier and two red-shaded lamps. The soft lighting combined with the intricate pattern of deep red and gold adorning the walls made it feel very much like a lover's cove.

The most prominent feature of the room was a single queen sized bed. Regal and inviting, its frame raised the mattress high off the floor. It was dressed in plush silken fabric in golden tones, its four posters reaching for the ceiling. Antique furniture, gilded mirrors and a gorgeous carved fireplace gave the room the appearance of guest quarters at some wealthy eighteenth-century French residence. Finn set down his bag near the bed, turning around once to take it all in.

"There's just the one," Emanuela said, feeling oddly inclined to explain why there was only one bed. She looked at him cautiously, just a few feet away, trying to feel him out. "Allie and I make these trips all the time and we tend to share a room. It was kind of short notice, I know. This place was fully booked and this is the biggest room with a balcony view. I didn't think you'd mind—"

"You're right," Finn said, looking dead at her. "I don't mind. I have no intention of sleeping anywhere but with you."

Her lips parted and she sucked in a breath, lowering her eyes. He cursed and snatched her to him. She gasped in surprise from the sudden movement but there was no time to think because he'd crushed her to him, taking her mouth with his. The force of the action knocked him against the door and her with him. He wasn't gentle and she didn't care. She was flush against him, almost on her toes, her arms wrapped around his neck to desperately pull him to her.

"Ah! Emanuela," he groaned against her lips. "Baby, you're gonna break my neck."

He pinned her to him with an arm around her waist. He slid his other hand into her hair, gripping the curls at the base of her neck and gently pulling her head back so he could control the kiss. She didn't complain because he was kissing her like he'd been starved for her. There were no soft presses, no tender pecks to coax her mouth open for him. He plundered her lips, sucking each one, biting the bottom before sucking her tongue into his mouth.

She tingled all over, her blood rushing through her, heating her entire body and bringing a blush to her neck and face. They were messy, their mouths devouring and noses pressing against each other's cheeks. His tongue retreated and she grazed it with her teeth, nipping his lips with hers. She could feel his response and ground hard against it, breaking their kiss to exhale on a shaky sigh.

"So greedy," he said, tugging her head back just a little farther to drag his open mouth along her neck. He licked the rapid pulse there, his tongue in tune to the swirl of her hips and matching her rhythm.

"I missed you," she breathed, grabbing his arm from her waist to guide his hand to her hips.

He released her neck to grip her ass in both of his hands; pressing her to him and up, over and over again, each time bringing her to her toes. "*Oh my God*," he moaned.

No other words were necessary. Everything had been building up to this. It was so much more than what she imagined each night they spent apart, but not nearly enough now that she was in his arms.

Emanuela panted at the direct contact of his arousal rubbing against her and the pressure building within her. She clutched his arms, feeling herself tense already, just moments from her release.

A loud knock sounded against the door. She yelped, grasping at Finn so she wouldn't fall. She nearly cried out her frustration. He kissed her again, gently this time, reassuring her and swallowing the sounds she was making.

"Sssshhhh," he whispered, kissing her soundly one more time. He set her back on her heels and straightened her dress.

The knock came again.

"Cleaning service," a courteous feminine voice rang out.

****

Finn adjusted himself to hide the evidence of their impassioned reunion the best he could. He gently tugged Emanuela by the hand, guiding her behind him before opening the door. "Hi," he said in his most charming tone. "I've only just arrived and I'd like to get out of my travel clothes. Do you think you could come back in twenty?" He gave the poor cleaning lady an arresting smile just for good measure.

Emanuela stifled a giggle at the woman's stammered response.

"I— Y-yes, I can do that for you, s-sir. Twenty minutes, okay."

"Thank you," he said politely, moving to close the door.

Emanuela's lusty laugh rang throughout the room that was thick with sexual tension just moments earlier.

He turned to look at her with a puzzled smile. "What?"

"Nothing," she said, doubled over, her face flushed from laughter. "It's just that she probably heard us. I lost track of the time. They clean the rooms from ten until two. I think we traumatized her." She laughed again. "She might not come back."

"Good." He reached for her again.

"Uh-uh." She pushed at his chest to halt the trail of his lips across her shoulder.

"I was kidding. She'll be back."

He was at her collarbone now. "In twenty minutes."

She giggled and shoved him away. "Change. I have plans for us today."

Finn eyed her. "Oh?"

"GO!" She laughed again.

He pulled away with a searing look, every bit as handsome as the last time she'd seen him. He'd traveled in casual gray slacks, loafers and a cool blue Henley, buttoned down and pushed up to his elbows. He was a bit disheveled, his clothes wrinkled and his wavy hair tousled in front where a few curls fell onto his forehead from her less-than-gentle ministrations.

He picked up his bag and leaned in to kiss her cheek. "Fine." His honeyed voice filled her ear. "But this is a rain check, not a cancellation."

Heat filled her cheeks again at his boyish charm, and he strolled into the bathroom.

****

They walked hand-in-hand along Dumaine Street, just a few minutes' walk from their hotel on Royal. The streets were filled to the brim by now with eager tourists on foot, in carriages, and cars, some even stopping to take pictures of their hotel. Emanuela was taking them in the opposite direction of most of the tourist traffic, away from the main attractions of the French Quarter.

"Are you hungry?" She ducked behind him to make room for others on the sidewalk for a moment, never letting go of his hand.

"Starving," he said, pulling her back to his side.

"I know the perfect place."

The buildings started to look older and less maintained and he tilted his head at her.

"Trust me?" she asked.

He chuckled at her childlike enthusiasm. Seeing her this way, dressed down and carefree, added a new dimension to whatever was growing between them. She was still sexy and charismatic and strong, but this relaxed side of her endeared her to him all the more.

"I trust you."

"See that bus?" She pointed to the city bus stopped

at the corner about a hundred feet away. People were still disembarking. She turned to him again. "We have to get on it."

She was definitely up to something. Finn had no time to speculate because she took off jogging, pulling him along with her. They filed onto the bus, two of the last people to get on, and Emanuela fished some coins from her wristlet and dropped them into the dispenser for both of them. There was standing room only, so she grabbed onto a pole. The bus pulled away, and he stood behind her, shielding her from bumping into other passengers.

The crowded bus meant that people were consciously looking out of windows or down at their phones, angling their bodies the best they could to avoid undue physical contact with other passengers. The terrain was flat, since most of New Orleans was at or below sea level, but there were a few bumps in the road and each one brought her body closer to his. He snaked an arm around her, settling his palm across her tummy, and kissed the top of her head.

"Where are you taking me?" he asked with mock concern.

She slid her hand over his to interlock their fingers and turned her head to the side to answer. "Nervous? I wouldn't put you in harm's way."

"I know. Not unless I asked you to."

She giggled. "I'm not one of those kinky women you dated before."

He lowered his face to her ear. "That's not how I remember it."

He heard her moan only because his cheek was pressed to hers. He thought about letting up on her but he was enjoying it too much. He increased the pressure of his hand, moving it slightly lower on her tummy.

"I seem to remember that you like to be bitten," he said in his lowest register, letting his warm breath moisten the curve of her ear. She shuddered against him, and he would have taken a nip of her ear for good measure, but the bus's stop bell sounded and the pair stood up straighter, remembering where they were.

They shuffled out of the way of people getting off, and Emanuela checked their surroundings. The cross street said Burgundy.

"Almost there," she said, relaxing into his hold once again. "Two more stops."

He looked out of the window at the stark change in scenery. The hanging gardens of the French Quarter were forgotten, replaced by the concrete landscape spread out before them. Rundown tenements and shotgun houses emerged on each side of the road, and small mom and pop establishments could be seen nestled between them and on street corners. Few tourists were about, mingling with the locals in search of authentic fare without the exorbitant prices and commercial feel of popular tourist haunts.

"This is us," Emanuela said.

The bus stopped at a corner across the street from a bright pink, two-story building. A big *Welcome to Festival Season at Gene's* sign hung from its second-story balcony. They followed other exiting passengers off the bus and he reached for her hand. They were both tourists here and, although he knew she was more than capable of taking care of herself anywhere, he felt protective of her. They used the crosswalk and headed right for the pink building.

A simple white sign said *GENE'S PO-BOY* in big block letters. Five large yellow signs nailed to the side of the building advertised an ATM for only ninety-nine cents and no fewer than *three* of those signs advertised the *Hot Sausage & Cheese Po Boy.*

"Just in case there was any doubt about what we were gonna order," Finn said.

The inside was much like any fast food establishment. There was no fuss about atmosphere or ambiance. The checkered floors could've used a scrub but weren't filthy, and the display behind the counter held big yellow signs just like the ones outside.

"Man, it smells incredible in here," Finn said, breathing in the smell of cooking meat and warm bread.

"I know. I'm salivating," Emanuela said.

He ordered their food and led them to a small table in the dining area. Her eyes widened. "Wow, these are huge."

"Half as big as you are." He grinned, digging into his massive po boy.

His taste buds went nuts. The damn thing was sloppy, the "dressings" making the sandwich's contents slide off repeatedly, but he didn't care.

"Oh my God," Emanuela moaned, swiping a bit of food off her chin and popping it into her mouth.

"Do that again."

"Shurrup," she said, her mouth still full.

"This is amazing." He started in on the second half of his sandwich. He couldn't decide what he loved more, the soft, buttery French bread with its crunchy crust, or the spicy sausage squished between all the dressings. "How'd you find this place?"

She'd nearly polished off the rest of the half

sandwich, licking the corners of her mouth before chasing it down with her drink. "Morris recommended it on my way to get you. It's his favorite spot for po boys and he's friends with the owner."

"And Morris? How'd you meet him?"

He waited for her to finish her latest bite, smiling at the way she tucked into it without vanity. She wasn't vulgar about it, just—*normal*. She was extraordinary in every way, so elegant and refined. Those things were still true now. It occurred to him, not for the first time since meeting her, how quickly they became comfortable with each other.

She looked thoughtful for a moment, then wiped her mouth to answer him. "Before Katrina, Morris had a small but very successful taxi business. He had six cars serving the whole city. It may not've been fancy, but he and his drivers built up a great reputation because of how well they treated their passengers, and because of their great recommendations for places to see. After the storm hit, he lost all but two cars, including the pretty one he drove us in."

Finn smiled, knowing first-hand how charming and warm Morris was from their ride earlier that morning. He was sad to hear what happened to him.

"I found Morris's letter by chance," she said. "It'd been mistakenly added to the testimonials section of our firm's website. I guess some intern screwed up but I saw it and removed it before anyone else took notice. At the time, I wouldn't have dared suggest to Philip that we help him out."

He looked at her at the mention of her boss's name. He hadn't mentioned his reservations about Philip. He wasn't certain of his own standing with her. They were just getting to know each other and he didn't see any pressing reason to bring it up.

"What did you do?" he asked.

"I sent him some money. I didn't have much yet but I couldn't just respond with some generic, *Sorry about your loss. Wish we could help.* The first checks were for two hundred dollars every month for that first year. Gradually, as I made more money, I sent more until he was back on his feet. Then, two years ago, I made an anonymous donation. I can't say for sure that it's what got his taxi business back up and running again, but a part of me hopes it's true. I contacted him when Allie and I first started planning this trip to see if he could be available for the whole weekend, at an increased rate, of course."

"Of course." He grinned and reached under the table to squeeze her knee. "You're so good. Like an angel helping people in need."

She blushed again. "I don't know about that. I just came across a hardworking man's unfortunate story and did what was in my capacity to help. Besides," she said, lowering her voice, "I'm not sure you'll still think so after our next stop."

He lifted a brow, trying to read her expression. *Naughty*, he thought, feeling his pulse race. "And where might that be?"

"You'll have to wait and see."

They disposed of their mess and headed back out into the hot New Orleans spring day.

Chapter Twelve

"Not what I was expecting," Finn said, looking around.

Almost every available surface, including much of the floor, in the small space was filled with Yoruba and Christian art, statues, and artifacts. Over a dozen voodoo dolls kept each other company on an altar of sorts, surrounded by gifts from former visitors, money offerings and even Mardis Gras beads. The heavy scent of incense and burned candles seemed to filter from the very walls. Finn raised his hand to touch a tall wooden statue that came almost to his shoulder, an unused cigarette in its mouth and lifted a brow at Emanuela.

"And just what *were* you expecting?" she asked with a tilt of her head.

His lips twitched, undoubtedly to spout a flippant response, but he was interrupted before he had the chance. A handsome, full figured woman with terracotta skin and a kind smile joined them in the foyer of one of the French Quarter's most storied voodoo temples. She wore a white peasant top with a deep neckline, revealing a generous bosom, and her dark curls peeked from beneath a red headscarf. Her long, full red skirt swept the floor when she moved.

"Welcome," her soothing voice greeted them. "I'm Priestess Felicie. Have you ever had a reading before?"

"Never," Emanuela said, and Finn shook his head.

They were enamored of the woman already. It was hard not to be, so captivating was her aura coupled with the mystery of the place.

"Well there's nothing to be afraid of," she said. "I'm going to start off with a snake reading to prepare you—"

Emanuela's soft gasp made the Priestess laugh.

"*Nothing* to be afraid of," Priestess Felicie said again.

A python, none too small, materialized from somewhere behind her. Emanuela willed herself to stay put. It may have been fear, despite the kind woman's reassurances, of what the snake would do if she moved suddenly that kept her planted where she stood.

Finn took a deep breath and watched, his brows stuck in their elevated position. The Priestess raised the snake above her head, its body writhing slowly, its tail curling around her wrist.

"Cross your arms over your chest," she told Emanuela.

Emanuela did as instructed, controlling her breathing, making an effort to will away her anxiety. The woman lifted the snake over Emanuela's head, raising and lowering the reptile until she'd walked a complete circle around her.

"This is an uncrossing." Priestess Felicie took Emanuela's hands and lowered them to extend out in front of her.

She looked into Emanuela's eyes, and calm came over Emanuela. Though she was still not fond of the snake, her apprehension was gone. The Priestess brought the creature forward and allowed it to curl around Emanuela's outstretched arms for just a moment. It slithered over her skin, cold and a little unnerving.

"The negative energy will leave you now so it won't be a distraction during our time together."

She smiled at Emanuela and moved to repeat the ritual on Finn. He didn't look afraid at all. He seemed more intrigued than anything else, open to whatever was about to happen.

Priestess Felicie smiled at him. "I can feel that you are very transparent. Everything is there on the surface to see." It wasn't a compliment. It was an observation. "Follow me," she told them, walking through a beaded doorway.

The inner temple was small, with even more gifts and artifacts filling the space. Several candles were lit throughout the room, and there was a clearing in the middle of the room where the floor was worn but very clean.

"Please sit," the Priestess said, indicating two cloth-covered chairs on the edge of the clearing.

Finn pushed their chairs closer together and patted Emanuela's knee when she sat down. The Priestess selected a glass jar full of a powdery yellow substance from a shelf and knelt on the floor. She poured the yellow powder onto the floor, using it to draw snake-like figures parallel to each other and spaced apart. "When our time together was scheduled, I was told I would be meeting with best friends."

"I'm sorry," Emanuela said. "She wasn't able to make it this time because she was tied up at work."

She smiled at Finn, who took her hand in his. Priestess Felicie completed the drawing with her powder. She seemed bemused but didn't respond right away, drawing a cross at the top of the space between the snakes, and three sunbursts down the center. Then, she stood and walked the short distance to her seat at a small cloth-covered table.

"I see no error," she said, looking at them candidly. "Except that yours is no ordinary friendship. There's more to it than that, but you didn't come here for advice about love or relationships."

Once again, she was making an observation and didn't require a response from either of them. Emanuela eyes met Finn's at the mention of the words *love* and *relationships*. She'd stiffened in her seat and her face flushed. They had yet to discuss who or what they were to each other. They were so happy to be in the same place that they were using the time to simply enjoy each other.

The Priestess interrupted her thoughts. "That is your *veve*." She indicated the drawing on the floor. "It is the voodoo spirit of courage."

"Courage?" Finn asked.

The Priestess smiled at him and looked at Emanuela. "I think we could all use a little more courage, don't you?"

Emanuela met her eyes and felt as though Priestess Felicie was speaking to her alone.

"I'd say so," Finn said with a smile.

Emanuela swallowed and looked at Finn. He was enjoying this. She had to admit that it wasn't what she thought it would be. The place certainly had its quirks—the many shrines or altars and the amalgam of seemingly random objects that made their home here. This was no spooky session of spells or conjurations. It felt like talking to an advisor or a close family friend.

"We're going to let the spirit of courage dwell with us for a while." The Priestess picked up her stones, gave them a shake within her palms and cast them on the table in front of her.

Emanuela didn't know what the series of lines and symbols on the cloth covering the table meant. It could have been a game of Backgammon for all she could discern. Priestess Felicie looked at the orientation of the stones with great concentration, her hands clasped for several long moments. Finn and Emanuela looked at each other just as the silence started to stretch, and then the priestess spoke again. "This journey you're taking is very important," she said, alternating her gaze between the pair. "You both have some important decisions to make. These decisions will require a great deal of courage to overcome any barriers that might stand in your way."

"Our journey *here*?" Emanuela asked, wondering if this weekend held some great significance. She felt Finn's thumb moving gently over the back of her hand in encouragement.

The Priestess smiled at Emanuela, her voice warm. "Your journey to my home is temporary. The journey I'm talking about has more permanence. If you want to take it together, you will have to search your hearts. It is there that you should seek your answers. Don't let your minds overtake you. Many a mind has ruined the desires of the heart. It seems to me that you both know your minds very well..." She paused a moment, lifting her head like she was receiving a message from some higher power. "Whatever is in your hearts, I hope you'll share it with each other, or the energy I sense between you will consume you both."

Though her words held some foreboding, the silence after she spoke to them was comforting. If the spirit of courage really did exist, it was sitting with them, holding their hands or their hearts or *whatever* it was that spirits did.

Priestess Felicie stood to extinguish the candles about the room. "You're welcome to enjoy the courtyard and the museum if you like."

They followed the priestess back to the foyer.

"Thank you for seeing us," Finn said. "I had my reservations but I feel honored that you shared your wisdom with us."

"Yes." Emanuela smiled. "Thank you so much!"

She wouldn't have taken the Priestess for a hugger, but hug them she did, and disappeared through the beaded doorway.

****

Jackson Square teemed with street vendors. The tantalizing smells of frying pastry dough, and a savory smorgasbord of New Orleans' most celebrated cuisine hung thick in the humid air. Brass bands marched around the outskirts of the square and down the streets of the Quarter, playing unique renditions of Jazz's most beloved songs. Artists of every kind hawked their wares, their voices lost in a bedlam of foot traffic, street performers and city sounds the moment Finn and Emanuela walked past them.

Though they'd stuffed themselves at Gene's just a couple of hours ago, Finn's mouth watered more and more with every vendor they passed. They came upon a food truck whose umbrella proudly displayed *Pandora's Snowballs* and Emanuela's eyes widened at the spectacular array of colorful flavors. Finn smiled knowingly and shook his head, following her to the end of the line.

They took a lazy stroll through the square, appreciating the sights and sounds as they savored their frozen treats. Emanuela's snow cone disappeared quickly and Finn couldn't resist a peck to her blue-tinged lips. Another kiss to her nose brought a giggle and then she was distracted by an incredible display of impressionist folk art, stopping to stare at the paintings in awe.

"Hi," she said to the artist. "These are stunning! Especially this one." She pointed to the piece that caught her eye.

"I'm Lily," the artist said with a smile. "That one is near and dear to my heart. The subjects are real people and the music they were playing that night had so much *feeling*. I just had to capture it."

Finn leaned in closer, admiring the way Lily was able to illustrate the glow of a French street lamp, and the way it lit up a clear New Orleans night as two jazz musicians played their saxophone and cello. "Amazing. I love their facial expressions. They're really feeling the music."

"Thank you," Lily said. "They were very much one with the music they played. I would have been content to just watch them play if it wasn't for my itchy painter's hand."

It was no surprise to Finn that Emanuela bought the piece. From the time they spent video chatting with each other, he remembered she had a love for impressionist art. Her immaculate walls were covered with beautiful pieces, and he thought about how great it would be to see them in person and hear how she acquired each one. The familiar pang of longing hit him again but he pushed it down, somewhere in his gut where it wouldn't ruin their time together. *I just have to wait for the right time.*

Emanuela gave Lily her address and a check so the one of a kind piece could be mailed to her, and then she tugged Finn along, eager to return to their hotel to get ready for yet *another* surprise.

"Are you tired?" she asked. The hotel was just a five-minute walk from Jackson Square, but she was mindful of Finn's leg.

"Just a little." He squeezed her hand. "I wouldn't mind taking a break with you for a little while before you subject me to whatever mischief you have planned." He gave her his most devastating smile.

She mis-stepped and his smile widened.

"Don't get any ideas," she said, turning onto Royal Street. "We have to look pretty for where we're going so you can't go messing up my hard work."

He couldn't imagine it taking any effort for her to look gorgeous, but he kept that thought to himself, following her through the tiny crowd of people taking photos of their hotel and inside to their room.

****

They sat on the communal balcony just outside of their room, people watching and talking quietly to each other. The space could seat six, and they had it all to themselves. Emanuela's chair was pulled up close to Finn's, their seats touching to form a small loveseat. Her thighs rested across his lap, her legs and bare feet dangling at his side. He caressed her smooth skin absentmindedly.

"I can't believe we're here," he said.

"Me neither. I can't believe any of it, really. I mean, what are the odds of a story like ours? Your story alone is pretty incredible."

"You looked me up. Well, of course you did. You're very thorough."

Emanuela averted her gaze for a moment.

"Don't be embarrassed." He bent to kiss her shoulder. "I looked you up too. A few times, in fact." He grinned at her surprised expression. "I had the basics down, of course. Any good entrepreneur is part stalker. I already knew you were beautiful." His hand moved just under the hem of her dress. "And sexy." She trembled, and he smiled into her neck.

Her hand caught and held his naughty one before he could get carried away. His lips continued to trail her neck and she swallowed. "It was a little different for me. I knew nothing about you before we met, and then suddenly you were everywhere. Everyone wanted a piece of Finnegan Kane's pie."

His chuckle tickled her skin. "I didn't know what to expect. Professionally, I knew you were impressive. I'm pretty sure you could make a book from the pages I read about you."

"Really?" His lips moved to her collarbone and her shoulder rose involuntarily.

"Mmmhmm," he mumbled against her skin, quickly losing interest in what he was saying.

"And?" She giggled, taking his face in her hands to stop him from burying it in her chest.

"And"—his eyes met hers—"I knew I felt a strong attraction to you, but I thought I would be able to handle a working relationship anyway. Why not? We live on different coasts and I just had to get through the weekend. Easy. I didn't think you'd rope me in the way you did the second you walked into that restaurant. I realized I'd been lying to myself, psyching myself up probably. But I'm glad it happened."

Her body went slack, melting against his chest. "I felt the same way," she whispered.

He didn't say anything else. He looked at her lips and relaxed his smile, smoothing the crinkles around his eyes. He watched them part in anticipation, then bent to kiss her. He loved the feel of her lips on his, so soft and full. It seemed like they were made for long, leisurely presses, for soft bites and gentle sips.

She was soft and responsive, embracing his face with her hands. He moved his hand from her leg and trailed it along her arm until it reached her neck, a whisper of touch that made her shiver as he continued to savor her for several long seconds.

A rowdy whoop went up in the air, joined by jeers and suggestive whistles. Finn and Emanuela pulled their faces apart to see a group of tourists egging them on from the street below. They smiled impishly and laughed, waving at their admirers and even posing for a few photos before the group moved on.

"We should get ready anyway," she said, mirroring his reluctance to end the moment.

"We should." He planted a soft kiss to her chin, then scooped her in his arms to carry her back inside.

Her laughter rang in his ears during the few short steps to their door. "Do you mind?" he asked. "My hands are full."

She giggled and twisted the knob to open the door. He set her down carefully and held her by the waist for a moment. "Go get ready before I decide to foil your plans for the evening, Miss Monroe."

His tone was playful, but he meant every word. She swallowed like she was trying to make up her mind about something. Then she gave him a quick peck on his cheek and stepped away, gathering a few things and disappearing into the bathroom.

****

She emerged sometime later wearing her bathrobe, though she was completely dry, and several rollers in her hair.

"You look breathtaking," Finn said, stepping out of the way of her playful smack before it could land on his ass.

"Just go take your turn," she snapped. "Time's a-wasting!"

She sat at the antique buffet in front of a large gilded mirror, skillfully applying her makeup. Finn came out of the bathroom, dry but for his damp curls. He sat on the edge of the bed in his boxers to put on his leg.

He caught her checking him out in the mirror and made a point to let her see him catch her staring. She blushed, turning her attention back to her face.

He grinned and positively *sauntered* his way to the armoire to pull out his clothes, making sure his path passed close to her so she'd catch every bit of his performance. She snickered and finished her makeup with a deep red lip before moving on to remove the rollers from her hair. By the time her hair was styled into full, flirtatious curls, Finn was dressed in slim black slacks that were fitted to his long limbs, and a white shirt unbuttoned at the top to allow a few short curls to peek out. His shoes were shined to perfection, the gray dinner jacket he wore on their first date slung over his arm.

His eyes lit up with amusement at Emanuela's appearance. "Well I, for one, think you look beautiful in anything. I just don't want you to feel self-conscious with me looking so fancy and you in your bathrobe."

"That's very thoughtful of you," she said. "I just need your help with something." She slowly removed her robe but remained where she stood.

He whistled low at the sight of her. She was sheathed all in black, her soft curves hugged by the smooth fabric. The neckline of the sleeveless dress plunged to show the collarbone he adored, and just enough of the valley between her small breasts to make his tongue snake out to lick his lips. Her feet were nearly nude, a single black strap across her toes and another around her ankles all that held the sexy stilettos in place. "Help with—"

There didn't seem to be anything amiss with her outfit. Then she turned around.

He inhaled sharply. Her dress was open, the zipper dangerously low on her back revealing a glorious expanse of golden brown skin and a flash of red that caught his eye.

She tossed him coquettish look over her shoulder and moved her hair out of the way. "Could you zip me?"

He tossed his jacket on the bed, the rumple of fabric sounding loud in the otherwise silent room, and stepped behind her. He made no move to zip her dress. He wanted her to feel the heat from his body, the burn of anticipation she kindled within him with her game. He trailed his knuckles down her back and she moaned, arching against his hand. Down his knuckles went...down, down, slowly down...until they brushed the dip above the curve of her ass and her body jerked reflexively.

Finn swore, feeling a rush of blood to his groin at her responsiveness. He was intrigued by the stunning contrast of the sheer red band of her bra across her back. He pulled one of her dress straps off her shoulder and halfway down her arm. A soft breast was visible through the sheer fabric of her bra, only her nipple and the topmost portion covered by floral appliqués.

"Jesus."

She flashed a smug little grin at his reaction, and he grabbed her by her arms, yanking her to him. She gasped, and he knew she could feel his arousal against her backside. He wrapped an arm around her, planting one hand firmly to her tummy to press her against him, kneading a breast with the other.

"Finn!"

He didn't stop. He increased the pressure of his massaging hand and sneered in her ear. "Little cruel, don't you think, dangling steak in front of a starving man?"

He quickly zipped her up and crossed the room to lift his dinner jacket from the bed. "Shall we?" he said gruffly, his lips a hard line.

He wasn't angry. He was channeling every bit of energy he had into controlling his lust. The only thing stopping him from taking her into his arms again was his word. He wouldn't disrupt her plans for the evening. All that would be damned to hell if they didn't leave right now.

Emanuela grabbed her evening bag and preceded

him from the room without a word.

Chapter Thirteen

They'd walked into a time capsule. The House of Blues on Decatur Street had been transformed into an impressive reproduction of the sensual grandeur of the Moulin Rouge. The usually exposed rafters of the little blues joint were covered by yards and yards of luxurious red tapestry striped with gold. Miniature lanterns dotted the perimeter of the cloth-lined ceiling and emanated soft golden light from their tiny glass windows. The walls of the place were cloaked in heavy scarlet curtains, golden tassels drawing them apart wherever there was an entryway or a staircase.

Finn and Emanuela presented their tickets to the man at the door, witnessing many hopeful walk-ins turned away. "Full house," the man said, or "Dinner jacket required." The tuxedo-clad hosts and servers were dressed more elegantly than some of the paying guests who came in business casual, but it did not seem out of the ordinary somehow, as though it was simply part of the experience.

Their tickets indicated special seating, so they were led past rows of tables draped in white tablecloth and red velvet seats, to their rounded table for two on the mezzanine balcony nearest the stage. Small, red-shaded table lamps sat atop every table. The effect was enchanting, giving the intimate room the feel of a magical red forest lit up with hundreds of glowing fireflies.

Finn would have pulled out Emanuela's chair, but a gentleman in a tux beat him to it. Her eyes flashed at a motion behind him. A scantily clad hostess, decked out in all of her white and gold, beaded and feathered showgirl glory, held his chair out for him and smiled. They thanked their attentive hosts and took their seats.

Finn gave Emanuela an amused glance, admiring the way the soft light of the table lamp highlighted her cheekbones. "Why do you always sit so far away?" Before she could deny it, he reached for her seat and pulled it next to him. "Better."

She blushed at the look of satisfaction on his face. "Behave."

A few more guests trickled in as the Galop from Jacques Offenbach's "Orpheus in the Underworld," famously known as the Can-can Dance song, began to play softly in the background. Champagne and house wine, red and white, flowed freely at every table. No fancy offerings were available, probably because management didn't want drunken guests jeering at the girls during the show.

"Remind me to never underestimate you," Finn said, looking around with wonder at people gussied up to varying degrees.

"This show was too intriguing to pass up." She offered him a look at her program.

Burlesque: A Tribute for the Ages, it said. The two-hour long show would pay homage to six of the world's most famous burlesque stars, with standup acts intermittently during the three course meals. The Galop exploded from the speakers, the lights went up, and the curtains of the stage opened. A dozen showgirls with elaborate headdresses, beaded bras and feathered derrieres danced onto the stage from either side. Between them, eleven tuxedoed gentlemen joined in. The ruffled skirts of yesteryear were forsaken. This was no classical revue, so modest costuming was unwelcome. Long legs circled and kicked high into the air, exposing bits of thigh between fishnet stockings and frilled bloomers. The men were high jumping and kicking their legs wide. The air in the space was electric and many guests clapped in double time to the exuberant sound of horns and strings. At the end of the opening number, the dancers executed their skillful dispersion, disappearing backstage. A dramatic drum roll sounded and another curtain parted.

"And now," an announcer said with sensational flair, "your hostess for the evening, *Rrrro-si-taaa*!"

A *very* tall, sexy figure floated onto the stage and the clapping grew louder. Her revealing costume was made entirely of bronze, her headpiece and arm cuffs lending her an imperial bearing. A projector screen lowered behind her during her deliberate stroll to the edge of the stage, her arms outstretched. Black and white footage of the late Rosita Royce played on the screen, and at the exact moment that doves were released in the footage, real doves flew over the audience and alighted on the hostess's outstretched arms. The audience roared. Hostess Rosita nodded to one dove, sending it off again and blew a kiss to the other before it too departed.

"Welcome," her deep voice crooned.

The realization that the hostess was in drag drew gasps and another uproarious applause. Rosita bowed several times before the audience quieted enough for her to continue her opening remarks.

The food mimicked the time, and they were served American takes on popular French dishes from the fifties. The first course, *Coquilles Saint Jacques*, served in scalloped oyster shells, was presented during Rosita's hilarious opening speech and Finn felt like teasing Emanuela. He waited for her to raise her fork to her lips and nudged her arm, causing a bit of the warm, buttery sauce to drip to her open neckline.

She glared at him and reached for her napkin, but he smacked her hand. "Let me."

He dipped his head to lick the delicious sauce from her collarbone. It was over in a flash, but her face heated through and she glanced around to see if anyone noticed what he'd just done.

"*Behave!*" she hissed, grateful for the dim lighting.

"You have some nerve. I know what you're wearing under this…" He trailed his fingers along her side and grinned at her shivering response. "I think I'll have some fun too."

Her eyes were apprehensive, beseeching him not to do anything embarrassing, so he let her finish her first course unmolested. They watched a lively tribute to Jennie Lee, known as "The Bazoom Girl." Emanuela remarked at how the buxom blonde was able to bounce and swing the way she did without sending her tassels flying and flashing her nipples to everyone in attendance.

"Jealous little cat," Finn said in her ear. "I think you need some more attention."

"No…"

She didn't sound convincing at all, and Finn was already dragging his fingers along her thigh, pulling her dress back by the hem, his fingernails raking her smooth skin. She gasped and reached down to still his hand.

"No one can see. These tablecloths are very convenient." He turned his hand to capture her fingers in his and pushed it along her thigh until they reached the mesh of her panties.

"*Finn!*"

"Just act natural." His grip on her fingers was firm as he moved them over the flimsy fabric. He licked his lips, watching her squirm in her seat, a fractured breath leaving her parted lips. Encouraged, he increased the pressure, keeping the movement of their fingers maddeningly slow until faint wetness seeped through to his fingers.

The servers were making the rounds to clear the tables for the main course, so he slowly removed their hands, pulling her dress to cover her thighs again. He lifted her fingers to his nostrils and inhaled deeply. He took two of her fingers into his mouth and withdrew them slowly, licking her fingertips before letting her hand fall to her lap.

Her breath hitched and he grinned. "Sweet."

****

Their server arrived to top off their glasses. The wine seemed to be on tap, and Emanuela was grateful for it. She was going to need a bit of a buzz, because they weren't even halfway through dinner and she couldn't do anything yet to alleviate the persistent pulsing between her thighs. A quick glance at Finn's expression told her he'd very much enjoyed teasing her, so she focused her gaze on the stage in an effort to ignore him.

The main course, *ossobuco alla Milanese*, was served, and her horrible attempt at aloofness was cut mercifully short. The tender braised veal melted in their mouths, and the risotto was flavorful from having absorbed the white wine and broth.

The stage curtains that were closed during the comedy routine between acts opened again to reveal a set that looked like an Arabian desert. The provocative strains of Maurice Jarre's famous "Night and Stars" from Lawrence of Arabia filtered into the space. The guests felt an inexplicable tremor through their spines, and then a very leggy lady slinked onto the stage.

They were mesmerized by the burlesque beauty's rendition of Lili St. Cyr's "Salome's Bath." Her shimmering bronze skin peeked from her belly-dancing costume in strategic places, her movements like a charmed cobra rising from its vessel. The last thirty seconds of the routine, like the ones before, included vintage footage of Lili herself on the screen behind the performer. It ended with the dancer in sequined panties and golden tassels, reclining in the prop bathtub. She was obviously the crowd's favorite. The room erupted with applause again, and the curtains closed to prepare for the next performance.

"That was hot," Finn said, looking Emanuela up and down.

She giggled. "It was. I couldn't take my eyes off her."

"I don't know where they sell them around here, but I've *got* to get you some tassels."

"I'm sure we can find out," she said, "so you can wear them for me." Her head fell back with the force of her laughter at his pained expression.

His retaliation was swift. Taking advantage of her vulnerable state, he bent his head to lick her exposed throat. She snapped upright and he sat back, self-satisfied and leering at her.

"Knock it off," she said, shifting in her seat.

"You started it." He shrugged and leaned in, lowering his voice to murmur in her ear. "And then you brought me here. I'm very impressionable, you know."

His breath caressed her ear and she shivered again. "That's *nothing* compared to the way you've been harassing me!"

"You can't just flash me like that and think it won't distract me the entire evening. Besides, I like seeing you squirm like this. You're always so composed."

"I am *not* squirming."

He reached for his glass, his arm grazing the side of her breast. She gasped and he leered at her again, casually sipping his wine. She tried to scoot away from him to allow herself some space and a chance to calm her heart rate, but he brought one big hand down to clamp her thigh and that was the end of that.

Baba au rhum was served, and Rosita took the stage to introduce the final act of the evening. The scent of rum wafted from the pretty little yeast cakes, and the swirling tufts of sweet cream in the center tasted divine.

"If the wine hasn't done it for me, this definitely will." Emanuela savored another spoonful.

Finn groaned softly at her treatment of the spoon. Her eyes shot to his. *My, how the tables have turned,* she thought, going for another bite. She milked it for everything it was worth, letting the small silver utensil glide between her full lips and come out clean. She licked her bottom lip, her teeth biting the soft flesh for added effect.

His eyes narrowed. "You'll pay for that."

She squirmed again.

"All of our lovely performers have done an extraordinary job tonight, wouldn't you agree?" Rosita asked, provoking the audience into enthusiastic applause. "I think the late and great divas would be proud of their tributes tonight, but probably none as much as the one you're about to see. It's said that Ernest Hemingway called her 'the most sensational woman anyone ever saw.' Ladies and gentlemen, I give you our homage to Miss Josephine Baker."

This time, the projector screen hanging in the background came to life early. Josephine Baker's pretty round face smiled above the stage, her slender body ornamented with a beaded bra and the famous banana skirt. The dancer on the stage below wore a similar costume and assumed Josephine's exact pose. The audience held their breaths a beat, and then another; and then the music started up. Isham Jones' lively "Original Charleston" filled the room and both Josephine and her dancing tribute sparked to life.

What followed were three and a half minutes of the glorious free spirited dancing characteristic of one of the greatest performers of all time. The audience's attention was rapt, divided between the projector and the stage, where both dancers moved their bodies in perfect sync to frenetic Charlestons, leggy Knee Rocks, and captivating variations of the Camel Walk. The act, and the show, ended with fifteen seconds of wild hip movement, then the screen dimmed and the dancer on stage strutted off behind the curtain.

After another rupture of applause, the room

emptied quickly. Guests were whisked away to the street to compete for taxis or stroll the French Quarter in search of bars to finish off the night. The hotel was an easy ten-minute walk for Finn and Emanuela. He draped his dinner jacket over her shoulders and they wrapped their arms around each other. Anticipation of what was in store for them the rest of the evening grew stronger the closer they got to their gated hotel. The charged air between them was back, fading their light conversation to electric silence.

****

He was fixated on her, walking down the softly lit hallway and up the stairs, as though he could see her naked flesh right through his dinner jacket and underneath her clothes. She stumbled subtly at the landing and he groaned behind her. He knew what made her steps unsteady, and the knowledge that she was primed for him brought his desire swift and strong. She turned to look at him and he grabbed her at the same time. He took hold of the lapels of the jacket and hauled her to him, backing them against the wall.

"Your legs drive me crazy," he murmured against her lips.

She sighed, moving a slender thigh between his legs to rub against him. He cursed and she took advantage of their parted lips to slant open-mouthed kisses along his jaw to his neck. His hands spanned her waist, migrating to her ass to give it a firm squeeze and press her against him.

"That feels so good." She pushed back with her hips to intensify the pressure and purred with delight.

Somewhere a door closed and they remembered where they were.

147

"Easy," he said softly, steadying her on her feet and turning her around by her waist.

He followed close behind her up the staircase to hide his excitement and allow the other guests to pass on the other side. He pressed her against their door while she fumbled for the key. She was shaking, holding onto the door for support, so he wrapped an arm around her waist and took the key from her to open the door. Once inside, he tossed the jacket somewhere on the floor and turned her at her waist to face him.

He waited for her to open her eyes. "Show me."

She brought trembling hands to his chest and pushed, prodding him to the high-backed upholstered chair near the fireplace. The back of his legs hit the chair and he sat at its edge. Her deep breaths made her breasts heave softly, level with his face, a fact that sent a delicious heat wave through his body.

A warm blush painted her beautiful skin and his mouth watered. He wanted to follow everywhere the pretty pink hue went with his lips, his tongue, his hands…

She took his hands in hers and brought them to her thighs. She held his questioning gaze with her steady one and drew his hands up. He got the message and glided his hands up her thighs, pushing the hem of her dress up, up, over her hips to her waist. His touch was firm, moving with deliberate slowness over her thighs, so close to her damp softness that he almost felt dizzy. Her sighs made him want to heighten the sensations she was experiencing, so he gripped her ass in his hands, applying pressure with his fingers.

"*Unh*," she moaned, reaching up to support herself on his broad shoulders.

He'd seized bare skin. The lack of material beneath his fingers filled his mind with images of her bare bottom, but he didn't turn her around. Not yet. His eyes lowered to the flimsy scrap of red mesh and floral appliqués covering the most sacred part of her, and he pulled her to him.

"Very nice," he said, burying his face there and inhaling deeply.

He breathed in the scent that was uniquely hers and moaned against her, his hot breath heating her through. He sucked, drawing in her essence through the thin material. She moved against his face and he increased the pressure. He glided the flat of his tongue along the slit between her folds, flicking the tip over her clit. He repeated the motion until the sounds she made turned desperate. He felt her thighs tense, every muscle in her body locked in limbo and waiting for release.

"*Please*." She clutched at his shoulders.

He knew what she needed, so he swirled his tongue around her clit and drew it into his mouth for one long suckle. She moved against his face, writhing and moaning, and he drank her up, lapping at her wetness until her orgasm passed and she slumped against him.

He smiled. "Don't get tired yet, baby."

****

The hint of promise in his tone sent tiny tremors through her body and she clung to him as he lifted her across his lap. She began to tease his ear, swirling the cavern with hot flicks of her tongue. She caught the lobe between her teeth and gave it a saucy tug. He jerked his head away, bringing his mouth down hard on hers. He licked her lips and thrust his tongue into her mouth, starting the frantic pulse beating through her body all over again. She had to move.

She squirmed in his lap, massaging him through his pants, and he groaned into her mouth. Awareness of his arousal only heightened her own. The hard resistance of his large frame against her body made her want to melt into him even more. Her quick fingers tugged his shirt from his pants, undoing the buttons so she could worship his chest with her hands, her fingers gliding through the short curls.

One of Finn's hands supported her back, the other on one of her breasts, massaging and squeezing in turns. A rock-hard nipple poked through the soft material of her dress and he pinched it between his forefinger and thumb. She moaned in his ear, covering his hand with hers and pressing it even harder to her.

"So, so greedy," he said, flexing his hips.

She ground her ass down on him and licked his neck. "I can't help it. It's been so long and you feel so good."

She kissed her way from his jaw to his chin and back to his lips, biting the bottom and pulling it with her teeth. They devoured each other for several minutes, the sound of their kisses mixing with their uneven breathing.

It was heaven, a recurring dream every single night they spent apart. Her memory had been vivid with the sight of him, of soft skin over hard muscle, filled with the gentle sound of his deep voice, the feel of her body curved to his. Only seeing him the way he was right now, absorbing her cries as he kissed her, and touching her in the flesh would ever do him justice. It *still* wasn't enough. She whimpered.

"Emanuela." He pried her wandering hands from

his torso. "I want to see."

She didn't want to separate from him, but somehow, she stood on wobbly feet and let him turn her around. He smoothed her hair out of the way, bending to kiss her cheek, her neck, her shoulder-and tugged her zipper down. He peeled her dress down inch-by-inch, trailing kisses down her spine to the dip at her lower back, and her body quivered.

"Jesus," he whispered, and she knew he'd found his prize.

He turned her around by her waist and she held her breath, watching him slowly appraise her form. She chose the risqué lingerie because the scarlet fabric had a sheen to it that made it shimmer against her golden-brown skin.

"Do you like it?" she asked, posing for him.

"You know full well that I do." His eyes raked over her again.

Her eyes mirrored his hunger. Weeks of sexual frustration culminated to this moment. He lifted her by her thighs and carried her to the bed, her legs wrapped around his waist.

He laid her down, then stood for a moment to remove his clothes and take off his leg. The sight of his stump didn't make her feel awkward at all. She smiled, happy to know he was comfortable enough to be himself with her. He climbed into bed beside her, kissing her senseless, the heat of his lips melting away her smile.

He curved an arm beneath her to unhook the clasp of her bra, stripping it from her body and tossing it to the floor. His hands palmed her breasts, his fingers toying with each stiff nipple before sucking them into his mouth. Her breath was forced from her in a long, frantic gasp. The sweet torture sent shockwaves through every nerve ending and her back arched from the bed.

"I've missed this." He whispered it in her ear, sinking his hands beneath her hips to peel off her panties, then running them possessively over her thighs.

"Me too."

She raised her fingers to trace an angular cheekbone, and the strong line of his jaw, softly caressing his lips. She lifted her head, gliding the tip of her tongue along his lower lip. He cursed, pushing her back against the pillows, driving his mouth down on hers. She was thrilled that his heightened urgency matched her own eagerness.

"I can't wait anymore." Finn pulled her beneath him. "Are you okay?"

She couldn't speak any longer. Every part of him hugged her and all she could do was moan. She wrapped her legs around him, raising her hips and digging her hands into his hair. She kissed him with all the hunger she repressed during their time apart, relaying everything she felt to him through the welding of their lips. His deep groan was the last thing she heard before he finally pressed into her.

A shudder traveled from her body to his as her body closed around him. She moved her legs higher, pulling him deeper. He pushed into her again and again, their moans blending into a single, agonizing sound. She lifted herself up to him, helpless with need and matching his frenzied movements. His thumb found her clit, and something like lightning shocks pierced through her for several seconds before her entire body seized up. She cried out, unintelligible words leaving her lips, every muscle tightening before light faded to black.

Beads of sweat collected on Finn's brow, his body tense and shuddering above her. He ground into her one last time, and she contracted around him to heighten his release.

"You're beautiful," he said, "so precious to me, Emmi."

She gasped at his panted endearment, and he froze against her. She recovered quickly, unwilling to let him be unsure of himself, not after what they just shared. She wrapped her arms around him and kissed him soundly. She felt tender with emotion, weak with completion. Perhaps she was high on the afterglow, but she felt the thing that had taken root in her heart a month ago grow in that moment. She was sure he could feel her erratic heartbeat pounding against his chest.

"It started to hurt, how much I missed you," she whispered. "I don't ever want to feel like that again."

Chapter Fourteen

The hour was late, and the room was dark but for the soft glow of light streaming from the partially open bathroom door. Emanuela was lying on her back, her head nestled in the crook of Finn's arm, peering up at his earnest features. Her impenetrable emotional mask was firmly in place, but he was staring into her eyes.

She was more vulnerable than she could ever remember feeling. The seconds ticking by were agonizing. *It's too soon.* She felt very aware—of the sound of late night partiers passing by on the street outside, of the gentle whir of the air conditioning, and of her nakedness. She drew the sheets up to cover herself and buried her face in Finn's side.

"Don't do that," he said, gently taking hold of her chin and turning her face to him again. "I'm sure this is difficult for you, and I don't want to make it worse, but I have to know what you're thinking. Don't hide how you're feeling from me. I know you're used to wearing your poker face when you feel the need, but not with me. Okay?"

She blinked, surprised that he picked up on her habit. He waited, his fingers massaging soft circles at her nape. Slowly, she adjusted her guarded expression to a frown and tried to put her thoughts into words.

"It's hard," she said. "I don't know what I am to you. I try not to feel silly because you've been wonderful and we've only known each other this short time, but I can feel myself getting in this too deep—" She swallowed and his brow creased, a shadow forming behind his eyes. "If you're not feeling what I'm feeling, if we're just having fun—"

"Emanuela."

Her face must have shown her silent mourning of her return from "Emmi" to "Emanuela" so soon, because his expression turned rigid. *"Dammit, I'm crazy about you!* I wouldn't have come all this way if I wasn't."

She gasped, her surprise evident, and he cursed again.

"I wasn't sure where I stood with you, either," he said. "I catch myself feeling jealous but I don't have a right to be. I don't have any claim to you. I've no right to be envious or protective or angry if someone else tries something with you, but I *want* the right to be, Emanuela."

An almost soundless whimper escaped her then. She pulled his fingers from her nape, guiding his hand to her chest.

"You're crazy about me too," he said, his words sounding more confident with her uneven pulse beating against his palm.

"Mmhmm."

She smiled up at him. They surveyed each other's faces for a long moment, as if seeing each other through new lenses. His aristocratic features were softened in this light, affection radiating from his face. It suffused her in warmth, and the cold grip of insecurity on her heart loosened and fell away.

She allowed herself to be completely exposed for

the first time since they met, and at first, it was terrifying. She sighed, relieved to know he shared her feelings with the same intensity.

She wrapped her arms around his shoulders to pull him to her, her fingers seeking the soft curls at the back of his head. The hand he held to her chest renewed its purpose, roving a firm breast beneath the sheets. They didn't speak a single coherent word again that night, making love anew and falling asleep in each other's arms.

****

They were snatched from their deep slumber by a brass band making its boisterous progression down Royal Street.

"Holy hell," Finn said, sitting up.

"It's begun." Emanuela stuffed her face into her pillow.

"What has?"

"Saturday," was her muffled reply.

The blaring trombone, sax and tuba grew louder, backed by persistent percussion, signaling the band's passing right by their hotel. Everyday sounds of morning in a busy city filtered into the room after the band passed, so there was no *way* they were going back to sleep.

"It's almost nine. I never sleep this late," he said, grinning at her like a Cheshire cat.

"Stop looking at me. I look terrible."

"I can't stop looking at you." He sank back down and pulled her to him. "You're beautiful. I like you a little mussed up, means I'm doing my job."

"Oh my God," she groaned, turning away.

To Finn, that was perfect. He angled his body to

hers so he cradled her back, wrapping an arm around her, fanning his fingers over her tummy.

"Good morning," he crooned in her ear.

"Good morning." She sighed, putting her hand over his to play with his fingers.

He touched his mouth to her neck and she shivered against him. He gripped her thigh and raised it to move his between hers. "I can't get enough of you."

He whispered more sweet nothings in her ear, his hard body pleading to be swept up in her softness. He melded their bodies and she gasped, pushing his hand down to glide his fingers over her clit.

"*Jesus.*" He kissed her shoulder.

She sighed and ground against him gently.

"Say you'll be mine, Emmi." He whispered it like a prayer, moving his hips to join her again. "I need to hear it."

"Yours," she said softly.

They were completely absorbed in each other. He cupped her breast in his other hand, she clutched his hips, and they spent the next twenty minutes oblivious to the world, their heavy sighs blending to block out any other sound.

****

They arrived at Café Du Monde just after ten o'clock. It was filled to the brim. The line moved quickly though, and soon enough they were seated outside the famous café, enjoying their iced au laits and beignets. Finn, true to form, moved Emanuela's chair to his side of the small table so they could sit next to each other, drawing a few amused glances their way. He used the excuse that the place was loud and they'd be able to hear each other better. He slung his arm around the back of her chair.

"I wouldn't've minded spending a few more hours locked in our room," he said, absently stroking her arm.

"I know, but I want to *talk,* and it's best that we do it in a public place surrounded by lots and lots of people."

"Okay, shoot. What do you want to know?"

She shifted, as if unsure of how to approach the question. "Well, we've talked a lot about work, and I've told you about my family, but I don't know much about yours." She gave him a tentative look. "I didn't want to pry because I know it's a sensitive subject for you, but I… What happened, Finn? You lost your parents when you were sixteen…"

"Almost seventeen," he said, wanting to show that he was open to her questions.

He had known this conversation would come, and he welcomed it, but he also sensed it would be one of many they would have on the subject and didn't want to inundate her on this trip.

She dusted a bit of the mountain of powdered sugar from one of the still-warm pockets of fried dough, and took a bite. "Mmmm," she hummed appreciatively, licking stray sugar from her lips. "Oh, Allie would *love* these!"

He smiled into her eyes, silently thanking her for a lighter moment to collect his thoughts. "Allie, the infamous baker? I'm sure she could make her own."

"She could, but I don't think she's made any since culinary school. I think I know what her gift will be."

"Culinary school? Didn't she go to business school with you?"

"Mmhmm. When I continued to graduate school,

she started at Le Cordon Bleu. Then she abandoned me for two years to cook in places I was *dying* to visit while I slaved away eating garbage."

He chuckled. He loved how easy it was to talk to her. Her sense of humor and her tolerance for his teasing endeared her to him even more. "She must be making it up to you. Those pastries you ate during one of our chats looked amazing, almost too good to eat."

"Canelés! My favorite. I've never had any as good as hers," she said with a smile. "One day you can visit me and help me eat an entire box so I don't have to finish them all myself."

The mention of Finn visiting her in New York made his heart drop to his stomach, his expression somber. Emanuela seemed to sense it too and fell quiet.

He cleared his throat. "I was a junior in high school. The night of the accident, our varsity basketball team had just won the state championship. The Sentinels. I wasn't the most sought-after guy on the team, but I was getting offers. My dad wanted me to go to UCLA. Maybe it was just exceptionally bad timing, or adrenaline from the game, but my confidence was way up there and I chose *that* night—in the car on the way home—to tell him I was turning down athletic scholarships. I wanted to study engineering at UW instead."

He licked his lips and looked at Emanuela. She was rapt, taking in everything he had to say.

"It wasn't the first time I'd disappointed him. Now that I think about it," he said with an edge to his tone, "it probably started when I lost my innocence. I don't know how old I was—maybe seven or eight—when I picked up on the reality of my parents' relationship."

"Kids are really perceptive," Emanuela said. "You probably sensed it much sooner and didn't understand what it was."

"I think you're right." He gave her a doleful smile. "I'd heard them fight before, but as I got older, I could understand the words. He'd hit us sometimes, but never where anyone could see the bruises. Drank a lot. My mom and I got really close."

"Finn." She took his hand. "I'm so sorry."

He squeezed her hand. Her heart was breaking for him, and he adored her for it, but he needed to tell the story. He needed her to know who he was.

"I remember you're the third Finn in your family," she said. "What was your mom's name?"

He smiled, seeing her face in his memory. "Diane. I get my eyes and my humor from her."

"Two of my favorite things about you."

"What if I'd said *hair and toes*?"

"Then those would be my favorite things."

They laughed, and he felt at ease again. "She'd known for weeks about my decision. My dad was angry when I told him, of course. Started yelling, saying he'd make me see things his way."

He swallowed and she squeezed his hand, grounding him in the present. As long as he held her hand, he could tell the story without getting sucked back to the past. "My mom tried to get him to calm down. Told him not to ruin a great night. We could talk about it later. And then he knew I'd already told her. He just *knew*."

He looked out at passersby, seeing them without really seeing them. "Then he just…lost it. It's almost funny," he said without humor, "the irony that he'd driven around drunk so many times without anything ever happening. But that night, he was so busy yelling at us, he sped through a stop sign at a four-way intersection. I didn't even feel it when the truck hit us. Don't remember it at all. When I woke up, they told me my parents were dead, and I'd lost my foot and part of my leg."

Tears welled in Emanuela's eyes, but they didn't fall. "It had to be difficult for you, trying to recover and mourn at the same time."

"I had a lot of anger," he said. "I welcomed it because it drowned out the other stuff-sadness, fear…anxiety. The priest at my parents' funeral told me to let go of anger or it would destroy me. My state-appointed shrink told me to *use* it, because it would keep me from giving up, trying to avoid the unpleasant."

"So, who'd you listen to?"

He smiled ruefully. "The shrink. I threw myself into recovery. In two years, my gait was almost perfect. Couldn't even tell when I was wearing pants that I had one leg. After that, I busted my balls just to graduate and get into UW. The work was challenging, and I liked that. But it wasn't enough to distract me from the thought that it should have been me who died instead of her."

"Finn…"

"No, I know," he said, raking his fingers through his hair. "It's a horrible thought, but it was honest."

"So…how did you cope after that? Was there anyone you could talk to?"

"*Well…*"

"*Multiple* someones?"

He winced. "I know it sounds cliché, but I was a kid trying to find myself. I was performing well academically, and I had a few friends, but dating was a source of stress for me. I got sick of the pity, and girls who couldn't hack it, and the ones who thought I wasn't...*whole* enough. Then I learned there were women who got turned on by guys like me."

"They fetishized you."

"I was okay with it," he said, wanting to be completely honest with her. "I enjoyed it for a long time. Most of it, anyway."

"*Most* of it?"

"*Ah,* things got weird sometimes."

One of her brows rose.

"Emmi..."

"What? Tell me."

"It's not really...it's kind of embarrassing."

"More embarrassing than the spanking?"

"*Way* more embarrassing than the spanking."

"Okay, now you *have* to tell me. Come on," she said, nudging him. "Give it up."

"Shit." He rubbed his chin. "Okay, the worst one had to be a woman I met in my twenties. She was cute and we hit it off fine, until she asked me to...penetrate her...with my stump."

Emanuela gasped. "*Finn!*"

"And urinate on her."

"*Oh my God...*"

He chuckled at her stunned face, her brows nearly at her hairline and her mouth agape.

"I didn't do it," he said. "The experience woke me up, that's for sure. I still took advantage of people's attraction to my impediment, but I figured they were mutually exploitive experiences and didn't lose sleep over it. I was more selective until I eventually lost interest. I guess you could say I finally found myself."

"Wow…"

"And now I've found you. This project meant everything to me until I met you. It was fate." He smiled, his ears reddening.

"I didn't know you believed in such things, Doctor Kane."

His gaze narrowed at her use of formality. "I didn't think I did, but after that night in your hotel, the thing that consumed my life for so long seemed almost inconsequential compared to you. I thought about you all the time." His voice deepened. "I think about you all the time."

Her breath caught and she reached for her iced *au lait*.

"Emmi."

Color filled her face, and her eyes lowered. "It's all so overwhelming, isn't it? Sometimes I can't even breathe."

He didn't care that they were seated under a crowded canopy, or that a few people were pretending not to stare at them because his shorts exposed his prosthesis. In that moment, he only worried about her. He took her chin in his hand to drive it home. "It gets to me sometimes too, but it lets me know I have the capacity to care about someone in a way I've never felt before."

"You don't think it's happening too fast? Maybe we need more time to—"

"The only time I want is right here, right now. Whatever you give me, for however long."

She looked at him and swallowed, unshed tears in her beautiful eyes. "Just—shut up and kiss me. Okay?"

So he did. It lasted just a few seconds, but the seconds were theirs. It felt like a promise, that there would be infinitely more seconds now because time was reset when he bared all to her.

He lifted his head again to see Priestess Felicie about to enter a building across the street. A smile graced her handsome face and she nodded once, seeming to bless the pair before walking into the restaurant.

****

The rest of the balmy Louisiana morning lulled by in its easy unhurried way. They strolled the French Market hand-in-hand, people watching and chatting up vendors. Emanuela filled her tote with local delicacies to gift Allie and the office with. Their walk through the market was smattered with frequent stops to indulge, often ending with new additions to her tote. They tasted Zapp's Voodoo Chips, an assortment of mini Hubig's fruit pies, bacon pralines and sweet potato cookies.

"Ugh, I'm gonna gain twenty pounds," she groaned as they waited for the St. Charles Avenue Streetcar. "All I do is eat with you."

Finn wrapped his arms around her and bent to her ear. "That's not *all* we do."

"*Finn!*" She grabbed the rogue hand at her tummy. "Be*have*."

He ignored her and kissed her neck. "I can think of a few ways to burn some calories."

She looked around, nervous that they were giving other tourists an eye and ear full. "You're such a menace. I have to watch what I say around you all the time or you'll twist it to your own advantage."

"Can you blame me? What is this thing anyway?" he asked, running his hands along her bare shoulders before releasing her to take her tote.

She liked the way her sun-kissed skin glowed in her peach romper. The scalloped lace details were flirty and feminine, and she felt younger than her thirty-two years with her hair pulled into a messy bun, her bangs loose and framing her face. "It's a romper. Stop looking at me like that!"

"It's very sexy," he said, taking her hand.

The look she gave him would have spelled trouble if they weren't out in the broad light of day. Her gaze locked on his form and traveled the length of him, drinking in the way his light gingham shirt hugged his chest and arms, and his slightly tapered chinos showed off his powerfully toned thighs. His complexion had deepened to a tawny shade, and a stray curl hung over his high brow. She bit her lip.

He squeezed her hand. "*Stop that.*"

"We had to hurry this morning so you wouldn't maul me and frighten the cleaning lady again. I think I earned that." The streetcar arrived, saving her from his no-doubt lecherous rebuttal.

They sat comfortably in the cool mahogany seats of the beautifully antiquated streetcar, the warm breeze filtering through its open windows. They enjoyed the scenery and talked quietly to each other. There wasn't a whisper of space between them during the hour-long ride. The streetcar moved slowly through the Central Business District, then curved along St. Charles Avenue through a tunnel of majestic oaks. They passed under their branches, and flowing Spanish moss brushed the top of the car. The route was dotted with historic monuments, grand antebellum mansions with their many columns and balconies, and the sweeping grounds of the Audubon Zoological Gardens. The landscape was so beautiful, the streetcar so reminiscent of another time, that the ride was very romantic despite the ever-present hum of tourists and traffic.

"This is nice," Finn said. The streetcar made its way back toward the French Quarter. "Were you planning to see any of the acts today?"

"You mean on the fairgrounds?" Emanuela asked, registering his nod in response. "Oh God, no! So few of the acts are even jazz and it's so crowded and hot. I've got something better for us, so I hope you brought your dancing shoes, baby."

He perked up at her sweetly worded challenge. "I'm just here for the ride. *Baby*."

****

Later that night, Morris dropped them off at Bullet's Sports Bar in the "backa tawn." It was a neighborhood upriver in the Seventh Ward, with its shotgun shacks and small businesses peppered with rundown houses and empty lots. A couple of celebrated musicians who left the city after Hurricane Katrina in search of better paying gigs had returned for the weekend, and a little birdie told Emanuela where one of them would be playing.

"Thank you so much, Morris! You're taking such good care of us," she said, exiting the beautiful cab.

"Just doin' my job, Miss Monroe. Y'all pass a good time but stay close, and call me when you're fixin to leave. It's good kids here but sometimes tourists make easy targets and they get tempted."

"We will. See you soon, Morris." Finn guided Emanuela into the bar with a hand at her lower back.

The place was in full swing, with tourists and locals alike in various stages of happy drunkenness, moving their bodies to the lively music coming from the band. The small, powder blue establishment didn't have a stage, so whoever the musicians were, they were playing from a space on the floor. Tables were cleared for the occasion, and there was standing room only. They couldn't see the musicians yet, but Finn seemed to recognize the song immediately.

"Oh my God, that's Cyril Neville!" He practically had to yell in her ear to be heard.

She grinned at him, his excitement making her a bit giddy herself. "You know Cyril?"

"Are you *kidding?* I love him! This is the best cover of 'Working Man' I've ever heard. I like it even better than the original and that's saying something!"

It was hot in the tiny space. Bodies were in motion, swaying, twisting, rocking-and some just bobbing their heads-nearly shoulder to shoulder to the magic of the electric guitars and drums. Finn all but dragged Emanuela through the crowd to get them as close to the band as he could. His efforts paid off, and he planted himself in a space at the end of the bar, pulling her to stand in front of him so he could hold her and take up as little of the limited space as possible. It was far too loud for any kind of conversation without yelling, but they were comfortable just enjoying the music and each other's nearness.

The sixty-six year old blues singer wore a fitted button up shirt and jeans, several chains, and a fedora over the bandana tied around his head. He was eccentric, the perfect blend of rock and soul, and there wasn't a better artist to come see that night. Finn's arms tightened around Emanuela. She felt his contentment in the moment, covering his arms with hers, and they rocked into the late night together.

Around one o'clock, Cyril revved up the crowd with a funky rendering of his hit "Brand New Blues," then injected his signature style into "Tipitina" as a tribute to Professor Longhair, New Orleans legend of rhythm and blues. Finally, he closed out the show with a special kind of tribute, sucking in the crowd, who came simply to have a good time, with his sincerity and passion.

"I'm 'bout ta claim dis stage, and claim the *night,* on be-half of the folks from the Sixth, Seventh, Eighth and Ninth Wards of *New Or-Leens,"* he said with great fervor. *"MY CITY!"* He led his band into a mighty, soul-laced rendition of Curtis Mayfield's "My Country."

The powerful sound and its message seemed to shake the ramshackle building, heightening the experience and unifying the crowd of strangers.

"God, what a night!" Finn yelled.

Emanuela twisted in his embrace to plant a kiss on his chin. Seeing him so happy and filled with wonder was something she wouldn't soon forget.

****

Finn held Emanuela in their hotel bed that night. "Tonight was incredible. I can't even remember when I've had this much fun."

"I can't either," she said, kissing his throat. "You were so excited. It was pretty cute."

"Cute?"

"In a manly, adorable way." She pressed her mouth to his jaw.

"*Adorable?*"

She maneuvered herself on top of him and he groaned. "In a very sexy way." She sighed, luxuriating in the feel of her taut nipples brushing against the curls on his chest.

She moved against him, feeling his body stir in response to the velvet softness of hers. Their open mouths found each other, breaths merging as their bodies became one, provoking their passion and urgently sating it again before they finally fell asleep, content.

Chapter Fifteen

They walked along one of many beautiful trails in City Park after spending the morning touring an old antebellum mansion. The air was mild in the shade of some mossy oak trees near a pond. They decided to sit on a bench and pass some time alone, away from the excitement of the fairgrounds and main attractions.

"I'm trying not to think too much about this being our last day together for a while." Emanuela snuggled in to Finn's side and rested her head on his shoulder.

He wrapped his arm around her, pulling her closer. "I know. I don't think I can go a month before seeing you again. The only thing that got me through those last two weeks was knowing I'd be here with you now, and *barely.*"

"I'm not sure how easy it'll be to see each other more than once a month. It's really overwhelming for me to think too far in advance. I'll just be in my head and ruin the rest of our time together."

He kissed the top of her head, thinking. "Okay. Let's not think that far ahead then. How about we just plan as we go?"

She nodded against his shoulder. "You and Simon found a few potential locations for your new lab space, so I'll have to come inspect them. I have to make sure you two aren't up to anything suspicious," she said, giving her words less of an edge.

"We have. We're looking forward to getting out of his garage and into a real lab. We aren't the only ones interested, so we'll need to decide pretty soon."

She was quiet for a long moment, and he could practically see her busy schedule running through her brain.

"I can do it in two weeks," she said.

"Are you sure? Can you just decide like that or do you need someone to sign off first?"

"Subtle." She moved her head to glare at him playfully.

He kissed her nose.

"It's part of my job description, Finn. The timeline is different for each project. What I do sometimes depends on what you do, so if you tell me there's real estate to look at, I book a flight. If there's some new development related to a product we're backing, it's possible that I may need to come see what you're up to."

"*Interesting.*"

"Uh-uh. Don't get any ideas. If you two blow something up, it's my ass on the line."

"Well," he said with false gravity, his hand snaking down her spine. "I'll do everything I can to make sure your ass isn't compromised in any objectionable way."

"*Finn!*" She grabbed the delinquent hand at her backside. "I'm serious!"

"So am I." He nuzzled her neck.

"You aren't." Though her expression was serious, her head tilted back to welcome his affection. "Besides, it's likely going to be you doing most of the flying. Your schedule is more flexible than mine."

He raised his head to look at her, considering her

words for a moment. He decided now was as good a time as any to tell her about Simon. "You're right. It wouldn't be a problem for me. Sy knows about us."

"How?" She searched his face. "Did you tell him?"

He bristled a bit at the accusation in her tone. "No. He suspected something was up during that big conference meeting we had when Philip was all over you. I'm not as good as you are at disguising my feelings, apparently."

"Ouch."

"I'm sorry," he said, kissing her fingers. "You didn't deserve that."

"I *didn't*, but I know what that must have looked like to you...I don't think I could stomach another woman falling all over you."

Finn's expression softened again, and he squeezed her hand.

"This thing with Philip..." she said, sitting up straighter. "We've been friends a long time. I have a feeling he might feel something more than friendship for me recently, but I can't be sure. He hasn't explicitly asked me out or done anything inappropriate. We've always had an easy-going working relationship, but I'll need to tread carefully. I just want you to trust that, if the time comes, I'll handle it."

Finn met her eyes, needing to see the sincerity he knew would be there before he could truly relax. He hated how the distance made him second-guess himself. "Do you feel anything for Philip?"

"He's obviously good looking, and I'll admit that there's a natural attraction there."

Finn watched her squirm. She obviously knew he wouldn't be crazy about that gem of truth, though he appreciated her naked honesty.

"I've never acted on it and I don't intend to," she said. "For a lot of reasons. I don't have feelings for him in that way, especially not since meeting you." She raised her eyes to his. "I don't want to do anything to mess this up."

Finn processed what she told him, and it seemed like an eternity had passed.

"I'm sure Philip is a good guy," he said finally. "I trust you, but it's no picnic being three thousand miles away while you work so closely with someone who might have feelings for you."

She visibly relaxed. "You won't regret it, Finn." She tilted her head to press a kiss to his tense jaw.

A crowd of festival goers could be heard in the distance, interrupting the quiet calm of their interlude. Finn cast a quick glance in the direction of the rowdy people starting to come into view, then looked down at Emanuela. "Let's get out of here."

****

They made short work of their clothes, kissing each other wherever their frantic lips could reach between each carelessly discarded item of clothing. Finn cursed, yanking at her shorts.

"Get these off," he said, against her lips.

He waited for her to tug them off, then spun her around. He bent her over and took her in one smooth thrust. They cried out in unison, and Emanuela grabbed hold of one of the bed's four posters, coaxing her body to relax despite her rapid pulse. He made love to her with a ferocity she hadn't yet seen from him. Part of her understood his animal need to possess her, to release the frustration of being swept up in something he couldn't control. She accepted his possession, submitted to it, rewarding him with the sounds he loved, until his powerful thrusts sent him panting over the edge.

He breathed against her smooth back for several moments, gently easing her tight hold on the poster, his heart pounding in his ears. "C'mere," he murmured, turning her easily and lifting her to the bed.

He looked into her glistening eyes and kissed each one, then her nose, and finally, her lips. This time he moved with deliberate slowness, guiding himself into her with his hands planted beneath her hips. He focused every cell of his body on pleasing her. His eyes never left her face as she rocked against him, holding onto him for dear life, until her beautiful face twisted up and she bit her lip.

"That's it, baby," he said, his forehead breaking into a sweat. "Come for me, Emmi."

She did. A long, soulful moan escaped her, her head falling to his shoulder until the tremors left her body. He held her even after she stilled against him, her warm breath moistening his skin.

"What was that?" she whispered, pulling away to look into his eyes.

"I don't know. I think I let the reality of the situation get to me and I took it out on you. I shouldn't have done that," he said, gently tucking a curl behind her ear.

"I'm glad you did. It's nice to know I'm not the only one dreading tomorrow."

"You aren't. Not by a long shot."

He swooped her up and carried her to the bathroom. They showered and spent the next couple of hours happily in their underwear in the air conditioned room, ignoring whatever old movie played on a local cable channel in the background. They cuddled, groped each other, traded more dating horror stories and shared a hundred kisses before it was time to get dressed for their final evening out in the Crescent City.

****

The Creole Queen rose two hundred feet above the water, her forty-foot length hugging the Poydras Street Dock behind the Hilton Riverside Hotel. About two hundred passengers prepared to board the beautiful paddle wheeler, the band waving at them in greeting from the upper deck.

"You look so beautiful," Finn said in Emanuela's ear, guiding her up the ramp with a hand at her lower back. "People are staring."

"Don't tell me that!"

They presented their tickets, allowing the smiling hostess to show them to the upper deck.

"It's true," he said over her shoulder, continuing up another set of stairs.

She did look wonderful. Her hair was pulled into an intricate bun atop her head, drawing all focus to her beautiful face. Her skin glowed from exposure to the sun over the last few days, her white trapeze dress glorious against her skin.

The host almost tripped over himself to greet them, his eyes glued to Emanuela, before he showed them to their table.

****

"You look beautiful too," Emanuela said when they were seated.

His salt and pepper waves were slicked back from

his face. He wore a crisp, light blue shirt that drew attention to his eyes. It was buttoned down a bit, rolled at the sleeves in his distinctive way, and tucked into his light chino trousers.

"You'll want to watch that," he said. "Someone at this table seems to think I don't behave myself in public."

"You *don't.*"

"Come over here." He pulled her chair closer.

"Why don't I just sit in your lap?"

"Woman, do not tempt me."

She grinned, but heeded his warning this time, not trusting that he wouldn't make a spectacle. They greeted the elderly out of town couple being seated at the table next to them as the river boat started to pull away from the dock. The twenty-four foot paddlewheel churned the water slowly, and the live band began to play.

They sipped sparkling champagne and signature cocktails, chatting cheek to cheek like they were the only two people on board. Servers came around with their grilled oyster salads just as the sun began to set, painting the evening sky in shades of pink, lavender and gold.

They fed each other bits of chili spiked soft shell crab and pecan smoked beef, whispering and giggling like teenagers. An elderly man at the next table kissed his wife's hand and graciously led her past their table to the dance floor.

Finn looked at Emanuela suggestively, drawing another airy giggle from her. He pushed his chair back, standing in front of her to offer a dramatic flourish and extend his hand. "Madame."

She laughed, shaking her head at his antics. "Mademoiselle, please."

She took his hand and let him lead her to the floor. He hugged her to his chest, clasping her small hand in his. The band transitioned to the next song, the pianist striking up the intro to Louis Armstrong's "A Kiss to Build a Dream On" like a soft berceuse. Finn and Emanuela swayed together, listening to the singer's deep voice rasp the words.

Emanuela sighed, letting her head fall to Finn's shoulder, turning her face into his neck. The clarinet and trumpet joined in the lilting lullaby, the tender lyrics wrapping around them and tying them together.

Finn released her hand and draped her arm over his shoulder so he could wrap both of his arms around her. They remained so entwined as the Creole Queen meandered her way along the Mississippi River and the New Orleans skyline slipped by beneath a canopy of stars.

****

"Emmi," Finn said, hovering over her, waiting for her to open her eyes.

She did, smoothing her hands up his chest, clasping her fingers behind his head. "Don't say it."

"Emanuela."

"Don't. Not yet." She lowered her eyes.

"You promised you wouldn't do that."

She dragged her gaze back to his and raised her hips.

He let it go, deciding instead to show her how he felt until she was ready to hear it. Their eyes never left each other again, and la petite mort claimed them.

He curved his body to hers and they drifted off to

sleep.

"Finn?" she whispered in the dark.

"Hmmm?"

"Thank you."

He kissed her shoulder. They spent the rest of the night on the same pillow, their bodies seeking each other even in sleep.

****

Their flights were scheduled to take off within thirty minutes of each other, so they rode to the airport together.

"Miss Monroe." Morris pulled her aside, and Finn went to check their bags curbside to give them a moment.

"Morris?"

"I didn't get a chance to give you this 'til now. I knew I'd have to wait until time for you to leave or you wouldn't take it." He handed her an unmarked, legal sized envelope.

"Morris…" Emanuela was apprehensive, refusing to take the envelope. "Whatever it is, I don't want it."

He ignored her. "I got some help with the math. That should be 'bout thirty percent of what you loaned me over the years." He held his hand up at her protesting. "Now Miss Monroe, I do know a little something 'bout how these things go. This here is rightfully yours."

She could see there was no point in further protest and Finn was waiting for her, so she took the envelope and, without thinking about it, pulled Morris into a hug.

"Take care, Miss Monroe."

"You too, Morris." She smiled at him one last time, then walked with Finn through the reflective double doors.

****

Her flight departed first, so Finn waited with her at her gate, holding her behind a column, away from the prying eyes of her fellow passengers so they could say their goodbyes.

"I'll miss you," he said.

"It's just two weeks."

"Tell me anyway."

"I will. I'll miss you."

She looked into his eyes, and he could see her discomfort at their very public display. She shook her head, rising to her toes to kiss him. It was brief, just a few seconds, but he knew how much the gesture meant coming from her, and hugged her close until it was time for her to board.

"I'll see you in two weeks," he said, kissing her cheek one more time.

"Two weeks."

His chest tightened at her obvious reluctance to pull away. But she did, at the final boarding call. She disappeared through the terminal, and then he turned on his heel, a thousand beautiful new memories accompanying him to his own gate.

Chapter Sixteen

"Do you believe in God?"

Finn set his empty dinner plate aside and looked at Emanuela, rubbing his chin with his fingers. They talked each night around seven, Pacific. He was home by that time, affording him some privacy, and a chance to talk to her for more than a few minutes between meetings, during the rare lunch when she *wasn't* working, or in the morning when he was still a zombie and she was sprinting out the door.

"First of all," he said with a grin, "I'm digging the outfit. Very cute."

She was tucked into bed at the late New York hour, peering at him on her laptop screen, which sat atop a dinner tray over her lap. She looked comfortable in her favorite faded Columbia T-shirt, her hair pulled into rollers with a silky scarf tied around her crown, her reading glasses perched on the bridge of her nose.

"I like to impress," she said. "Now answer the question."

They'd been back on their respective coasts for a few days now, and they—mostly Emanuela—had quizzed each other at length. Their first night away from each other, Finn thought it was something fun she came up with to help distract them from how much they missed each other. When she continued the questions the next night though, his heart started beating faster at the idea that she was sizing him up as someone she saw herself being with long-term. The questions alternated between profound, philosophical, and even downright silly, but he took care to answer every single one honestly and thoughtfully.

He knew she wasn't ready to hear how he felt about her out loud, and though he was pretty sure she was in love with him too, he wouldn't push her. He tried to remember that her feelings for him and this entire situation overwhelmed her. This question about God was the first on this, the third night of the Emanuela Monroe Comprehensive Evaluation, and he couldn't help but smile. If this was her way of seeing if he measured up, he would go along with it.

"Finn!"

"I do," he said, confidently.

He watched her fine brows go up in surprise. "Really?"

"Really. As a scientist, everything I know is quantifiable. I can measure it. God is not something that can be measured. So, to me, it's unscientific to say he doesn't exist because there is no way to prove it."

"But there's no proof that he's real, either."

He could tell she wasn't being combative, that she wanted to dig deeper, and he wanted her to. "Maybe it just comes down to what you feel. I think we have souls, and I feel that God exists in that part of me. It's similar to the way I feel about you. I know what we have is something really special, even though we've known each other a short time. I can't seem to explain it. Time doesn't matter to me where you're concerned."

"Wow. I like that answer."

"Why? Would you have felt differently if I'd said

that I didn't?"

"Maybe. I don't know...I guess not. I mean, I know you're a good person. I know that you're grounded and you're honest. We have the same ideas about what is moral and what isn't. I guess I just wondered in case..." She floundered, blinking rapidly. "Because we both want children."

"We do," he said when it seemed like she was hesitant to keep going. "You were concerned about religious differences complicating matters if we wanted to raise children together."

"I— Yes. Is that weird? Maybe this line of questioning is a bit much so soon."

"No. I'm happy you want to ask me these questions. I'm already in—invested in you, Emmi," he said, catching himself. "It would be a waste of our time if we weren't considering a future together, given the distance. Besides, I'm happy you've been thinking about having my babies."

She blanched. "Ugh, I've had enough of you."

"God, I hope not. Emmi?"

"Hmm?"

"I'm older than you."

"I know."

"A lot older. Ten years."

"What's your point, Finn?" She removed her glasses and set them on her nightstand.

He understood her annoyance. Their age difference had never come up before, and she probably wondered what brought it on. He didn't know how to put it delicately, so he just came out with it, hoping he didn't freak her out. "If we had a baby tomorrow, I'd be sixty by the time Little Kane goes to college. And you'd be—"

"Fifty," she said. "You'll be sixty-four and I'll be fifty-four when Little Kane graduates. Sixty-eight and fifty-eight by the time Little Kane can get a rental car. Am I missing anything?"

"Emmi—"

"I know there's an age difference, Finn, but it's not your age that matters, is it? I'm the one who needs to settle down soon if she wants to have kids before everything dries up."

"Emanuela," he said, gently. "I mentioned it because I want you to know, I'd love to have a family with you, but even if we both dry up, I'm happy just to have you."

"Finn—I—" She clamped her mouth shut.

"I know," he said. "You don't have to feel the same way right now. I just wanted you to know."

"It's not that…"

"You promised," he said. "If we're gonna do this thing, you have to talk to me, Emmi. I'm about level intermediate when it comes to guessing."

She took a deep breath and let it out slowly. "Okay. I've told you about Greg."

"You broke up with him when he proposed."

She winced. "The thing is, I almost said yes." She looked at him warily.

"It's okay. Go on."

She licked her lips. "Everything was perfect, you know? On paper. He was a good guy and he loved me. I wasn't getting any younger, and I really wanted kids… It would've been so *easy* to say yes to him."

"Why didn't you?"

"At first, I blamed it on my fear of inheriting my

183

mom's mental illness. I was afraid of what it'd do to our kids…that I'd be a burden." She fidgeted with her fingers.

"And then?"

"And then…I finally admitted that I didn't love him. I was with Greg for two years and I didn't feel the way I do with you. Thinking about kids then felt like pressure, and now— I can see it, and it's a little scary."

"Why?"

"I think I'd convinced myself that I was content with my life for the most part before I came to Seattle. Now it feels like I'm not sure about anything anymore. It's hard for me…to feel that way." She swallowed. "I like to feel in control. When I'm with you, I don't feel like I have control of myself—of anything, really."

Finn exhaled on a long sigh. "It must've been hard for you to admit that."

Emanuela looked away for a second, silently confirming his observation.

"Thank you, Emmi. I won't take it for granted."

"I know." She smiled, visibly relieved.

"Is it my turn or is this some kind of quick fire round?" he said, quirking a brow.

Her lips twitched. "You can go now."

"*Thank* you. Miss Monroe, where would you like your career to take you in coming years? You don't strike me as a woman who'd be content as someone's second in command indefinitely."

"Well…believe it or not, I don't want to be Philip when I grow up."

This was a surprise to Finn. "No?"

She shook her head. "I wanted to work for him because he became so successful at such a young age.

He seemed knowledgeable about *so* many things, and he was passionate about every bit of it. I figured someone like that would be a great teacher, and I was right. But my passion isn't in acquisition."

"You don't feel the thrill of it all?"

She laughed. "Of *course* I do. It's fun; don't get me wrong. And the money is good. That was a big draw too, obviously. Living here isn't cheap. But I don't see myself doing this forever."

He smiled. He loved that she continued to surprise him. "What do you see yourself doing?"

"I really like to help people. I liked this job because it felt like I could give people with great ideas a chance to make it. Of course, it's not just giving a handout. It's a business, after all. But my big dream is to head a nonprofit organization."

"Wow," Finn said, a wide grin on his face.

"What?"

"Nothing. I don't know why I'm even surprised. The way you helped Morris was amazing. I still can't believe you were able to do it for as long as you did." Pride sprang up in him. "What kind of nonprofit do you want to start?"

"I haven't exactly figured that part out yet." She bit her lip in thought. "I mean, I loved helping Morris. Helping struggling small businesses get back on their feet would be rewarding, but it's still more of a business transaction than a charitable venture. I guess I haven't found my niche yet." Her brow creased with a small frown.

"That's okay. I'm sure you'll find it and you'll be able to use what you've learned working with Philip to do some good in the world."

"I hope so," she said, wistfully.

He laughed.

"What?" she asked, eyes wide.

"Here I am, a pauper trying to make something of myself, and there you are, my beautiful Midas, trying to give everything away. I'm not sure this is gonna work out after all."

"That's too bad. I thought you might have something I could work with." She shrugged and let go a dramatic sigh.

"Well, now I feel dirty."

"I can work with dirty. But I'll need some time to prepare."

"How much time?"

"Maybe a week and a half?"

"Looking forward to it," he said with a grin. "It's quite possible you now know everything there is to know about me."

"I'm sure I'll think of something else. Say goodnight to me. I have a long day tomorrow."

"Oh?"

"Philip's back from the business summit," she said, looking at him tentatively. "He'll want to meet and catch up on everything."

Finn simply nodded. "Does he know? That you don't want to be the next Philip Hurst?"

"He knows." She sighed. "He's trying to change my mind, of course."

"Of course."

He could understand Philip wanting to hold onto Emanuela. She was quick and she had a way with people. He tried not to think of any other reason Philip would want to keep her around. He knew he shouldn't get carried away, but it gave him hope that her heart wasn't firmly planted at Hurst Capital.

"Get some rest. I'll talk to you in the morning," he said, smiling warmly at her.

"Goodnight, Finn." She kissed her fingers and pressed them to the screen.

"Nite, Emmi."

****

Finn's cell hummed in his pocket. It vibrated once for a couple of seconds and then stopped, so he knew it must be a text message. It was still early, barely nine o'clock, and only two people ever text messaged him, one of whom was sitting right next to him. He grinned.

—*You believe in God, so are you religious?*—

It seemed she wanted to continue her questionnaire this morning.

"Everything okay?" Simon asked.

"Everything's great," Finn said. "Unrelated."

"Cute, but we're about to start an important meeting!"

"I know, Sy. Relax, the ball's in our court this time. *They* have to impress *us.*"

Simon sighed. "You're right. Of course, you're right."

Finn responded to Emanuela's text:

—*No. Are you?*—

Almost immediately, his phone buzzed again:

—*Not really. Love God, but not much experience with organized religion. :)*—

Simon glared at him, and Finn quickly tapped another message:

—*In a meeting. Talk soon, beautiful.*—

His phone hummed a final time:

187

—Me too. Later, handsome.—

Finn grinned again and put his phone away.

"My God," Simon said. "You two are *children.*"

Before Finn could respond, their nine o'clock appointment walked into the conference room, and he and Simon stood to greet them.

****

Emanuela reclined in the office chair, long legs crossed, shoes kicked off near the corner of her desk. She gnawed on the end of a pen and skimmed a hefty pile of documents. Her cell pinged and she glanced at the screen with a smirk. Her smile grew wider, and she typed a quick response, then put her phone back down and returned to reading.

"I think I'm not working you hard enough," Philip said from the doorway, a broad smile on his handsome face. "You look way too comfortable."

She sprang upright in her chair. "Philip! Welcome back!" She tossed her glasses and the proposal she was reading half-heartedly onto her desk. "How was Japan? Did I miss anything good this year?"

"Whoa whoa *whoa,*" he said, stretching his palms out toward her. "Would you mind if I sat down before you bludgeon me with questions?"

Emanuela grinned. "Please."

He looked her over, taking a seat on the couch. "You're looking well, Em. Maybe it was a good thing for you to skip the summit this year, although you make much more entertaining conversation than Brian," he said, crossing his legs. "It was a long flight."

"Thank you. I can imagine. Glad it wasn't me stuck on a fourteen-hour flight with Brian this year. Did I miss anything good?"

He chuckled. "Ah, let's see… There were the usual LP and GP blokes going back and forth about their predictions. I can't recall how many dinners and networking events we attended, if I'm honest. There were some interesting faces this year. Niklas Zennström was a keynote. You'd have enjoyed that one, I think."

"The Skype guy?" She could hardly conceal her excitement.

"*One* of the Skype guys."

"Wow, I think he's made more investments than even you have."

"Well he's considerably smarter than I am." He smiled. "But it's his work in environmental research that caught my interest. He's very involved in combating climate change. I think it's really admirable—and *brilliant.* I don't think we've invested in enough companies like that—green innovation companies. What do you think, Em?"

"About green innovation or about Niklas being smarter than you are?"

"Both."

She thought of something, and her head jerked to the side a bit.

"Out with it," he said.

"Well, I think we're already well on our way with our latest venture. I haven't had a chance to catch you up on that yet but I think you'll like where we're headed."

"You're obviously referring to our friends in Seattle."

"Mm-hmmm. They met with a few interesting people this morning, as a matter of fact. I thought I would brief you before we catch up with them later to

see how everything went." She was brimming with
enthusiasm. It was catchy, she could tell, because his
lips twitched and his dark eyes seemed to radiate
toward her.

He shifted on the couch, getting comfortable.
"Brief away."

****

—I have to go or I' gonna be late.—
—Just tell me what color.—
—Behave!—
—Please?—
—Fine. Blue.—
—Light blue? Dark blue? Help me out, Emmi.—
—Navy, OK? See you in a minute.—

****

Emanuela took her seat at the spacious boardroom
table with Philip and a few members of the team he
recognized from other meetings. She was the last to
arrive for their video conference, and he grinned at the
knowledge that responding to his messages had held her
up. She squirmed almost imperceptibly, obviously
aware of him undressing her with his eyes. He forced
his gaze away from her tempting form and tuned in to
the meeting.

"We're very excited to announce our first hires for
SimLife Laboratories," Simon said proudly. "Phil
Leahy is leaving Genencorp here in Seattle to join us in
the research and development of artificial skin using
recyclable materials. It's so great what he's been up to!
Crab shells, for instance—"

Finn cleared his throat to stop Simon's inevitable
sidebar into the wonders of organic materials for
modern applications. Emanuela cut her eyes to Finn's

briefly, visibly stifling a giggle.

"Forgive me," Simon said, turning red. "I get excited at times and forget that I'm on borrowed time."

"No need, Simon!" Philip said. "I'm very interested in what you have to say. Perhaps after this meeting we can have a word?"

"Absolutely!" Simon perked back up again. "Finn?"

"Sure." Finn took over. "We just completed negotiations this morning with Ikeda Terumoto, formerly of RoBiology in Silicon Valley, to help develop a means to power medical devices, including our smart limbs, using natural bodily systems. In addition to these projects, our lab will do regular contract work as the primary source of revenue."

"Great!" Philip slapped a palm on the table. "I think five-year contracts would be ideal. We only need two or three to keep the lab busy year-round. If you have anyone specific in mind, let's review them and we'll get talks started as soon as possible."

"We appreciate that," Finn said, thankful that he and Simon weren't going to be micromanaged.

Having the freedom to choose their research and the staff employed by their lab was something Finn was adamant about from the beginning. He wanted to do meaningful work that he enjoyed; otherwise, he never would have started this project.

—You OK? Lost you for a minute.—

Finn glanced up to see Emanuela's subtle smile. Philip and Simon were engaged in yet another tangent of discussion, so Finn and Emanuela had a few seconds to message each other unnoticed.

—Great. You look beautiful.—

She looked across the table, nodding a dismissal to her bored subordinates before tapping her response.

—What's your favorite color?—

Finn suddenly needed to clear his throat again, shaking his head at a scowling Simon to let him know he was fine.

—Navy.—

Her grin nearly split her face in two.

—Wish you were here.—

—Me too.—

Philip and Simon shared a few more minutes of the most animated exchange anyone had ever seen between two adults, and then Philip wrapped things up. "The next and most obvious step is to get you guys into a real lab! I'll leave you in Emanuela's more than capable hands for that. One of her many talents that I lack, is the ability to walk around big, empty spaces and envision something magnificent."

Emanuela glared at him and shook her head. "He makes me do all the grunt work and tries to make it sound good," she said, smiling. "I look forward to cashing in on that rain check for dinner, Simon."

"So do I!" said Simon.

They all exchanged goodbyes and the screens went black.

****

"I really like those guys," Philip said after a moment, moving to sit on the table's edge near Emanuela's chair. "Especially Simon. He's very catchy. He could sell me a bridge, I'm sure of it!"

"It's hard not to like him."

"What do you make of Dr. Kane? He seems to be a man of few words."

"Fewer words than Simon, maybe. But he's just as passionate about his work. Maybe more."

"I can see that. Shame I haven't had a chance to meet them yet. We should have them out. Perhaps we can prevail upon your lovely Lydia for the task?"

She stood and prepared to leave, trying not to let the elation show on her face. "Of course."

"I think we can wrap up for the day." He glanced at his watch. "Unless I've got you locked in this tower for some dire reason?"

"No, not this evening anyway," she said with a laugh.

"Great, then you can have dinner with me."

Her spine stiffened. She hadn't anticipated Philip asking her out so soon. He'd only just returned, after all, and they were getting into the swing of things again. She opened her mouth to stammer a reply, but loud feedback pierced the room from the speakers before clicking to silence.

Shit! Emanuela thought. *The call was never disconnected!*

"Damn, that hurt," Philip said, smiling at her until he noticed her bewildered expression. "Em? Are you okay?"

"I can't go to dinner with you, Philip," she said, averting her eyes. Then she walked from the room.

Chapter Seventeen

She knew Philip would follow her. She considered leaving for lunch, though she wasn't particularly hungry, to avoid being a sitting duck in her office, but she didn't want to run away. This thing with Philip needed to be dealt with, but *how?* He was her friend—a dear friend—and she wanted to go about it carefully. She thought that there would be more time to get her thoughts together.

Stupid, she berated herself. *He tried to ask me out over a month ago! I should've known.* Well, to be fair, it was just a hunch. Her instincts told her weeks ago that Philip wanted more than friendship. He knocked on her door, and her heart jumped.

"Em? Can I come in?"

She nodded and he stepped in, closing the door behind him. He silently sought permission to sit down, and she nodded again, trying to settle her nerves. He was quiet a moment, clearly gathering his thoughts. She couldn't make direct eye contact with his questioning brown eyes. They seemed to pierce right through her clothes, seeking entry to her soul, so she focused on the pattern of lines on her palm instead.

"I have to say, I'm a bit confused, Em." He raked a hand through his hair. "Am I way off base, here?"

"I—No, not exactly," she said. "But things have changed…"

"Have they?" He stood, shifting his weight from one foot to the other. Then he moved to sit in one of the seats in front of her desk. "I swear there's something between us. There's always been *something*, hasn't there? I forced it away because I value our friendship and it's bad for business—You were so *young*, and I wasn't ready for anything serious. It would have been serious with you, I'm certain of it."

He was a fount of information, pouring himself out like he'd been holding it in for centuries. "But then just a few weeks ago I started feeling optimistic. I let myself hope—because I could have sworn you felt it too. I *know* you did. We were standing *right* there."

He pointed to the place they'd stood weeks ago near her couch where she'd fired off all the reasons they needed to fund the Kane proposal. "If there's one thing I've managed to be good at, it's reading women," he said with absolute certainty. "So what changed? Are you afraid?"

There was a plea in his tone that brought Emanuela's eyes up without her control. She immediately regretted it, because as soon as they locked with his, she saw that this conversation would be much more difficult than she anticipated. She thought, at most, she would bruise his ego—cause some awkwardness for a few days. She saw something in his eyes that told her it was much, much more. Her throat felt sore. "I admit that I'm…that I've been attracted to you. I can't control that, but I never intentionally did anything to make you think that I was—that we should—"

She stopped herself, cursing her ineptitude with the spoken word at the most inopportune times. She realized nothing she could say would be adequate. He wasn't describing the physical attraction they'd had all along. That was something simple. Easy. What plagued him was much more complicated and it floored her. "I had no idea."

"I know," he said gently. "We're a conflict of interest in every possible way. I'm aware of that. I have been careful with you. I never wanted you to feel uncomfortable around me or in this office. The optics would have gone badly and I couldn't forgive myself if all your hard work was reduced to being involved with me unprofessionally. I told myself I'd give you time—time to establish yourself here, and then time to get over Greg. Then I would use my undeniable charm to convince you to give me a go."

She wanted to smile, but the whole situation was making her chest hurt. She felt pressure there, afraid that what she said next could very likely destroy the friendship she'd grown to cherish. She forced herself to meet his eyes. She thought somehow she owed him that much. "I value our friendship too. I'm so grateful for it and I would be—it would hurt if I lost it."

His eyes softened, and he started to say something, but she needed to get the next part out. "I started seeing someone right around that time. It happened quickly but it's gotten—serious—and I don't want to do anything to jeopardize it."

She winced at the distraught look miring his handsome face. She would give anything to become suddenly endowed with eloquence, an ease of speech that could help lessen his pain. She wasn't granted such a mercy though, and was left staring at him, pleading with her eyes for him to understand and not resent her.

The silence was uncomfortable. She willed herself not to fidget, to resist the urge to look away from the hurt in her friend's eyes. Had she been aware of the depth of his feelings, she wouldn't have delayed the conversation for so long. It wasn't her fault, but she still felt terrible.

He finally shook his head and stood. "The only person I'm disappointed in is myself. I missed my window *again* because I was too slow to move."

Emanuela didn't know how to respond to that, so she gave him a small smile in return. He rounded her desk and she followed his movement with her head, tilting it back as he came to stand beside her chair. He took her hand and kissed it.

"I wish no ill will for your relationship, Em," he said. "But if the day comes that you are no longer attached, I'll not move so slowly." He walked to her door and opened it, turning to offer his most devastating smile. "Stop worrying. Our friendship remains intact."

She smiled at him once more before he strode out her door.

****

Finn was trying to keep his resolve. The only reason he replaced the phone into his pocket for the tenth time in more than an hour was because he promised Emanuela he would trust her. He took it out again, checking to see if he'd missed a call or text from her. Nothing. With a frustrated sigh, he put his phone back into his pocket and prepared to board the ferry from Mukilteo to Whidbey Island. It vibrated at the last second, and he fished it from his pocket again, not bothering to check the caller ID.

****

"Hi."

Emanuela's heart twisted at the strain in his voice. It was just the one syllable, but it was packed full of anguish. She knew he was miserable the rest of the afternoon waiting for her to call, but she couldn't put off the conversation with Philip any longer, and she hoped Finn would understand.

"Hi," she said, softly. "Are you okay?"

"No."

"I'm so sorry you had to hear that, Finn. I talked to Philip—right after, which is why I'm just calling you now—and everything's okay. I took care of it." His sigh was ragged. "Finn?"

"Did you tell him? About me? About us?"

"I—no. I told him I was seeing someo—"

Finn released a string of curses. "Emanuela—"

"It's none of his business, Finn! He asked me out. I told him no. I told him I'm committed and I don't want to mess it up. What more do you want me to say?" She was quickly getting upset, feeling exhausted and strained herself, and a little like she was being attacked.

"That you're with me. That you're in love with me."

Emanuela gasped.

"Why can't you say it?" he asked, an edge to his tone.

"You're not being fair."

"Maybe not, but at the moment, I don't care."

"Finn…"

"He's in love with you too. But you knew that."

"I didn't know that," she said. "Not until today. How did you—"

"Oh *come* on! Any idiot could see he's crazy about

you! Always touching you, calling you pet names—"

"So I'm an idiot because I didn't see it?"

"You know that's not what I meant!"

"Finn, I can't do this right now. I just broke someone's heart and I feel pretty shitty about it, okay? I don't have feelings for Philip but I consider him my friend. I hated doing that and you're making me feel like I didn't break it badly enough for your liking."

"Emanuela—"

"*What?*" Her voice cracked.

"I'm sorry. God, I'm so sorry." He cursed again. "I'm going crazy here. I miss you, and hearing him ask you to dinner just made me feel even farther away than I already am."

"I know how hard this is, Finn."

"Do you?"

"Of course I do! I'm in it, too! The situation isn't any easier for me."

"Did you let him say it?"

Emanuela sighed.

"*Did* you?"

"He didn't *try*! If he'd tried, I would have stopped him."

"Jesus, Emmi. Why?"

"Be*cause,*" she said, exasperated. "People say it all the time, even when it isn't true. I don't want you to say it right after we make love or right after we fight. Emotions are all over the place. I want you to be sure."

"I *am* sure."

"How can you be sure right now? We're fighting."

"Yes."

"You're angry."

"Not anymore. And even when I was, I lo—"

199

"*Don't!*"

"*Dammit, Emanuela!*"

She burst into tears.

"I do, Emmi," he said, softly. "I love you. Right now, I don't know whether I should throw my phone or climb through it somehow and hold you until you believe me."

"I—thank you."

"Don't thank me," he said, tenderly. "I just wanted you to know. I *needed* you to know."

She sniffed. "I'm sorry."

"I won't rush you. I don't want you to feel pressured to say something you don't feel or do something you aren't ready to do. But I can't keep things bottled up. I'm not wired that way. I need an outlet, so unless you want me to proclaim my undying affection to Simon—"

Emanuela laughed. It sounded hearty, almost hysterical, even to her own ears.

"Emmi?"

"I'm not prone to emotional outbursts, but I was so *stressed out.* I thought I was going to lose a friend and have to quit my job."

"And now? Are you okay? Will you and Philip be okay?"

He was trying. For her. She smiled. "I'm okay, and I think my friendship with Philip will be okay too. He was hurt but he seemed to take it well, considering the mixed signals."

"Because you think he's hot."

She laughed. "*Well…*"

"Don't tease me, Emmi. I'm hanging on by a thread here…and you made me miss my ferry."

"I'm sorry. I promise I'll make it up to you," she said in an unmistakably seductive tone.

"You're killing me."

"Not yet."

****

"I'm afraid of heights, Em."

"I know."

"And I hate popcorn."

"I know."

"So why the hell are we doing this again?"

"Because I like those things and you're here for me, remember?" Emanuela reminded Allie as they buckled their lap belts and prepared to ascend into the darkening New York skyline. "Plus, you can't run out on me if we're in midair."

Emanuela loved the feeling she got in the pit of her stomach from riding Ferris wheels. It was the closest sensation to taking off in a big commercial airliner. Its steady climb and aerial views stripped the worries of the world away, if only for fleeting moments. It made her feel weightless. Comforted.

The Coney Island Wonder Wheel churned to life, and Allie clenched her teeth, gripping the cool steel handlebars. "The last time we did this, your mom showed up out of the blue."

Emanuela took the redhead's trembling hand in both of hers and sighed. They were overdressed for the half-full ride, theirs one of the last turns it would take that evening. The sun was finishing its descent.

"What's wrong, Em? Why the S.O.S.?"

"Philip loves me," she said flatly, looking down at their hands.

"Seriously? Em! You brought me here for that! I

could KILL you!"

"What? You *knew?*"

"Of *course* I knew! Don't give me that look. I would have told you if you really wanted to know. We both know you didn't, so there's no story here."

Emanuela looked out at the navy skyline. *Navy.* She smiled.

"What the *hell,* Em?"

"I love him, Allie," Emanuela whispered, still looking straight ahead. "I love Finn, and it scares the shit out of me."

"Oh my God. I *knew* it!" Allie grabbed Emanuela into a hug.

Emanuela raised her head to look into Allie's face. "You did?"

"I'm not *stupid* Em, come on! How long have we known each other? You started off telling me *everything* about the guy—which I appreciate, *believe* me. Then suddenly you stopped. You kept seeing him, which you didn't keep from me, so it made no sense! I knew you weren't hiding it from me so much as keeping something for yourself...I get it. Took you long enough to tell me though. I was about to disown you!"

Emanuela giggled, then fell silent.

"He's not your mother, Em."

"I know."

"He isn't Greg, either."

Emanuela gasped, and Allie fairly snorted. "Oh come on! I know you like to play the martyr and blame yourself, but Greg wanted a pretty little thing to show off at business parties. You aren't a trophy."

"You can't know that."

"Well, I knew about Philip, didn't I?" When Emanuela simply nodded, Allie continued. "You have to tell him."

"It's *so* soon," Emanuela said. "It's happening so fast, and then where do we go from here? Everything I know will have to change. I don't know if I'm ready for that."

Allie pulled her best friend close to her again and touched her head to hers. "That *is* scary. Shit, Em.— *Shit!*" she said again, the big wheel descending once more. "I don't think anyone's ever really ready, you know? We just jump in hoping we'll make it without drowning. You're one of the best swimmers I know. I don't even need to know if the Good Doctor can swim."

"Have I told you how amazing you are?"

"Not enough, frankly. It's a good thing I've got great self-esteem."

Emanuela laughed, then sighed. "What now?"

"I dunno. I guess it's like any big decision you make in life. When the time comes for you to need the answer, you just *know*. You know if it feels right or if you should move on. But for the love of God, you better tell me in advance this time! I need to know where to send those damn canelés."

Emanuela felt Allie's grin against her cheek. "Deal."

Chapter Eighteen

Finn craned his head a bit, a lecherous grin spreading across his face.

"Stop staring at my ass and tell me if it's straight!" Emanuela snapped, teetering on the edge of a barstool.

"A little to the left."

She turned to look at him on her computer screen with a suspicious scowl. "You *just* said it was too far left."

"No, you. Move a little to the left. You're almost out of view."

"Will you *behave??* I want it to look nice!"

His lips twitched.

"The *painting!*" she said, impatiently.

With a lift of his hands, palms out in surrender, Finn finally stopped teasing her. "It looks great. Now, every time you feed your coffee habit, you'll see it and think of me."

"I will." She hopped from the stool and dragged it back to the counter so she could sit down to continue their conversation. "I still can't believe that trip happened. It already feels like it was ages ago."

He understood completely. Their two weeks away from each other were drawing to a close, but the days seemed to drag as though there were unseen forces stretching each hour until it felt like a month.

"I still think you should reconsider the hotel. We

both know you aren't staying there and Simon already knows about us," he said.

"I know, but this is supposed to be a work thing, Finn. I can't use work funds to travel for leisure, so the hotel room stays booked."

He groaned. "I only get to have you for one day. It's madness!"

"Well, I don't see why I should have to fly all the way out there only to turn right around and come back the next day."

His eyebrows went up, wondering what she was on about. "Emanuela…"

"I wouldn't want to overstay my welcome—"

"*Emmi!*"

"I'm staying through Saturday, Finn!" She giggled at his exasperated expression. "I have to be back at work on Monday so it's just the one extra day."

"I'll take it," Finn said, quickly. "Two days are better than one. And two nights." He grinned when her face heated. "Can't wait to see you."

"Me neither."

****

Emanuela squirmed in her seat. The familiar drop in her tummy after each decrease in altitude was joined by a swarm of tiny winged creatures her chest, and she crossed her legs in an effort to keep still. She looked out at the glistening water and white-capped mountains surrounding downtown Seattle from the tiny window of the seven fifty-seven. Finn was down there waiting for her. To take her home. *His home,* she corrected herself. Still, she couldn't shake the thought that someday— soon perhaps—this could be her home too. She looked out again, squinting her eyes against the early morning sun. It didn't occur to her until that very moment, but it didn't scare her anymore. Whatever reservations she had about the unknown future had quietly turned to hope.

****

"Hey, Beautiful," Finn mumbled into Emanuela's shoulder.

They embraced on the curb just outside Seattle-Tacoma International Airport. Whatever she replied was muffled against his throat because she was covering his neck in quick, happy kisses.

"Emmi, not in front of the kids." He grinned at her after they finally pulled apart.

She flushed, taking notice of the mother and two small children to their right, the two little ones giggling and pointing at their public display. Finn opened his passenger's side door, loaded her carryon into the trunk, and they were off to The Edgewater Hotel. He waited for her in the car while she checked in and changed her clothes. They needed to meet Simon to check out possible lab locations in thirty minutes, and they both knew they'd be late if he went in with her.

The passenger door opened and Emanuela slid into the seat.

"Jesus," he said in reverence.

He hadn't seen her in professional clothing this close since the last time she came to Seattle, and was painfully reminded of how dead sexy the sight was. His appreciative stare traveled from her expertly lined eyes to her neat chignon, and he made a mental note to muss up her hair later.

She giggled and leaned in to kiss him. "Thank you."

Finn held his breath, trapping her scent in his nostrils. "Emmi."

"Hmmm?" she said, pecking at his jaw.

"You're killing me."

"Sorry." She grinned, sitting back in the seat. "Shall we?"

He took her hand, needing physical contact with her in some form, and navigated them toward Seattle's biotech research and business hub in South Lake Union.

****

The next several hours were spent touring potential properties for SimLife Laboratories. Finn and Simon were very involved, indicating to the agent, the contractor, and to Emanuela the renovations that would need to take place to accommodate lab space, offices and equipment. It was a grueling morning, particularly for Emanuela after her long flight, but she never let it show. She was fully engaged, taking photos and asking questions until each property was seen.

After lunch downtown, which turned into a three-hour affair where the trio decided on the property most suitable for their needs, possible suppliers for laboratory equipment, and a hundred other details, they finally called an end to the work day.

Emanuela glanced at her watch. "Wow, four o'clock already! I'd say we've covered considerable ground, wouldn't you?"

Simon beamed. "I'd say more than that! I'd say you've earned yourself some of the best cooking this city has to offer."

"Oh?" she asked, feigning ignorance.

"Jamie is something else," Finn said. "He's pulling out all the stops for dinner tonight, just so you know."

"Well, I look forward to it," she said.

"So do we!" Simon smiled. "I'll see you two soon. Don't lose track of time or my husband will be heartbroken."

He winked at them and kissed her cheek. It was his first acknowledgment of her relationship with Finn, and Emanuela felt suddenly shy. "I—we won't," she said.

****

Despite a frantic reunion against Emanuela's hotel room wall—and another in the bathroom, they arrived at Simon's beautiful home right on time at six-thirty. Emanuela and Jamie fell in love with each other at once.

"Oh, she's gorgeous!" he said.

She stood dutifully still until he finished giving her a playful once-over. She hadn't bothered with a shower cap, and there had been no time to blow dry or straighten it again, so the soft, spiraling curls were left to frame her face. Jamie hugged her as if they'd known each other for years.

"Thank you. I love your home, especially the windows," she said of the eight-foot panels that let light in from nearly every direction.

"See, honey?" Jamie called to Simon. "I *told* you those windows would bring this place out of the Stone Age!" He leaned in to confide in Emanuela. "I love him to death but he's oblivious to anything remotely fashionable. He doesn't buy new clothes unless I throw his old ones away."

"Oh, I know!" Simon yelled, making his way down from the upstairs kitchen to greet them. "He thinks I don't know." He glared at Jamie playfully.

Emanuela laughed, looking at Finn.

"They're such an old married couple," Finn said. "They're gonna be like this all night."

"I hope so."

Simon hadn't exaggerated Jamie's talents. He was quite the culinary artist. At thirty-three, he was already editor of a celebrated food and wine magazine. Emanuela swore by the digital version, to Jamie's delight, and best of all, he hailed from New York. He claimed his accent was only obvious when he got animated in any way, which, as it turned out, was a lot.

After dinner, Emanuela paid her compliments to the chef. "I must have eaten salmon a million times, but that had to be the best I've ever tasted. What did you do?"

He was only too thrilled to share his method, but Simon and Finn didn't need to hear it again. They gathered the dishes and took them into the kitchen, leaving their significant others to fawn over each other.

"Well the marinade is mine, so I'd have to kill you," Jamie said. "But the secret is really in the technique. I use a cedar plank to grill it. It's a play on the traditional way Natives of this area cooked their meat. It's not the same, of course, but it'll do in a pinch."

Emanuela laughed, thinking of Allie. "My best friend would *love* you. You have so much in common."

****

Simon and Finn prepared to bring out Jamie's dessert, observing the fast friends from the kitchen.

"Would you look at that?" Simon said in astonishment. "I don't know if I should be happy or jealous."

Finn shook his head, watching the pair carry on.

"I'm not surprised at all. Jamie is amazing, and they're about the same age."

Simon looked at Finn. "It would make it easier for her, if she were to move here eventually, to have a friend."

Finn saw no reason to beat around the bush, not with Simon. "It would. We haven't talked about it yet because I don't want her to feel like we're rushing things, but she's it for me, Sy. I suspected it from the first day she came here and now I'm sure of it."

Simon patted Finn's shoulder. "A blind man could see that, my friend. You two are walking smoke signals."

"Is it really that obvious?"

"Well, she's a little better at poker than you are but not much. I'm happy for you. Just take it at your own pace. There's no rulebook for these things. You know I adore her, and Jamie is close to stealing her from you himself."

****

Jamie made a rustic salmonberry galette for dessert, the beautiful berries a local delicacy. When they were finished eating, they moved to the wrap-around terrace to enjoy the clear, mild evening with some wine.

"So how did you two meet?" Emanuela asked. Looking at them now, she couldn't see Simon or Jamie with anyone else, but she had to admit they seemed an unlikely pair.

"What? You don't think I'm a catch?" Simon asked.

She was horrified, thinking she may have offended him.

"It's okay," he said with laughter in his tone. "I know we must seem like an odd couple. We probably are. Somehow it works for us."

Simon kissed the top of Jamie's head and she smiled. She was quite comfortable herself, snuggled up to Finn on the wicker loveseat with his arm around her.

"I'm the one who got Simon into cooking," Jamie said. "He's brilliant, don't get me wrong, but before he met me, he couldn't boil an egg properly."

"On with the story, Jamie, unless you want me to tell it!" Simon said.

Emanuela giggled and looked up at Finn, the way she'd done all evening, wanting to see his reaction to every little thing. He grinned and kissed her nose.

"All right, *all right!*" Jamie said. "You're gonna love this." He was obviously talking only to Emanuela. "He was on a date with someone *else* when we met!"

Emanuela was scandalized by this fact, her eyes wide, lips parted.

"It was their first date and it was going *horribly.* Ask me how I knew."

"How'd you know?"

"Because they were getting cooking lessons and I was their teacher!"

"Oh my God!"

Finn and Simon exchanged amused glances, their lovers all but ignoring them.

"I *know!* And this guy was such a *schmuck*—I'm sorry, Sy, but he was—talked about himself the entire time. He wasn't even paying attention to the lesson which, by the way, Simon paid for and I was *not* cheap!"

She laughed many times before he finished the

riveting story. The poor, self-centered "schmuck" had unwittingly insulted Simon's job, renounced marriage as a sham and, worst of all, burned the pricey steak Jamie had so expertly taught them how to make. Simon tried to make the most of the ordeal, remaining polite and charming. Little did he know how he'd captivated the young chef, after revealing how awkwardly brilliant he was when he'd explained the science behind certain cooking techniques.

"I would've married him six months after we started dating," Jamie said. "But we weren't allowed to until 2012."

"Which was?"

"Two years after we started dating. We'd been living together for a year. Here, of course. My place wasn't nearly as nice as this."

"Serendipity," Emanuela said in amazement. "What an incredible story."

"Not unlike yours," Simon said.

She looked down, knowing that Simon had no idea just how much that word described her and Finn. He squeezed her thigh, and she knew he was thinking the same thing.

It was with some reluctance that Finn and Emanuela said goodbye to their hosts, but it was getting late and they still had a ferry to catch. She embraced Simon before turning to Jamie. "It was so nice to finally meet you."

"It was lovely to meet you, gorgeous!" he said, kissing her cheek. "Take care of her, Finn. I want to see her again so don't go screwing it up, okay?"

Finn laughed and kissed Jamie's cheek. "I have no intention of screwing this up, Jamie, believe me.

Thanks for dinner. I'll see you Monday, Sy."
    "Take care!"

Chapter Nineteen

It was after ten o'clock and the ferry to Whidbey Island at the late hour was typically short and smooth. They would be there in fifteen minutes.

"Are you okay?" Finn asked.

They sat snuggled up in his parked car below deck. Even during the warmer months, the evenings were chilly, and Emanuela's cardigan was more fashionable than practical.

"Better than okay," she said, tipping her head back to kiss his chin. "I finally get to see where you've been shacking up."

"Well, technically it's not shacking up until you get there, but I'm willing to let you make an honest man out of me."

She gasped. *It's just a joke, calm down.* She watched his grin wane. Holding her gaze, he brought his hand to her chest and held it there. Her heart hammered against his palm, her hand instinctively coming up to cover his. She was sure he could feel what she was feeling at that very instant.

"Crazy about me," he murmured.

She couldn't interpret his expression right away. Even in this light, she could see there was much more there than the smile that brought fine lines to the corners of his eyes. A flicker in her mind brought her back to the lounge in Chicago all those months ago.

God, it seemed like so much longer than that. She had seen past his easy smile all the way to his soul. She sensed how important his project was to him and remembered hoping it would make him happy.

Is that what she saw in him now? No. His eyes looked too doleful for it to be mere happiness. Joy, then? She was wise enough to know the difference, but the trace of uncertainty, just a tiny puncture in his confidence that turned his smile a bit lopsided, hinted that wasn't quite right. She frowned with the effort to place it. Optimism? *What?* she asked with her eyes. And then something happened, an almost imperceptible glimmer in his eyes, and she figured it out. *Hope.*

She had no clue how long they sat there like that, staring at each other in breathless silence. It felt like some sort of limbo, an indeterminate space of time in a suspended reality. Frozen. And then her pulse picked up beneath his palm, faster than it was when he first placed his hand over her heart. The peace she felt in the moment was strange, considering her erratic heartbeat, but before another thought crossed her mind, her whisper permeated the silence.

"I love you, Finn."

A sound escaped him like nothing she'd ever heard, something between a choke and a sob, and then she was plucked from her seat and into his arms. The tension left his body in a long, unsteady breath before he lowered his face to hers.

She must have kissed him a million times since that first time in the restaurant, not caring that God and everyone bore witness, but it was nothing compared to this.

It felt like the melding of their lips beckoned their

souls to commune, and it was so good that they wouldn't stop, couldn't stop. Their breaths were absorbed between them, their hearts begging connection, beating their joy against each other's chests through their tight embrace.

Emanuela knew what it was, back in their hotel room in New Orleans, when she spilled her heart to him before her mind could stop her. She never lost control that way. It was something she took pride in. Besides, admitting it to herself would mean committing to a future that was uncertain and it frightened her. In truth, it still did, but when she saw the look of hope in his eyes moments ago, she knew she could no longer hold him at arm's length.

It wasn't until the captain announced their arrival at the Clinton ferry dock that they finally pulled apart, breathless and grinning like fools. Before she slid from his lap and into her own seat, she whispered in his ear. "Say it."

He took her chin in one hand. "I love you, Emanuela. I think I have from the moment I met you but I didn't know what it was. And I know that I always will."

****

It was a comfortable forty-minute drive to Finn's rented beach house in Penn Cove. They didn't feel the need to fill every minute with conversation the way they did during their chats while they were apart. Something as ordinary as driving home together was an experience they hadn't yet shared, and they relished the moment, making easy conversation when something came to mind.

"This is it." He drove through an iron farm gate

and up a long, worn stretch of driveway to a beautiful timber lodge style home built of Douglas fir. It was dark, but the exterior lighting was enough to give Emanuela a decent view of the porch and an idea of its size.

"Wow," she said, tilting her head for a better look. "It's bigger than I thought."

"Wait until you see the inside." He leaned over for a quick kiss and got out to collect her bag.

Once they were inside, he held her hand to guide her on the grand tour. There were exposed beams and rafters throughout the single-story home, fourteen feet high where the ceiling came to a point in the living room. Rustic married modern, and though the space was considerably large, it still felt cozy. The walls of the office and two standard bedrooms were made of logs, the shared spaces very contemporary. There were large windows throughout the house to allow for natural light and magnificent views during the day. A stunning, free-standing natural granite fireplace separated two seating areas, while recessed lighting and a classic, open kitchen tied it all together. Emanuela smiled.

"What?" he asked, pulling her into his arms in the living room.

She tilted her head to look up at him. "I've caught glimpses of this place during our chats, but it's more vivid in person—I like it. It's very you."

"You haven't seen all of it yet."

She yelped, swept into his arms before she could blink again, and he led them toward the south end of the house. He carried her into the master bedroom.

"Wow," she said for the second time since her arrival.

Exposed rafters imitated the ones in the living room, rising high above the spacious bedroom and meeting at a point at its center. A ceiling fan hung down the middle from a beam running the length of the room, and another gorgeous granite fireplace graced the wall across from the queen-sized bed. The master bath was on one end, and double French doors leading outside were on the other, of the room.

Finn didn't put her down. Instead, he sat on the bed and held her in his lap. She slowly appraised the room—their room at the moment, his adoring gaze on her face. Her lids grew heavy after she took it all in.

"Don't take this the wrong way," she said on a yawn, "but why are you staying in such a big house all by yourself?"

"None taken," he said, kissing her nose. "My staying here was supposed to be temporary. I was just crashing until I found a place in the city. Easier commute to Sy's house. It's easy for me to get around—no stairs. And I fell in love with the view. There's none like it in Oak Harbor unless you live on this stretch of beach. The rent's not much higher than a decent place in the city, so I stayed."

She quirked a brow.

"Trust me," he said, "you'll understand in the morning."

"Okay." She yawned again. "I'll take your word for it."

He chuckled and lifted her again, carrying her to the bathroom so they could get ready for bed.

"I have legs, you know." She was being flippant, even in her exhausted state, but she secretly loved it when he tossed her around.

"I'm painfully aware of that, Emmi." He let her down, smacking her bottom for good measure.

****

Emanuela awakened to the distant sound of waves and birds. After she came out of her groggy haze, the room was dark, but for a faint natural luminosity that allowed her to see after her eyes adjusted. The space beside her on the bed was empty, but still warm.

"Finn?" she called softly, but there was no response.

She sat up and reached for her phone. 5:13. She rubbed her temples and climbed out of bed, about to wander through the house in search of him when movement outside the French doors caught her eye. She grabbed the throw blanket from the foot of the bed and wrapped it around herself, walking out to the deck to join him.

"Hey you," she said from behind him. "What are you doing up already?" She opened the throw and wrapped her arms around his waist.

"Habit, I guess." He turned his head to grin at her. "I usually get a phone call from my girlfriend around this time, but I'll just let it go to voicemail this one time."

She smacked his butt and his grin grew wider.

"I like to watch the sunrise," he said.

"Mmmm," she mumbled into his back.

They stood together for a moment in the darkness before dawn, listening to the windy sound the waves made as they climbed ashore, then sizzled softly before receding again. Gulls flapped noisily about somewhere overhead, greeting each other with their high-pitched caws and sea lion-like barks. Emanuela narrowed her eyes, identifying the shadowy shapes of trees in the distance as far as her eye could see.

"So when does this spectacular show start?" she asked, shivering a little at the breeze off the water hitting her bare legs.

Finn reached for her, pulling her in front of him for a hug. "Not for twenty minutes or so." He kissed the top of her head. "What are *you* doing up? You were so tired."

She pulled away just enough to look at his face. "I didn't mean to pass out like that."

"I was surprised you lasted the car ride, honestly. We did a lot yesterday."

"I know, but I'm leaving tomorrow and I wanted to make the most of our time together." She pouted. "I told you I love you."

"You did."

"Then I fell asleep."

His chuckle vibrated from his body to hers. "Well, we're here now."

She registered his challenge with a grin and rose to her toes, touching her lips to his. Their mouths parted instantly, making way for the gentle caresses of their tongues. She sighed into his mouth. She *loved* this, the way he tasted, the way he smelled first thing in the morning. She enjoyed him in every way, but something about their lazy, unhurried exploration of each other during the earliest hours of the day warmed her through like nothing else.

"Emmi," he said against her neck, "let's go back to bed."

"I—but I thought we could stay here. I want to see the sunrise with you."

He pulled away to look into her eyes. "You'll freeze," he said, giving her an out.

"You won't let me."

He groaned, taking her hand to lead her down a few short steps. He took the throw and spread it onto the cool, firm sand a ways from the deck, and pulled her to him by the waist. She shivered at the feel of his hands gliding along her legs, up the back of her thighs, and underneath her shirt to remove her panties and toss them aside. He pulled her shirt up over her head, quickly removing his own lounge clothes and leading her to the throw. She straddled his lap, carefully letting him stretch his legs behind her. Her thighs hugged his waist, their bodies pressed together, his arousal against her backside. She shivered.

"You're cold," he said, moaning at the flick of her tongue in his ear.

"I love it when you make that sound," she said, ignoring his concern. "It's so sexy."

He groaned long and low, right on cue at her seductive words wetting his ear. *"Emmi…"*

She ground against him hard and slow, clinging to his shoulders. "It's okay, I'm ready too."

Without another word, he lifted her by her hips and eased her onto him, dragging the most delicious moan from them both. He twitched inside of her, her own muscles contracting in response. He started to lift her by her waist, but she caught his hands, kissing each one before dropping them at his sides.

"Let me," she said.

She brushed her lips over his for one long moment before pushing his chest, prompting him to lie on his back. The movement pulled him from her a bit, and he moaned again. The knowledge that she could draw such guttural responses from this strong, incredible man made Emanuela feel a kind of power in that moment, and she wanted more.

He jerked when her thighs hugged his torso, and she brought her cool hands to his rigid stomach. "Jesus," he whispered, lifting his head to look at her.

She moved, her hips swirling a slow hula, and he dropped his head back helplessly at the sweet torture. His hands were wandering her body wherever he could touch her—moving along her thighs, kneading her breasts, gliding up and down her waist. He was so deep, and with every circle of her hips, she felt his stomach tighten with pleasure.

"*Ungh*," was his ragged response each time she pulled him back into her.

She was getting more excited, watching his handsome features twist in pleasure, her slickness joining the sounds of her heavy breaths, and his soft expletives. She wanted to control the pace, to keep her movements deliberate and slow, but the pulse beating within her had grown until it was unbearable, and she lost her rhythm. Her eyes slid shut and her head fell back as she rode him, sweat breaking out on her forehead despite the cool air.

The sensual tension gripped every muscle in Emanuela's body, and she was about to come undone. Finn must have felt it too, because he lifted his head and watched the signs of exquisite pleasure play across her face and immediately convulsed against her, his hands gripping her waist. "*Oh my God.*"

"*Finn!*" She was paralyzed above him, her thighs gripping his waist, her body wracked with the spasms of her denouement. He pulled her to lie on top of him, her chest heaving from her labored breaths, and peppered her face with kisses. After a moment, he tugged the corners of the blanket on each side, pulling it over them until they were covered.

"Look," he said, turning his head toward the water.

She raised her head as the first shades of yellow rose from the water across the cove. It sparkled, flecks of gold dotting the surface, brilliant orange and red illuminating the patches of clouds in the sky. It was easy to make out the curve of the beach across the water. The shadows she saw earlier became trees and beach houses dotting the land, and boats of varying sizes tied to their docks. The Olympic mountains stood majestically in the background, and she stared in awe until it hurt her eyes, squinting as she turned to look down at Finn.

"Didn't I tell you?" he asked smugly, squeezing her ass.

She giggled, blissfully happy, and kissed him again. "You did. But we should probably get out of here before someone sees us."

He held her still when she moved to get up.

"What?" She beamed down at him.

"You love me."

She grinned. "I do."

****

They slept late, then drove ten minutes from Finn's house to a popular stretch of beach in West Penn Cove. They arrived right at eleven, at low tide. People were scattered about, digging for oysters and clams and picking mussels. Finn stopped at the tackle shop in town to get boots to ensure his prosthesis stayed dry, and waterproof shoes for Emanuela.

They collected enough mussels to fill their bucket in no time.

Later, they rubbed elbows, flirting and laughing, scrubbing at the mussels in his kitchen sink. Such a normal activity may have been mundane for anyone else, but they were content, even excited, to perform domestic duties together. Although, he was the superior of the two in this respect, and eventually ordered her to a barstool to enjoy her pinot so he could continue working. Before long, he whipped up quick, Venetian style mussels sautéed with tomatoes, fresh herbs, lemon zest, garlic, and brandy. They sopped up the delicious sauce with the fresh, crusty bread they picked up on the way home. When their dishes were cleared away, they snuggled together on the patio swing, her legs across his lap.

"So, Chef Kane," she said, "what other talents are you hiding?"

He looked at her, his smile wavering a bit, seeming to contemplate something for a moment.

"Finn?"

"Hang on a sec," he said, lifting her legs so he could get up.

"Wha—"

"I'll be right back."

She sat up straight. She was under the distinct impression that whatever prompted him to get up so abruptly wasn't entirely pleasant. Before she could run the possibilities through her mind, he was back with a single piece of paper and a pen. She raised an elegant brow at him in question.

He seemed apprehensive for a moment, but handed

them both to her. "I need you to sign that."

"Excuse me?"

"Please, just sign it and I'll explain after."

Her curious gaze moved from his eyes to the paper. She scanned the page and brought her eyes to his again, this time in disbelief. "Seriously? A non-disclosure agreement? Finn—"

"I know it's crazy, but it's something I've given a lot of thought...I wouldn't ask if I didn't think it was absolutely necessary."

She was in business mode now, her instincts kicking in. "You're aware that this agreement won't stand in the event that you disclose something illegal to me?"

She registered his nod and signed the agreement, handing it back to him. He folded the paper and tucked it into his back pocket.

"Thank you, Emmi."

"I trust you, Finn, but you're freaking me out."

He smiled and reached for her hand. "C'mon, I wanna show you something."

He led her to the office, motioning for her to sit at the desk, then clicked on the monitor. She sat patiently, watching him navigate to an untitled folder and open it. Inside, there must have been a hundred photos of men, women, and children of all ages. He clicked on one, and the round face of a very wise looking adolescent girl filled the screen. It wasn't her pretty braids or her larger-than-life smile that caught Emanuela's attention. It was the purple, toy-like prosthetic arm posed in a wave, that made Emanuela's eyes widen in shock. Considering what she'd just signed, Emanuela knew it wasn't a toy.

"That's Maddie," Finn said. "She's twelve, from Haiti. Wants to be a doctor. Lost her arm in the big earthquake several years back. That's her second arm. The first one was pink."

"Finn—" Her mind reeled.

Finn closed the photo and opened another, and another, and another. A patient who lost a hand in a factory accident, a mine worker, a birth defect...

"Oh my God," she said, overwhelmed.

He told her about the 3D printer in Simon's garage, the program he wrote to custom design each prosthetic device, and the encrypted email system he used to keep his work under the radar. He told her about how he'd wanted to say something for weeks, but the timing was never right. She took a moment to process what she was seeing.

"Say something, Emmi."

She rubbed her temples, finally tearing her eyes from the screen to look up at him. "I— This is...I can't *begin* to tell you how big a conflict of interest this is, Finn."

"I know." He dragged his fingers through his hair.

"And the *ethics* concerns trouble me even more. I mean, *I* know how good you are, but these devices haven't been certified in any way— Some of those patients are so *young*."

"Believe me, I've taken all of this into consideration. Many times. If it helps, I've tested them myself to determine what they're able to withstand. I make sure to provide clear instructions to each patient for how to operate them safely. These aren't robotic devices, Emmi. They're very simple, meant for normal, everyday tasks."

"I believe you, Finn," she said earnestly, reaching for his hands. "I believe every word, and I know how much this must mean to you." She sighed, knowing she was about to ask something impossible of him. "It's incredible what you've done. If I had any other job I'd stop there, but you know I can't."

He nodded. "I can guess where this was going."

"I have to ask that you don't print any more devices until I can work something out. Your smart limbs haven't hit the market yet, and if—"

"Emmi." He went to his knees in front of her. "I'm telling you this as your lover, not as your colleague."

"Finn…"

"I know the risk, but so many people rely on these devices. If I stop sending them, who *knows* where they'll get them? If they get integrated into the same product line as the neuroprosthetics, the patients would never be able to afford them! I don't want people who've already suffered tragedy to get hurt even worse because they don't know what they're doing, or because they're being screwed by the system."

"You're decided then," she said, knowing his answer before he said it.

"I am."

"And Simon?"

"He knows. He signed the same agreement."

She nodded, taking his face in her hands. "*You* are—I don't know if I should be hitting you or kissing you."

"Maybe both?"

She smacked him in the shoulder, then bent to press her lips to his. "You make me crazy," she whispered, "but I've never been more proud of you."

****

They stayed in that evening, feeling their time together coming to a close. They didn't want to spend the final hours anywhere else but snuggled up in Finn's cozy bed, the heat from the fireplace keeping them warm.

"So," Emanuela said, his face nuzzling her neck, "are you hiding any other shady business besides shipping limbs overseas?"

He groaned and she giggled at the vibration against her throat.

"I'm just making sure you aren't part of a mob or—*ah!*" She gasped, her nipple caught between Finn's teeth.

She slid her fingers into his hair, the teasing remark on her tongue instantly forgotten. She held him to her, squirming at the expert hands roaming her body beneath the covers.

"Hold still, or I'll have to hold you down," he said in his deep, velvet tone.

Her sighs grew heavier, his open mouth trailing along her tummy, his tongue swirling her belly button. Her body jerked in response, and he growled.

She moaned. "Not fair."

He ignored her, positioning his head between her thighs, his hands planting her hips firmly in place. "Tell me again."

"I love you," she whispered. She repeated it many more times before she fell asleep that night.

Chapter Twenty

"Morning, Sunshine," Emanuela said through her Bluetooth device.

"Well, not yet."

"I'm sorry. I thought you'd be up watching that beautiful sunrise of yours by now."

The clock on her console read 8:14. She'd been driving along Eighty West for about an hour and could no longer resist the temptation to call him.

"Yeah, well you ruined that for me, Emmi. It's not the same without you here."

The image of a warm, more vulnerable Finn with his tousled bed-head waves filled her mind and she smiled. "I doubt that very much," she said, momentarily distracted until she succeeded putting her car in cruise.

"How much farther do you have to go?"

"A few more hours still."

"I wish I was there with you."

"Me too, but it's better for my mother when I ease her into things," she said. "Besides, she'll have a ton of questions, and this way we won't have to pretend we aren't talking about you."

"*Ah*, I see. How is she?"

"She's good. Going on six months now without any new episodes. I'm sure she'll be beside herself when I tell her about you."

"And your dad?"

"*Well...*"

"I thought as much."

"Don't take it personally. He dragged Greg with him on an eight-hour fly fishing excursion that started at four in the morni—"

Finn lost it, and she couldn't blame him. A city slicker like Greg up to his waist in the great outdoors was a mental image so ridiculous, Finn's fit of laughter filtered through the phone and bit her, sending her into a round herself.

"Hey, it's not *that* funny," she said when she could speak again.

"Oh, it's *exactly* that funny." He chuckled again and then quieted. "I like fishing."

"I know."

She did know. Because he'd told her over the phone—or maybe video chat. She couldn't remember. She was sick of both methods of communication.

"It's been three weeks," Finn said.

She sighed. "I know. It's been busy at the office, especially with Philip away—"

"He's still punishing you?"

"Avoiding me. At least I think he is. He emails regularly and conferences in on occasion, but he's been attending more forums this season than usual."

"Emmi—"

"It's okay, I can handle it."

"You shouldn't have to."

She didn't begrudge Philip his time away to sort himself out. She understood, and was making use of the time herself. "This is good for me. I work well under pressure, and I think I've shown that I'm capable of keeping the firm afloat while he's away."

"Of course you are."

She didn't need the reassurance. Her work spoke for itself, but it mattered to her to hear such conviction from Finn. "Thank you, for having so much faith in me."

He gave her what was quickly becoming her favorite response. "Ditto."

She smiled. "It just occurred to me that you are about to meet everyone important to me in less than a week."

"That has occurred to me more than once."

She laughed softly. "Don't be nervous. They'll love you."

"All I know is that I love *you.* Just lay it on thick with your parents, okay? Make me look good."

"I'll do the best I can."

"Smartass. Call me tonight. I know you'll be busy catching up, but I just want to hear your voice."

"I will. And Finn?"

"Hmm?"

"Ditto."

****

Emanuela turned onto the smooth, black road leading to her parents' Tudor style home just after eleven o'clock. The neighborhood mimicked an English country village, with plenty of lush green lawns, trees, and stately homes of free-flowing brick and traditional timber. She took a deep breath and pulled into her parents' driveway. The earth still damp from a summer rain, the smell of fresh pavement and newly cut grass blending in the warm air to welcome her home as they'd done so many times before. She grinned, hearing the front door open seconds after she shut the car door.

"Hi, Dad." She trotted up the steps to hug him. "Did Mom have you keeping watch by the window again?"

Ethan bent to her ear. "Just for the last thirty minutes or so, but it's okay, I had something to read." He stood back and pulled the newspaper from his back pocket with a waggle of his brows.

She shook her head in amusement, following him through the door. Her mouth watered at the tantalizing smell of meat cooking, and her stomach grumbled right on cue.

"All right, come on," Ethan said. "Let's get something else in you besides coffee."

"What smells so good?" she asked, following him through the house to the back yard.

"What else? Venison!" Ethan opened the sliding door. "That city living messed up your nose."

She wrinkled her nose in response.

"Ethan, you leave her alone." Mira made her way toward them from the grill. "There aren't any deer in the city until Christmas."

"*Mom.*" Emanuela gawked at her mother's sexy blue halter dress beneath her apron and the three-inch sandals on her dainty feet. "Whoa. You look hot!"

"Thank you, baby," Mira said with a little extra sway to her hips before wrapping Emanuela in a warm hug. "Trying to keep things spicy."

"Ugh, *Mom.*"

"Oh hush." Mira looked her daughter over with blatant curiosity. "Your skin is glowing, baby. And you look a little fuller—"

"Mom…"

Mira cocked her head to the side. "What else is

different about you?"

"Nothing." Emanuela tried not to fidget under her mother's keen eye.

Mira opened her mouth to say something else when Ethan cut in. "Let her get settled in before you start dissecting her, woman. You know she gets skittish when we ask too many questions."

"Mmmm," Mira mumbled. Her gaze burned into her daughter's for a long second before she turned away.

Emanuela sighed. Her mother would dig into her later, but for now, she listened to her parents recount their romantic train ride through the Adirondacks the weekend before, and Mira chatter away about the wonders of meditation for her sometimes overactive mind. Catching up was more than enough to carry them through their midday meal.

"So," Mira said after they'd cleaned their plates a second time. "Are you going to tell us who's got you so excited about us coming out next weekend, or are we supposed to guess?"

Emanuela's eyes snapped up and locked with her mother's.

"What are you talking abou—" Ethan said, but Mira quickly shushed him.

Emanuela groaned inwardly. If she hadn't frozen like a deer in headlights, she wouldn't have given herself away.

"She met someone," Mira said. "And since we haven't been introduced to anyone since Greg, I'm guessing it's pretty serious."

Ethan looked at his daughter. "Emanuela?"

A slow grin spread across Emanuela's face. *Busted.*

"How do you always do that?" she asked Mira in astonishment. Without waiting for a response, she answered her mother's question. "Do you remember the project we took on a few months ago? The one with the scientists from Seattle?"

"The gentlemen with the robots?" Ethan asked.

Emanuela smiled blissfully at Ethan's words, and then saw the look of anticipation on her mother's face and continued, "Something like that. As it turns out, I met one of them—Doctor Kane—last year during my trip to Chicago. His proposal crossed my desk a few months ago and since I'm lead on this one, we've been working pretty closely all this time—"

"How closely?"

"Ethan!" Mira said. "Let her finish!"

"We hit it off really well when we met again for this project, so we started seeing each other right away and I… We're—"

"You love him." Mira held Emanuela's gaze.

Ethan was incredulous. "Don't be ridiculous. She's known the guy for five minutes!"

"*Ridiculous?* I know our daughter. She's been grinning like a kitten since she got here, and when is the last time she pushed this hard for us to visit her in the city? We embarrass her. She hates public displays."

"She was with Greg for two *years.*"

"She never said she loved him."

Emanuela swallowed, at a loss at her mother's powers of perception.

"She didn't say she loved this doctor either," Ethan said.

"I love him, Dad."

He threw his hands up in surrender, grunting at the

smug look on his wife's face.

"Well, we look forward to meeting this…" Mira looked to Emanuela for an assist.

"Finn."

"What is a Finn?" Ethan asked, ignoring Mira's glare this time. "What kind of name is that? Is he European?"

"It's a family name, Dad. Short for Finnegan. But there's something else."

Ethan looked at her expectantly.

"Go ahead, baby," said Mira.

"They aren't robots," Emanuela said. "The devices Finn developed are called smart limbs. Prosthetics with the ability to communicate with the brain." She licked her lips. "Once they're out on the market, he'll be able to use one himself. For his leg."

It took a moment, but when the information sank in, even Mira looked stunned. "You're saying he's missing a leg?"

Emanuela stiffened. She expected they'd have questions, but she didn't expect to feel so…on *edge*. Protective. "I'm saying he sustained an injury that resulted in some limb loss. He uses a prosthesis so he can have the same functionality as everyone else."

"What happened?" Ethan asked. "Is he a vet?"

She saw something in her father's eyes she hadn't seen in years. Fear. Something clicked and she understood. "It happened a long time ago. A car accident when he was a kid. His parents died and his leg was crushed. But he's as capable as you are." She grinned. "Maybe more."

Ethan looked pained and Mira burst into laughter.

"Ethan," she said between laughs, "you look like

she just told you she's seeing a Martian."

"Sorry, Dad. Couldn't resist." Emanuela snickered, then sobered. "Dating Finn has its challenges, but I'm happier than I've ever been. Like you and Mom."

Ethan looked at Mira and his expression softened.

Emanuela understood. All the years, good and bad, were flooding her memory, too. They converged to this single moment in time, and her parents looked the happiest they'd ever been.

Ethan smiled at his daughter. "Just give me a minute, Baby," he said. "Maybe two, with that name."

"So you'll be nice?"

He sat back, crossing his arms over his chest. "I'm always nice."

Mira and Emanuela shot him the same dubious glare and he chuckled. "I'll be nice! What *is* it with you two?"

After sharing another laugh, Mira ordered Ethan into the house so she could have a moment alone with their daughter. "Come on, baby," she said, getting up from the table. "Let's go put our feet in."

They sat at the edge of the natural pool in the spacious back yard, shoulder-to-shoulder, their legs dangling over the side and their feet enjoying a soothing soak. The water lilies were in full bloom, bursts of soft pink and pale purple among the lily pads dotting the surface. Little ripples could be seen now and then when nature's smaller creatures came to share the pool.

"I'll talk to your father," Mira said. "He's a cynic, you know that. I don't blame him after what we've been through over the years. But I'm so happy for you, baby. Sometimes I worry about you working so much."

Emanuela smiled, looking down at her feet, slowly kicking them back and forth in the water. "I know. I never minded it before. I *like* working. It's just…" She licked her lips and thought for a moment. "I don't want to do *this* job forever. I guess I thought I would be content with the way things are for a while longer, until I figure out what I wanted to do. But lately it's not enough for me anymore. I still enjoy it, just not as much."

Mira laughed. "Oh, baby. It's never going to be enough again."

Emanuela winced, but Mira continued, "I know what it's like to have it all, at least to people looking at you from the outside. But *inside,* there's this nagging feeling there's more. It eats at you and eats at you until it's the only thing on your mind and you'll never be happy until you try and find it. The difference between you and me, besides one of us being crazy—"

"Mom…"

"The difference *is,* I didn't know what it was that I was looking for. I was chasing after this nameless thing and it was ruining my life. You're *different,* Emanuela. You know what *more* is for you and you aren't going to get it doing the same thing you've always done. Sometimes you have to switch it up. Shake your world."

"That's exactly how it felt, Mom. Like my world got shaken up. When the dust settled, I didn't recognize my surroundings anymore." She could feel her mother's eyes on the side of her face and turned to face her. "I've been doing a lot of thinking. About marriage and babies—but I couldn't figure out the last piece of the puzzle until I made the drive up here. I haven't told anyone, not even Finn."

Mira's eyes widened then, and Emanuela poured out her heart and mind until the sun reached its highest point in the sky late that afternoon.

****

"Hey you."

"Hey, beautiful." Finn's deep, gentle voice enveloped her, his contented smile flashing bright white on her computer screen.

"We have to whisper because I swear the walls here are made of tissue and spit," Emanuela said with a soft laugh.

"Good to know. You look good in my shirt."

"I know. That's why I took it."

"Keep it. It looks better on you. How was the drive?"

She looked at him thoughtfully for a few seconds. "It was really relaxing for me. Kind of therapeutic. I did a lot of thinking."

His brows went up. "Oh?"

"Yes. I promise I'll tell you what I've cooked up, but I want to do it in person, when you come to New York."

Just as she'd promised in New Orleans, she kept her expression unguarded. On the contrary, she felt almost luminous. Open.

"I have no idea how I'll last the week." He blew out a long, slow breath. "But I trust that you'll tell me what's on your mind when you're ready. I've managed to survive *three* away from you so far, so I'll let you make it up to me when I get there."

"Oh, well *thank* you. You're very generous."

"I know."

Chapter Twenty-One

One Week Later

Finn was grateful for the luxury sedan Hurst Capital dispatched for him and Simon. He didn't think he was able to tolerate small talk from a cabbie, so the staunch professionalism of the well-dressed driver suited him just fine. Without the distraction of meaningless conversation, Finn's thoughts were free to take over completely. He barely registered the cacophony of the busy world just outside of the backseat window except to will the sea of traffic away.

You've made it this far, he told himself. *What's another couple hours?*

He sighed. Torture, that's what. He had no idea how to make it through an entire meeting pretending to be nothing more than a friendly acquaintance when he hadn't seen Emanuela in a month.

Simon seemed to sense his anxiety and reached out to squeeze his shoulder. The driver let the partition down to give the time, 1:20, and announce that they were about five minutes away. Before he could think better of it, Finn pulled out his phone to call Emanuela.

"Hey you," she said in the velvety, singsong tone she saved just for him. "Are you finally here?"

"Nearly. Just a few more minutes. Wanted to give you a heads-up."

He couldn't hide the strain in his voice, and after a brief silence, Emanuela spoke again. "Tell Simon I need a favor."

****

Once they got through building security, Finn left his laptop briefcase with Simon in the lobby. He followed Emanuela's directions, and now waited alone in front of a service elevator, swallowing against the pulse beating in his neck. Thankfully, no one seemed interested in using the stairwell, the only other feature in the quietest corner of the forty-eight-story building, or they'd have wondered at his fidgeting. He stuffed his hands into his pockets and shifted his weight to his right. Finally, the doors opened.

The sight of Emanuela in her icy blue sheath dress, standing in the fluorescent light of the stark white elevator, caught his breath. She was the closest thing to an angel he'd ever seen—an angel with a lanyard around her neck and her arms folded across her chest. She grinned.

"Are you going to stand there and stare at me all day? I'm playing hooky to see you right now, so the least you can do is—"

It took only two of his long strides before he was on the elevator, cutting off air to her lungs, crushing her to him with one movement of a powerful arm around her waist. Their hearts beat against each other for several long seconds, their eyes hungrily reacquainting. Finn reached his free hand between them for her lanyard, pulling it over her head and scanning her ID before shoving it into his pocket.

Without waiting for the doors to close, he leaned forward and kissed her. Every cell in his body screamed with the urge to let go, to let down the elegant sweep of her hair, to give in to his needy mouth and the restlessness he felt in his hands. Even now, his fingers ghosted along her bare arms, her shoulders, her neck. She sighed as he took her face in his hands and let his mouth rove her flushed features. He wanted to make up for the time apart, but once he started, he wouldn't be able to stop. Already, the elevator had ascended a dozen floors and he could feel their moment slipping away.

Emanuela wrapped her arms around him inside of his suit jacket, rubbing his back, letting him bury his face in her neck. Whatever sound he made was muffled against her throat, but he didn't feel the need to say anything. His mood was obvious, his desperation to hold her again.

The moment ended all too soon. He kissed her neck then, pulling away with a crooked smile. "Hey you."

"Hey back."

"I missed you."

"Me too."

"I am so *sick* of missing you."

She rubbed the sides of his arms. "Me too. I promise we'll talk about it, okay? But right now—"

"You have to go."

"*We* have to go."

The elevator reached the twenty-fifth floor and the doors began to open. She dropped her hands, taking a step back. "Make a left at the end of that hallway and you'll end up in the café. You can take those elevators back down to the first floor. I'll see you soon."

"Yes, boss." Finn pecked her nose and stepped from the elevator.

"Finn?"

He cocked a brow at her.

"Behave."

"I love you," he mouthed through the closing door.

She grinned, and a silent *"Ditto"* left her lips.

****

"Miss Monroe!" A startled Lydia nearly collided with Emanuela after rounding the same corner from adjacent hallways.

"Hey Lids, were you looking for me?"

"Uh, yes, actually. Doctor Kane and Doctor Faulk just arrived. Mr. Hurst is already out there."

"Okay, I'll just be a minute," Emanuela walked toward her office.

"Oh!" Lydia said, scurrying back to catch up with Emanuela. "I printed that information you asked for. It was pretty substantial, so I made a little booklet for you. On your desk."

"Great. Thanks, Lids—"

"Miss Monroe?"

Emanuela stopped in her office doorway and looked at her assistant with curiosity. "Yes?"

"I-is there anything I should know? I mean, should I start looking for another job?"

Emanuela gasped, and she suddenly felt very inconsiderate. She was so distracted with work and trying to sort out her future, it hadn't occurred to her that her shrewd assistant of four years would draw conclusions from the information she was being asked to look into. Emanuela planned to have this conversation when she had it all figured out, but she couldn't leave Lydia in the dark any longer. She wasn't ready to divulge everything just yet, but she wouldn't lie, either. She respected her far too much for that.

"Yes," she said, carefully. At Lydia's petrified stare, Emanuela quickly tried to reassure her. "I don't want you to worry, Lids. I know you have a family to take care of. Come see me Monday, first thing, and we'll work it out together, okay?"

Lydia nodded, obviously relieved. "Thank you, Miss Monroe."

****

Finn survived Philip's emphatic handshake, but wondered how many people were walking around New York City with dislocated shoulders.

"Damn shame it's taken so long to finally meet you in person," Philip said, "but I can tell you I've been looking forward to it for some time now."

They were in the conference room, where a few employees filtered in and out, enjoying some of the light refreshment provided on the long table. The wall of windows running the length of the room offered an amazing view of the financial district below, and peeks of the harbor between business towers.

"It's a pleasure!" Simon said, matching the young mogul's enthusiasm. "I know how busy you are."

Philip flashed his brilliant smile. "Nonsense! It's not every day I get to meet true innovators."

Charming son of a bitch. Philip was just a couple of inches shorter. *With great hair*, Finn admitted begrudgingly. He was handsome—beautiful, even—and his suit must've cost more than a month's rent in the city. Even as he stood there, talking about absolutely nothing with Simon, charisma rose from him like scented vapor.

Finn was only too happy to have his attention

diverted, nodding to a couple of familiar faces that came and went. There was Brian the Asshole, the twenty-something benevolent geek from their video-conferences, and a few others. *Where are you, Emmi?* He wasn't in the mood for small talk but, thanks to Simon, no one seemed to notice.

Right on cue, Emanuela's crystal clear, confident voice filled the room. "Mind if I join you?" She smiled and walked toward them, carrying a pretty substantial box.

All three men moved to give her a hand, but Finn's longer strides brought him to her first. He lifted the box easily, and nearly leaned in to kiss her when her eyes got huge and her posture went stiff. *Shit!* It was like second nature to him, and his heart pounded in his ears at his near blunder. He recovered quickly, giving her a wink only she could see. "Where would you like me to put it?"

She stepped away from him. "On the end of the table is fine." She turned to hug Simon.

"So good to see you again, Emanuela!" said Simon.

She grinned. "Glad we're still using first names. No need to try and impress this guy." She tilted her head in Philip's direction. "He's already stuck with you." She hugged Finn, avoiding eye contact, and moved away again.

"Help yourselves, gentlemen," Philip said.

He sat next to Emanuela, indicating the seats across from them for Simon and Finn. They ate fruit and assorted cheeses, making small talk to break the ice. Then Philip piped up again. "Shall we open the box?"

Simon clapped. "Great idea! Why don't you do the

honors, Emanuela?"

She nodded and stood to open the box at the end of the table. It was previously opened, so she untucked the flaps and reached in to remove what looked like a very real human arm.

"It's frightfully accurate, isn't it?" Simon asked.

"Surreal," said Finn.

"That's not all," Philip said, obviously enjoying their reactions to seeing their prototype fully developed. "We've created an interactive website so patients can customize their prosthetic limbs. It was Em's idea to widen the spectrum of skin shades. It offers a range broader than any other on the market for even better personalization."

"I'd love to see that," Finn said, impressed with their attention to detail.

"Absolutely," she said with a smile. "May I?"

"Of course." Finn pulled out his laptop, flipped it open and typed in his passcode.

She tapped away at the keyboard, and he tried not to notice her stiff posture, or the return of the impenetrable mask she wore when uncomfortable. This wasn't any easier for him, but he wished she'd relax. Her nerves were giving *him* nerves.

"Excuse me." Philip rose from the table with his cell in hand. "I've got to take this. Please continue. I'll just be a moment."

Finn offered Philip what he hoped was a courteous nod, then returned his gaze to the soft lower lip Emanuela held captive between her teeth. He wanted nothing more than to give it a nip himself, but first, they had to make it through this meeting.

When Philip left the room, Simon shook his head.

"Walking. Smoke. Signals."

****

A few hours later, Finn, Emanuela, Simon and Jamie were well into happy-hour thirty stories above the city on the roof of The Skylark lounge in Midtown. Philip had apologized when their meeting ended, expressing that he would have liked to have drinks with them but had a dinner to attend in another part of the city. It was just a formality, of course, since Emanuela knew about the dinner ahead of time, and already made plans for the evening. The lounge was the perfect place to catch up over cocktails, with intimate couch seating for conversation, and fantastic views of the skyline and the Hudson river in the distance.

Jamie was laughing his ass off at Finn and Emanuela's expense. "I wish I'd been there! My *God.* That must've been the most awkward meeting. And Finn can't lie for shit."

"Jamie…" Simon cast an apologetic smile at Emanuela. "I can cut off his drinks if you want."

"No, it's okay," she said. "I can laugh about it now, but it wasn't very funny when it was happening."

"It *wasn't.*" Finn tossed a balled-up napkin at Jamie, who only laughed harder. He spoke low in Emanuela's ear. "I don't see why we needed to pretend in the first place, Emmi. We aren't doing anything wrong."

"I know, but I don't need everyone in my business. I've never made announcements about my personal life before, and I'm not going to start now."

"What are you two lovebirds tittering about over there?" Jamie asked, making Emanuela giggle.

Simon smacked his arm. "Leave them alone,

honey. They haven't seen each other in a while."

"Well it's been just as long since I've seen you, gorgeous, so come over here and talk to me."

He was pouting full stop and it made Emanuela laugh. She kissed Finn's chin and left his embrace, taking her second cocktail of the evening to sit with Jamie across from Finn. Jamie shooed Simon away to make room for her, and Simon went to share the couch with Finn so their significant others could carry on.

"Kicked to the proverbial couch again, my friend," said Simon.

"'Fraid so. I like seeing them together though. Just feels right."

"I have to admit they look good together. Jamie might be a bad influence on her though. She's too sweet for him."

Finn frowned. "You don't mean that. I think they balance each other out. I think Jamie balances you out."

"And she balances *you* out. Perfect equilibrium."

"It's almost too good to be true."

Simon's brows went up. "Trouble in paradise?"

"No, nothing like that," Finn said, watching Emanuela.

She was letting go of soft peals of laughter at Jamie, who was fully animated and talking with his hands, describing the hilarious ways in which Seattle and New York were *completely* different.

"I thought it would be easier—not that I assumed long distance dating would be easy," Finn said.

"Dating isn't easy, even without three thousand miles between you."

"True. Maybe I'm just not good at dating. I want to be married, Sy. What is the proper convention? Six months? A year? Two?"

"Screw convention, Finn. You two have managed to keep this thing going for four months when many haven't accomplished that living in the same city. That *means* something! It means you're committed. I know I'm not really an expert on women, but she seems like a lady who knows what she wants. I'm sure she'd tell you if you asked her."

"I have. Of course I have, Sy." Finn sighed. "I know she loves me. She's hinted at the things I want but— I guess I'm looking for a sign. I need a sure thing at this point because I don't know how long I can keep this up. I'm old." He tried to smile, lighten the mood.

Simon was about to respond when Emanuela's agonized tone cut their quieter conversation off in mid-air. "*Ugh*, I wish I'd never told you!"

Jamie didn't seem to be trying very hard to recover from another fit of laughter at whatever she'd unwisely disclosed, refueling each time he caught a glimpse of her chagrined expression through his tears.

"Oh, thank God you're loud," a crisp, feminine voice said from a few feet away. "Makes it easier to find you."

"Allie, you made it!" Emanuela stood to hug her friend. "I was going to introduce you to Jamie, but that was before, when he was human and not a laughing hyena."

"*Em!*" Allie said under her breath. "What's gotten into you?" A devilish grin painted her beautiful face. "Or *hasn't...*"

"Ugh." Emanuela tugged Allie behind her by the hand to introduce her to the men, who were now standing.

"Save it, Em. It's pretty obvious." Allie extended her hand to Simon. "You must be Simon." She flashed her pretty smile. "Alison Whitney."

"I must *be!*" he said. "Nice to meet you, Alison."

She nodded and turned to shake Finn's hand. "And you are *definitely* Finn." Her gaze traveled his suit-clad form without a shred of shame. Emanuela pinched her slender waist. "*Ow!*" she yelped, then grinned. "Right. Sorry."

"I'm definitely Finn," he said, his lips twitching. "Emmi's told me a lot about you."

"She's told me exactly as much about you, but I could hear more."

He chuckled, shaking his head and sitting back down.

"You're gorgeous," Jamie said, quickly appraising Allie's model-like frame and flowing, deep red mane. He turned to Emanuela. "Seriously, do you *know* any ugly people?"

Emanuela simply grinned and shrugged. "Allie, Jamie. Jamie, Allie. Now sit down, I'm starving!"

They chatted well into the evening. Cocktails turned to wine, and they had their fill of the lounge's rich truffle fries, beef sliders dripping in gooey gruyere, and spicy tuna tacos. It was a comfortable seventy degrees by then, and Simon and Finn had both shed their jackets, with Finn's sleeves pushed up to his elbows. Emanuela was buzzed, practically sitting in Finn's lap by the end of the night, and Jamie was absentmindedly running his fingers through the tangled mess of hair Simon sported at the late hour.

"God, I'm glad I'm a secure woman because you people are hopeless!" Allie said, standing up and preparing to leave.

"We're making you feel like a fifth wheel." Emanuela stood to accompany her friend out and see that she caught a cab.

Allie lifted a finely arched brow. "I'm nobody's wheel." She tossed her hair over her shoulder. "I am a *siren.*"

"All right, Siren," Jamie said, taking a slightly tipsy Allie's arm. He looked at Emanuela. "Let's see her out, then you can go back to canoodling."

Allie bid the others farewell, exchanging cheek kisses before letting Jamie and Emanuela escort her out. They made easy conversation on the elevator ride down. Jamie shared that he and Simon would remain in the city for a few more days. His grandparents had immigrated to a sprawling Jewish community in central Queens in the fifties, and three generations of his family were settled in a few of the cushier neighborhoods of Queens and Brooklyn. By the time they secured a cab, Allie had exchanged numbers with Jamie and promised to have coffee before his time on the East Coast came to an end.

Allie turned to kiss his cheek. "I like you, Jamie. I'm glad Em's gonna have you."

"Hey, I'm standing right here, you know," Emanuela said, but she sobered up at the maternal look on the scarlet-haired beauty's face. "Oh, Allie. You're drunk."

Jamie waved Emanuela away. "She's gonna have *both* of us." He kissed Allie's pale cheekbone and guided her into the seat by her elbow. "Goodnight, babe."

****

It was after midnight by the time Finn and Emanuela made it to her condo on West Ninety-Fifth Street. She'd made sure to have his carryon delivered from Simon's hotel, and it awaited them in the security office on the first floor.

"You have a *doorman*," Finn said of the elderly tuxedoed man stationed at the main entrance.

"I do, but I don't want to talk about that man."

"No?" Finn followed her onto the elevator, his ears prickling at her suggestive tone.

No sooner had the doors closed then Emanuela had him cornered, snaking her arms around his neck and pulling him to her. "Uh-uh," she said against his lips.

He wrapped an arm around her waist, beside himself at the joyful little sounds coming from somewhere in her throat, her lips eagerly mapping his face. He knew what floor she lived on from their many conversations, so he pulled away for a moment without releasing her, pushing the button for the twelfth floor.

"Someone's missed me," he said into her neck.

She giggled and slid a thigh between his legs. She gently moved it against his pants and grinned at his answering groan. "I'm not the only one." She sighed and kissed him again.

The month apart seemed like an eternity, so they reacquainted themselves with the feel of each other's lips, delicate and full meeting supple and strong. Soft touches became long presses, and by the time the elevator arrived, both were breathing heavily, sharp longing coursing through their bodies.

Emanuela adjusted the recessed lighting so the open living space was softly lit. Finn abandoned his carryon and jacket near the door, then let her pull him

251

by the hand into her living room to stand in front of the wall of eight-foot windows.

"I wanted to show you the view," she said. "It's my favorite thing about living here, seeing the city lights at night."

He was behind her now, wrapping her in his arms, cuddling her neck a moment to enjoy her scent. He looked out at the glittering towers in endless midnight blue. He couldn't make out any stars, but what looked like millions of lighted windows twinkled so high up, they seemed to light the sky on their own. The place felt more alive at night than any other city he'd seen by day.

"I can see why you love it." His deep voice hummed through her body and he felt every tremor. With a groan, his hands left her tummy and moved up to cover her breasts.

She gasped, arching her back and filling his hands. "Your sunrise is probably better."

He remembered the sunrise they watched together and turned her around to look into her eyes. "No sunrise will ever compete with that one, and I'm prepared to ruin all other nighttime skylines with you too."

Her shiver was anything but subtle this time, and he kissed her again. They helped each other out of their clothes, eager but not hurried, trailing kisses over newly exposed flesh until they stood naked before each other. He lifted her, hooking her legs over his arms, her thighs hugging his waist, and pressed her back to the window. She gasped, her warm flesh meeting the cool, thick glass, wrapping her arms around his shoulders for support. He grinned at her ragged breathing, knowing full well she enjoyed his blatant display of masculinity.

"Is this okay?" she asked, eyeing his leg.

"I'll be fine. I probably won't last long anyway. Missed you too much."

"You can make it up to me later. But one of these days, we should make it to a bed first," she said breathlessly against his lips.

He moved against her and moaned. "Maybe next time."

Chapter Twenty-Two

The sun hadn't yet risen when Finn woke up. He knew instantly that he was alone in Emanuela's bed and missed her warmth already. After an athletic romp against a window in her living room, they spent the better part of the night making love, and sleeping curled into each other in turns.

The room was quiet, and no sound came from the bathroom. Having no interest in being apart from her so soon, he tugged on his boxers, put on his leg, and went to look for her. He didn't search for long, and what he caught her doing in the living room sent him laughing into the palm of his hand. He startled her, of course, and she yelped, turning from the window to look in his direction.

"I didn't mean to wake you," she said, her cheeks turning red.

"You didn't." He looked pointedly at the glass cleaner and cloth in her hands. "You're one of *those* people."

She frowned. "Those people?"

He bent to kiss her nose. "If you couldn't sleep, you could have tapped my shoulder or something. I would've found some way to help you out." He pulled away with a wide, salacious grin.

"That's precisely why I *didn't* wake you."

"Here, let me." He took the items from her and

moved to finish the job, spritzing the solution over the window where she couldn't reach and wiping it clean. When he was finished, she put the cleaning supplies away and joined him on the couch. He eyed her svelte form in his wrinkled shirt, pulling her across his lap. "I was gonna ask why you're up so early, but I guess I don't need to."

The living room was immaculate but for the coffee table, which was covered in organized piles of what looked to be important documents. A few highlighters and pens were scattered about, and the coffeemaker whirred quietly from the kitchen.

Emanuela sank into his embrace, resting her head on his shoulder. "I've been working on something really big. It's taken up most of my free time lately, and I'm worried that it could blow up in my face."

His brow creased at her tone and her reluctance to look him in the eyes. There was a lack of absolute confidence when she spoke that wasn't like her at all. She definitely wasn't talking about Hurst Capital. He lifted her chin with two of his fingers and looked into her eyes. "Emmi?"

She hesitated a moment, then took a deep breath. "Last weekend, I told you I'd done some thinking—a lot of thinking, actually."

"You did."

He'd wondered what was on her mind during her drive to her parents' house, but decided not to push her. She was obviously nervous about whatever it was, so he rubbed her thigh, both soothing and encouraging her to keep talking.

"You're always telling me that time doesn't matter for us because it doesn't change the way we feel—and I believe that. I've never felt like this about anyone else," she said. "As long as you're alive, I don't want anyone else."

"Emmi—"

"I know." She stopped him with a touch to his lips. "You're always so generous. You tell me what you're feeling all the time."

"You're right," he said, kissing her fingers and linking their hands. "No more interruptions."

"I want everything with you." She looked into his eyes, bringing their joined hands to her tummy. "*Everything.* But we'll never have those things if we keep talking about it without *doing* anything—if *I* don't do anything. I realize now that it should be me."

"You do?"

She shrugged. "It was always going to be me. I knew that and it scared me. I had a plan when I finished grad school. My job at the firm was never supposed to be permanent, but the money was good and Philip was an amazing teacher. So I thought, 'Why not stay here until I figure out what I want to do?' I was starting to feel like my dream wouldn't happen because I was past thirty and parts of my dream still hadn't become clear."

Finn laughed softly at that, and she gave him a playful shove. "Laugh all you want but it's different for you. You can probably make babies until your teeth fall out."

"You don't have to have it all figured out right now, Emmi." He tucked one of her many errant curls behind her ear. "As much as I want you to have my babies, I won't pressure you. I can support us until you figure it out. If it comes to it, we can see someone—a fertility doctor or a voodoo priestess or a fairy godmother—"

"It won't come to that," she said. She spoke with a self-assuredness he hadn't heard from her since they sat down. "All this time, I've been trying to figure out a way for us to be together without feeling like I'm losing my career."

He frowned, but Emanuela quickly spoke again. "Say what you will, Finn, but three thousand miles is a hell of a commute. We both know we can't keep flying back and forth forever. I could ask you to move here but I've seen you in your natural habitat—"

She giggled, her back arching at Finn's retaliatory tickling.

"You'd be a fish out of water," she said when she could speak again. "Besides, Simon and Jamie are there and I couldn't ask you to leave your only family."

"You have family too. You'd be giving up a lot."

"I would," she said. "But I've come up with something that could make us both happy and give me something fulfilling to do. The hours wouldn't be as demanding and I could—we could—start a family of our own."

This all sounded wonderful to Finn, but there was a catch in her voice. "What is it?"

She took a deep breath and slid from his lap. She reached for a stapled document on the coffee table and handed it to him. "I have a proposal for you."

He lifted a brow at her, accepting the papers with a distinct feeling of déjà vu. His mind took him back to his beachfront deck where he asked her to trust him before she signed a nondisclosure agreement. Several of their conversations over the past few months ran through his mind. And then he knew.

"Emanuela."

"Hear me out—"

"You wrote a *proposal?*" He couldn't believe what he was reading, his eyes skimming the first page.

"I-yes, but this way there'd be no reason to hide it, Finn. I know everything there is to know about running a nonprofit. Think of how many more people you could help with the donations it'd receive?"

"And the ethics concerns?" he said, feeling his jaw tense. "Are those no longer relevant?"

It was the biggest point of contention for him, but she was already picking up a few more documents, riddled with highlighted segments in different colors, and handing them to him.

"Of course they are." Her voice was gentle, not a hint of her business veneer in her tone. "There are measures we can take to prevent the printed prosthetics from being sold for profit. The first is getting your program copyrighted. That will keep anyone from being able to use the code you wrote to create a similar program and print for-profit products."

He shook his head and looked up at her. "That only stops someone from using my code in its entirety. What's to stop someone from taking sections of the code to do the same thing?"

"That's why we get a patent."

"You can't patent a program, Emanuela."

"But you can patent what it *does,*" she said. "You can patent the process. We include the program in the background information when we file. That way, the code you've written and the function of the program in printing the final products is protected."

The sun was rising as she stood there, and he

thought about what a spectacle they must make—him in his underwear and her naked beneath his rumpled dress shirt, pitching a proposal to him in her living room.

"Say yes, Finn. We could live on the same coast, in the same city. My job would be all the more fulfilling knowing that I'm being entrusted to take on your dream, expand it to reach more people in need."

It was a long moment before he finished going over the documents. When he did, his voice returned to its rich, honeyed tone. "You've really thought this through."

"I have."

"You've even found donors?" he asked in amazement.

She nodded. "But nothing is final until you say so."

He couldn't believe his ears. "How?"

"You'd be surprised how many biotech companies could use tax write-offs," she said. "It isn't very sentimental but it's pretty standard. It's more than enough to get started, and with proper branding, we'll have regular donations coming in soon after."

"I have no idea what that means." He was starting to feel the time difference.

She took the papers from his lap and set them back on the table. "C'mere."

Finn allowed her to pull him up and wrap his arms around her waist. She took his face in her hands, and looked at him with every confidence in her eyes. "*I* know what it means. There are a lot of things you understand that I don't. There will be things—details—that I am equipped to handle that you aren't. I just…"

Her hands fell to his upper arms. "I trust you. If being with you means no longer living here, I know that, even if it's not easy, it's going to be okay. So by the same token, this is what I'm good at. If you trust me, I can make this work for us, Finn."

He saw the plea in her eyes, and realization hit him hard. This was everything he'd been waiting for. The sign he asked for—the sign that she was ready to make a real life with him. He knew the effort she put into planning her future with him was far more significant than some grand romantic gesture. She was entrusting him with her life and it meant everything to him. He decided then and there that he'd take care of the grand romantic gestures.

"I trust you, Emmi."

A clear path was laid before them with those words. It was a moment both exciting and frightening in magnitude, and Finn didn't have the energy to tackle the new questions shining in Emanuela's eyes right then.

"Later," he promised, kissing her nose. "For now, let's just go back to bed. We don't need to be anywhere for a while and I've got to get a little thief out of my stolen shirt."

He bent and swept her up in his arms, the coffee forgotten.

****

They dragged themselves out of bed around eleven o'clock and showered together—which proved challenging, and eventful. Finn assured her that he was content doing whatever it was she normally did on a Sunday, so they spent the afternoon in Chelsea, sightseeing and eating their way through the Market. Afterward, they wandered through the art district, stopping by a few galleries along the way before returning to Emanuela's condo to get ready for an evening with her parents.

"You look handsome." She waggled her brows, her eyes traveling the length of him with deliberate slowness. He was stylishly casual for an evening out in July. His gray chinos and navy shirt hugged him just enough to hint at the well-toned muscles beneath.

"Thanks, beautiful. You look good enough to eat," he said, biting the air at her playfully.

She wore a red cotton halter dress that stopped just above her knee and a thin navy belt. Her hair was pulled back into a ponytail that flipped over her shoulder as she maneuvered away from Finn.

"I know," he said, adjusting his tone to mimic her. "*Behave.*"

"I'm starting to feel an attachment to this jacket," she said about his sport coat. She slipped her feet into her sandals. "So many good memories."

His lips parted at the sexy gleam in her eye, but she'd already walked out the door. He cursed under his breath.

"I heard that," she called from the hallway.

"*You* behave," he said.

She locked her door, and they were off.

****

"They're coming," Emanuela said.

They waited for her parents outside of Mattie's Caribbean Café in Harlem. The sidewalk in front of the restaurant was filling with hungry patrons, mostly from Uptown. It was seven o'clock and the place was packed. A steady flow of people picking up their meals, walked in and out of the doors.

"They're grabbing something to drink across the

street," she said.

Finn looked across the street, then tilted his head at her. "That's a liquor store."

She grinned. "Mm*hmm*."

A few minutes later, a well-dressed older couple made their way across the street. The man looked to be about mid-fifties, with sepia skin and coarse, close-cropped hair. He carried a conspicuous bag of clinking glass bottles in one hand, and held the woman's hand with the other. She didn't look much older than Finn, although that was impossible. She had a mesmerizing walk—a regal posture with a natural sway to her hips that was just a touch above subtle—and she was drop-dead gorgeous. The couple drew closer, and he was stunned at the woman's resemblance to Emanuela.

Emanuela moved to embrace her parents.

"Sorry we're late, baby," Mira said. "Your father got us a spa date at the Mandarin and I didn't want to leave!"

"Obviously," Emanuela said with a grin. "I want you to meet Finn. Finn, my dad, Ethan and my mom, Mira."

"Well now," Ethan said, shaking Finn's hand. "So *you* are a Finn."

Emanuela exchanged a disbelieving look with her mother, but Finn didn't mind. He'd heard all about Ethan's reaction to his uncommon name.

"Short for Finnegan," he said. "Name's been in my family for centuries, I'm afraid. An Irish tradition that won't die."

"I happen to like it." Mira stepped forward and hugged him without any hesitation, then pulled back to have a good look at him, still holding his arms. "It has character. A suitable name for such a handsome young man. And brilliant, too, we're told." She gave him a beautiful smile before letting go of his arms.

His ears burned in embarrassment. "Thank you. I can see where Emmi's beauty comes from."

"All right, enough of that," Ethan said. "Let's go on inside before this place fills up again."

Emanuela beamed at him, her smile matching her mother's, and they followed her parents inside. It took a while to be seated, but they lucked out on a table toward the front near a window. Finn had never been to a place that encouraged patrons to bring their own booze, but he was more than happy to go along with it.

"You okay with soul food, baby?" Mira asked him.

"Might need to go easy on him," Ethan said. "I've seen mighty men fall after a good helping of down home cooking."

"Dad…" Emanuela groaned. "Can you keep the wisecracks to a minimum?"

"I love soul food," Finn said. "I'm not that familiar with the Caribbean variety, but I could eat my weight in shrimp and grits."

Ethan looked surprised and Emanuela grinned. "He's cultured, okay? Can we order now? I'm starving."

Ethan ordered for the table, a feast fit for an army, so everyone got to taste a bit of everything. There were Mattie's famous sides like callaloo, rice and peas, and fried, overripe plantains; West Indian classics like stewed chicken and oxtails; and traditional favorites like candied yams and mac and cheese. Finn spooned a healthy portion of fried okra onto his plate and Emanuela wrinkled her nose.

"Don't be such a brat," he said, kissing her nose.

His chair was so close to hers, they nearly shared the same seat. He found every excuse to touch her, brushing her arm while she was speaking, dropping a hand to her knee for a squeeze, or draping an arm behind her chair.

"Where are you from, baby?" Mira asked Finn, and he noticed for the first time that she'd been watching them.

"I was born and raised in California, but I moved to Seattle for college and got hooked on the air up there."

"Oh, it's wonderful," she said. "I haven't been back in twenty years."

"That's about how long I've been there. A lot's changed, but the air's still great."

"How old are you, Finn?" Ethan asked.

"Forty-two."

"Ever been married?"

"Dad…"

"It's okay," Finn said, squeezing Emanuela's knee beneath the table. He had an inkling about where this was going and took a sip of wine to settle his nerves. "No." He looked directly into Ethan's eyes. "It's not because I wasn't ready to settle down. I think a lot of men get married because of some unwritten rule that it's just what you do when you turn thirty. In some ways, my impediment helps me, because I tend to find out right from the beginning if a woman is right for me."

Ethan nodded. "Emanuela told us about your condition."

"What? That I'm white?"

Mira and Emanuela burst into laughter.

Ethan's brow lifted.

"I'm sorry," Finn said when the women could breathe again without crying. "It's just when people say condition, I picture something dire. Being an amputee can be challenging, even downright painful on occasion, but I consider myself lucky."

Ethan looked at Finn thoughtfully for a moment, leaning back in his chair and folding his arms over his chest. "What about your family? Who supported you when your parents passed away?"

Emanuela's hand slipped into Finn's. He could handle himself, but he appreciated her silent show of support. "I lived with my grandfather—maternal—until I recovered and finished high school. After that, I went away for college. He died when I was twenty-nine. I have some cousins in the Midwest..." He licked his lips. "I don't have much in the way of family now, but I was very close to my mother before the accident. She's who I learned the most from, and Emmi is just as important to me as she was, Mr. Monroe."

Mira studied him intently again, but he didn't mind. Emanuela's parents were looking for assurance that their daughter was cared for. Mira must have been satisfied by his honesty, because she turned her attention to Emanuela.

"Why don't we go freshen up, baby." It sounded like a statement, not a question.

Emanuela frowned. "We're not pack animals, Mom."

Finn stifled a laugh at Mira's no-nonsense expression. Emanuela groaned and gave his hand a squeeze, getting up to accompany her mother to the ladies' room. "Fine, but you two have *five* minutes," she said.

Finn couldn't help his grin. Mother and daughter quirked their flawless brows at them for good measure, and walked toward the back of the restaurant, garnering admiring glances from other patrons on the way.

"You heard her," Ethan said, relaxing his posture. "Emanuela is a lot like her mother. They value my opinion, but they've never waited for my approval before deciding to do anything. So humor me, son. Put my mind at ease."

Finn could see how much Ethan loved his daughter—his very capable, self-assured and brilliant daughter—and simply needed to know that she would be cared for. He smiled. "I think I can do that."

****

"What did you *say* to him?" Emanuela asked Finn.

They followed a few paces behind her parents along the fabled stretch of Fifth Avenue from Rockefeller Center to Central Park. It was almost nine o'clock. The summer sun had finally set, and both couples enjoyed window shopping and people watching, walking off their heavy dinner.

"Why do you sound so surprised?" he asked. "I didn't think he was so bad. Not at all, actually."

Ethan and Mira stopped so she could admire a gorgeous diamond collar necklace in one of Saks' tantalizing window displays. Emanuela took advantage of her parents' distraction and turned into Finn's embrace.

"Because I *am,*" she murmured into his neck. "My father usually has no less than a hundred questions for anyone I introduce. Even if they're answered to his satisfaction, he still might not like you."

He pulled her away from him by her waist to look at her. "I don't know exactly what sold him, Emmi. All I did was speak to him man-to-man. It wasn't an interrogation. It was a conversation. Maybe you succeeded in scaring the shit out of the others and he could smell their fear," he said, feigning horror.

She smacked him in the chest. "Fine, don't tell me."

He pulled her back to him and brought his face to hers. "I will, when it's the right time."

"Promise?"

"I promise." He pressed a lingering kiss to her lips to seal the deal.

A very deliberate throat clearing broke the pair apart, and they looked up to see her parents eyeing them with amused interest from just a few feet away. Emanuela's cheeks heated at the surreptitious, "Mm*hmmm*" coming from Mira's lips, and Finn could only chuckle.

"I think it's safe to say she'll no longer be condemning our public displays," Ethan said.

"Oh my God," Emanuela groaned. "Come on, let's keep going."

"Let's," Mira said, taking Finn by his arm. "But I'm stealing your walking partner for a while."

****

They made their way onto Forty-Seventh Street in the diamond district. Emanuela and Ethan were half a block ahead, and Finn slowed his pace to match Mira's. They'd been chatting amongst themselves the last twenty minutes.

"I was sorry to hear about your parents," she said. "Do you think the loss of your mother…forced you to grow up before you were ready?" She looked up ahead at Emanuela. "When I was at my worst, she was just a teenager, so I wonder sometimes if she felt cheated of some of her childhood."

Finn understood. "It's one of the things Emmi and I have in common that still amazes me. I'm not sure we grew up faster, but we were certainly less naïve than many of our peers. I think that's one of my favorite things about her. She has your worldly wisdom."

Mira smiled. "I think you've done a remarkable job becoming the man you are in spite of all the setbacks you've had. I can see why my baby loves you."

They checked to see how far Ethan and Emanuela had gotten when something in a window display caught Finn's eye.

"That's lovely," Mira said.

"I don't know much about this stuff," he said. "But this looks like her. Understated and elegant—kind of like you."

Mira gasped. "*Kind of?*"

"A lot like you," he said with a boyish grin.

"Hurry up, you two!" Emanuela's voice rang out from just down the street. "We want gelato from Dad's favorite place on Fifth."

His heart slammed in his chest. "Jesus," he said, looking at Mira. "Where'd they come from?"

"They always did have the best timing." She took one last lingering look at the display window before calling out to Ethan. "That place is a hike and my feet are starting to hurt."

"It's fine," Emanuela said, grinning up at Finn. "Just do the thing."

"Okay." He walked the short distance to the curb,

stepped into the street and held out his hand.

A yellow cab pulled up moments later and Emanuela smirked. "Shall we?"

Chapter Twenty-Three

One Month Later

"Hey you," Emanuela answered her cell. "How's the world tour going?"

Finn and Simon had begun making their scheduled appearances at the top ten engineering universities in the country, and Emanuela and Finn had become experts at phone tag.

"So far, so good!" he said. "We're finishing up the West Coast leg. Cal Tech tomorrow, and then we shoot for your side of the country in a few days."

"It's so exciting! I watched your presentation at Berkeley last night. I thought Simon was very compelling."

"*Simon?*"

"He's such a great public speaker, really knows how to capture his audience. There's something sweet about his mad scientist persona," she said, rambling on without mercy.

Finn groaned.

She snickered. "I'm sure you were very good too, but I was a little too distracted by how good you looked to really pay attention to what you were saying."

"I'm going on the record as being outraged about your treating me like a piece of meat, Emmi. Off the record, I'll keep in mind from now on that, while I'm trying to inspire the masses, you're out there undressing me with your eyes."

"Shamelessly, I'm afraid." She reached for a magazine on her desk. "Especially now that you're a superstar. World tours, magazine covers—"

"That's out already?"

"Mmhmmm." She looked at Finn and Simon on the cover of Popular Mechanics Magazine. They were provocatively styled in white lab coats opened over designer duds. They wore skinny ties and slicked-back hair, standing with their feet apart and arms folded. Their expressions were fixed like James Bond, sexy and stony. Most of the left leg of Finn's tuxedo pants was deliberately torn off, exposing the fine line on his thigh where the smart limb's "skin" met his own. It was a stunning image and Emanuela couldn't stop staring at it.

"Wow, that was fast," Finn said. "Feels like we just shot that."

"Their offices aren't far from here. You two should get a copy in the next week or so. It's really something else."

There was a pause.

"I miss you, Emmi."

"I miss you too. If there was anything else keeping you from me, I'd be jealous." She smiled down at the cover again. "But since you're off cavorting with *hundreds* of people instead of just one, I'll let it slide."

"Oh, well, I appreciate that."

****

"Miss Monroe?" Lydia poked her head into Emanuela's office half an hour later. "Mr. Hurst would like to see you."

271

Emanuela pursed her lips. Philip usually called her himself or stopped by her office if he needed something. "Did he say what about?"

"No, he just asked me to tell you to stop by his office as soon as you get a chance."

"Okay. Thanks, Lids."

She saved her work, locked her computer, and headed to Philip's office. Things seemed to be returning to some semblance of normal between them. Their old camaraderie wasn't completely restored, but being in each other's company was feeling more comfortable. He looked directly at her more instead of somewhere off to the side when he spoke. They were back in sync, delegating to each other during meetings as seamlessly as they'd always done. She released a soft breath and knocked on his open office door.

"Come on in, Em," he said, after looking up at her briefly. "Have a seat."

She smiled and took a seat in one of the chairs in front of his desk. When he didn't say anything after a few seconds, she spoke up. "Lydia said you wanted to see me. Is everything okay?"

He finished scribbling some notes, then sat back to look at her a moment, his face expressionless. "How long have you been seeing Doctor Kane?"

Her face fell. "Excuse me?"

"Something seemed off about you two during our meeting," he said in a measured tone. "There was this energy—tension." He motioned a hand in the air for emphasis, getting up from his chair and rounding his desk to sit at its edge in front of her. "I suspected you were uncomfortable with him, and made a mental note to ask if he'd been bothering you. But as the meeting went on, I began to wonder if it was something else entirely."

Emanuela quickly adjusted her initial look of surprise, carefully replacing it with her stoic mask, but remained silent.

"You don't deny it," he said.

"Why do I need to deny anything? Am I on trial?"

"Of course not." He sighed, getting up to pace in front of the large windows behind his desk. He turned his back to her and looked out at the city below, stuffing his hands into his pockets. "I couldn't be sure of what I was picking up on, so I had Andy in IT check him out."

Her mouth fell open. "You *violated* his privacy? Philip!"

He turned to look at her. "I had access to his hard drive, but I kept the investigation to a minimum. I could have discovered more than I did."

"So I should commend you then? For keeping your violation of his privacy to his personal email account?"

"There was no violation. I have a right to monitor emails as I see fit, based on the privacy agreement he signed. You know that, Emanuela."

Ah, the fine print. It never bothered her before because it never affected her directly. It was just part of the job. Nothing personal. Except that it was very personal.

"*As you see fit,*" Emanuela said. She nodded rapidly in disbelief, her body and mind at odds with what she was hearing, and released a heavy sigh. She was obviously no longer talking to her boss, and questioned whether she was talking to her friend. "Why didn't you just ask me? As long as we've known each other—as close as we've been—you felt you had to go behind my back?"

He stared at her for a pregnant moment. "As a friend?"

"As a *friend*." She spat the word as though it burned her tongue before it passed from her lips.

Philip at least looked ashamed. "I sensed something was going on with you two during the meeting. He was watching you like a hawk—*You* looked pretty damned uncomfortable, Em. And I don't know, a switch went off. I couldn't tell from your interactions whether it was mutual or one-sided. Given the way things between us had changed, it would have put you in an awkward spot to bring it up in conversation. When I saw the truth in those emails—"

He looked up at the ceiling for a moment and then back at her. "I was so looking forward to meeting him," he said, not actually saying Finn's name. "A man I had so much admiration for came out of nowhere and—"

"It's not a contest," Emanuela said. "I'm not a prize."

He threw his hands up. "You're right, Em. And I'm sorry, but I cannot unlearn the information I've obtained. The fact of the matter is that your boyfr—*Doctor Kane's*—dealings could reflect poorly on this firm."

"His *dealings?*" She felt her stomach drop, immediately registering what Philip was referring to. "He isn't selling these things from the trunk of his car, Philip! He's producing safe medical devices and giving them to people in need! *Children!*" She shot to her feet then, too wound up to remain seated.

"So why has he gone to such lengths to keep his

charitable work from being discovered?" he asked. "And why have you never mentioned it, Em? Surely if it's such a selfless cause, there should be no reason for the secrecy."

"I signed a nondisclosure agreement. He has his reasons—reasons that I think are valid—Admirable! Since you're so resourceful, perhaps you should *discover* them for yourself," she said, throwing the word back at him with disdain. "You might find that his reasons surprise you."

She glared at him from across his desk. His jaw tightened. Obviously, his pride was taking a beating. In all the time they'd known each other, he had never been the subject of such contempt in her eyes. But she was unmoved, crossing her arms over her chest.

His lips tensed. "Perhaps, but whatever his intentions, there is still the matter of optics."

They obviously weren't speaking as friends any longer.

"I'll handle it," Emanuela said, coolly.

"See that you do."

****

Emanuela rubbed her temples in agitation. She was driving poor Lydia crazy all afternoon, working with her on a plan to legitimize Finn's charity and make Hurst Capital look good. After countless calls to former clients and business acquaintances, setting up meetings with event planners and searching for an appropriate venue, they finally had a solution Emanuela believed Philip would go for. She left Finn a voice message urging him to call whenever he was able, but she hadn't heard from him yet. He was probably busy networking, or preparing for the next stop on his and Simon's talking tour.

She sighed. She hated having to tell Finn that his charity was about to go public in a very big way—much sooner than either of them had anticipated. She only hoped her plan would be successful enough to make it up to him somehow.

"I'll go ahead and draft a program template for you, Miss Monroe. I can have it for you within the hour," Lydia said.

"You're a *life* saver, Lids. Hey, before you go—"

Lydia looked up at Emanuela, gathering her notes. "Miss Monroe?"

"I-if this event is approved, it will be my last task for Hurst Capital. I'll be resigning shortly after."

"Oh," Lydia said, her face downcast.

"I know it's happening fast," Emanuela said. "For me, too. I didn't intend to resign for a few months, but circumstances have come up that—" She took a deep breath, uncertain of how to proceed with her explanation since she hadn't quite thought it through yet.

"There's no need to explain, Miss Monroe," Lydia said. "I have a friend at Titan Insurance Agency who says there's a position opening there soon. All I'd need is your recommendation and—"

"Of course! I'll call over there today and put in a good word for you."

Lydia gave her a solemn smile. "Thank you so much, Miss Monroe. I'm really going to miss working for you."

"You just let me know if you ever decide to move cross-country," Emanuela said, half serious.

"I will, Miss Monroe."

****

"Emmi," Finn said when Emanuela picked up her line. "Sorry I missed you. We just finished touring some of the labs here and we're breaking for lunch now."

"Sounds like you're having a great time."

He frowned at the tension in her voice. "What's wrong?"

"I don't know that there's an easy way to say this, so I'll just say it straight out."

He stiffened. "Okay."

"Philip was monitoring your emails during your visit here a few weeks ago."

Finn sucked in a breath.

She must have heard, because she spoke again quickly. "He kept it strictly to opened correspondence in your inbox. He assured me nothing else was compromised."

"Great. Then I guess it's okay."

"Finn—"

"Why?"

Emanuela sighed. "He thought I looked uncomfortable and suspected that maybe—that you were—"

"Sexually harassing you? Is that it?" He scoffed. "I'm sure he did. I'm also one hundred percent sure he's lying."

"I believe him."

Finn cursed.

"He was way out of line for what he did," she said, "but he thought he was looking out for me."

"You're defending him?"

"I'm not! I'm pissed too, Finn! He obviously

should have asked me himself, but considering the circumstances..." Her voice cracked. "I'm so sorry. This is all my fault. And that's not even everything."

Finn sighed in exasperation, but didn't say anything further.

"He knows about your charity work," she said.

"Obviously." His tone was biting but he couldn't help it.

"He voiced the same concerns I had when you first told me."

Finn's disbelieving laugh was his only answer.

"I didn't expect this to happen, Finn. I worked hard on the plan I shared with you, but I didn't want to move on it until you had time to think about it. The nonprofit hasn't even been registered yet."

"What does that mean?"

"It means the timeline has changed. I don't want to rush you, but I have a plan that will get your nonprofit up and going faster than we hoped. Hurst Capital will host a fundraising event for your charity. It'll be formal, to attract influential people with deep wallets. It's the best thing I could come up with that will make the firm look good, but only benefit your work. It's fool-proof, Finn. Let me make this up to you."

Pressure built between his temples. He appreciated her efforts, but no matter how diplomatic she worded it, he was being manipulated because a very powerful, very *insecure* man decided to snoop through his emails. It was insult to injury and frankly, he was pissed. "Fine. Whatever you need."

"I'll just need a name for it so I can get it registered and start moving on this," she said quietly.

"Give me a few hours."

"Okay."

The silence seemed to drag for an eternity.

"Finn—"

"I have to go," he said stiffly, and he hung up.

****

A couple of hours later, Emanuela stood in Philip's office, too wired after her tense conversation with Finn and too annoyed with her boss to even bother to sit down. He was reviewing the rough draft of her plan, which looked even more promising, she had to admit, with the program mockup Lydia designed.

"Is it satisfactory?" Emanuela asked when Philip finally looked up.

"It is." When she didn't immediately turn on her heel to leave, he spoke again. "Em—"

"You knew it wasn't harassment, didn't you?"

He sighed, his shoulders sagging. "Yes."

She nodded. "I'm tendering my resignation."

"Emanuela…"

She couldn't even meet his eyes. Instead, she looked somewhere to the side of him, speaking robotically. "Two weeks from this event, I'll no longer be working for Hurst Capital. I've compiled a shortlist of qualified replacements whom I'm confident will meet your expectations."

Philip searched her eyes. "Your mind is made up then."

She nodded once and, without another word, left his office. Her legs were a wobbly mess, her stomach twisted itself into a pretzel, and the beginnings of a migraine throbbed in her head, but she swore she heard him quietly sobbing before his assistant closed his office door.

Chapter Twenty-Four

Emanuela tapped away at her tablet, and Finn raked his fingers through his hair. They'd been at it for about an hour, batting potential names back and forth for the non-profit he wasn't sure he was ready to present to the world yet. The process was meticulous, each name needing to be checked through multiple databases to make sure it and anything remotely similar hadn't already been taken. It was a grueling day for them both, and the added tension from what Philip had done was like a third party in their conversation. It reminded them both of the reason they were sitting there in the first place. Emanuela looked slightly more optimistic this time, checking the final name in each of the databases.

"Well?" he asked, waiting for the verdict.

A few more taps and her chest rose and fell in a deep sigh of relief. "It checks out! Thank God."

She smiled at him, clearly pleased with their accomplishment. He'd given her a brief explanation for the meaning behind each of the potential names to help her determine an angle for branding.

"The name is perfect," she said, happily. "Best for last. I'll get a rush on registration first thing in the morning. There's quite a bit of paperwork—tax exemption and all of that—but I'll take care of it. The final step is to get a website up and running. People feel more confident making donations to organizations with an online presence."

He trusted her expertise completely, but he was growing tired of the tedious work at the late hour, and was ready to call it a night. When he didn't respond, she eyed him with a frown.

She pushed her tablet and several documents on her countertop aside. "I didn't want it to happen like this either, you know. I'm just trying to make the best of the situation."

He scoffed.

She sighed. "You know what? I've had it. I don't blame you for being withdrawn during this process, but I don't respond well to passive aggression. Why don't you just say what's on your mind, Finn?"

"*I* don't respond well to a spoiled, entitled grown man hacking into my personal email account because he's obsessed with my girlfriend."

She rubbed her temples. "What do you want me to do, Finn? I had no idea he was going to do that, and I was just as angry as you when I found out."

"Were you? Because, judging by the way you jumped to his defense—"

"I did not *jump* to his defense! Why are you turning this around on me? He was completely out of line for what he did, and I said just that when I confronted him about it. It wasn't illegal, and he's still my boss. There isn't anything else I can do."

He cursed beneath his breath. "You did defend him. You had no idea what his motive was or whether he went into my hard drive or not, but you seemed pretty confident—"

"Because I was. Initially."

"That's very naïve."

"We were *friends.* It's not naïve to give your friend the benefit of the doubt. He thought he was protecting me."

"Right. From sexual harassment, was it?"

"Finn…"

"The man told you he was in love with you, Emmi! You're perceptive—you should have seen right through him!"

"That's pretty condescending. And cynical. I'd rather be naïve than expect the worst from someone I trust."

"I don't have the pleasure of knowing him as well as you do, so forgive me if I don't trust him the way you obviously do."

She frowned. "What the hell is that supposed to mean?"

He sighed, immediately contrite. "Nothing, okay? We're both tired, so maybe it's best we talk tomorrow."

"No way."

He groaned. She wasn't about to let him off the hook.

"Explain yourself," she said. "Because if what you meant is the same thing going through my mind right now, I don't want to talk to you tomorrow."

"God, Emmi. I didn't mean it."

"It's interesting, isn't it?" she asked with a humorless laugh. "You can believe that you love me— that I love *you*—when we've hardly been seeing each other for five months, but it's naïve that I'd believe someone I've known for years."

"It's different with us, Emanuela."

"Why?"

"Because you love me. Because you know I don't have any ulterior motives."

"Do I? Maybe it's *naïve* to trust you after so little time. Maybe you're miffed because I admitted to being attracted to him and it's been eating you ever since."

He flinched. "I shouldn't have called you naïve."

"But you did."

Finn rubbed his chin. "Put yourself in my shoes. You took his word for it because of your friendship without considering how his feelings had changed…without considering how that looks to me from so far away."

Her face fell.

"Part of me understands why he did it," he said. "I'd probably be tempted to do the same thing in his position. But you can trust me, Emmi."

Her body relaxed, and she released a calming sigh. "I know. We've both been on edge for hours and we're taking it out on each other."

"I'm sorry," he said.

"Me too. I should have been more sensitive to how you were feeling. Are you okay?"

He really looked at her then, noticing the faint circles around her eyes for the first time, and he wanted to kick himself. He was so distracted by his own anger and annoyance that he didn't appreciate how hard she was working to turn things around in his favor.

"I'm fine," he said. "I'll talk to Philip when I'm ready, but I don't like being pushed. I don't like that something *he* did is forcing our hand."

"I don't like it either, but it was already part of our plan, Finn. It actually works out much better than what I proposed. A gala is more significant than a few donors. I didn't plan on quitting my job this soon, but we were arguing about whose mattress we'd keep and—"

"You *quit?*"

"Things got pretty heated between Philip and I. I told him I'm resigning two weeks after the benefit gala."

"Emmi—"

"It's okay. It's just a few months ahead of schedule. I can be a tourist—rent something in Seattle until you make an honest woman out of me."

Finn was pretty sure he could read every thought going through her mind, and he would have laughed out loud if he didn't know how vulnerable she was allowing herself to be for him. "Emmi, I would marry you tomorrow if you were ready, but I'm willing to wait until you are."

She gasped, trembling visibly, her eyes becoming great big glassy pools.

"Emmi?"

"How soon can you get here?"

****

Seven Weeks Later

"Don't be ridiculous, Em." Allie fell into step with a throng of evening rush-hour foot traffic along Spring Street in Soho, practically shouting at Emanuela through the phone. "We're not *not* celebrating your birthday. Quit moping just because the Good Doctor can't make it or I'll feel insulted."

"I'm not moping." Emanuela sat at her desk trying to think of an excuse to cancel their plans for the evening. "I'm just tired. Let's do something this weekend instead."

Allie stepped onto the curb. "I tuned you out after you said you weren't moping. I might not be able to give you screaming orgasms—or whatever it is you do when you have them—what *do* you do, by the way?"

"*Allie!*"

"Fine—but you're not ditching. Did you bring a change of clothes like I told you?"

Emanuela mumbled incomprehensibly.

"Good," Allie said. "Look hot. I don't want to upstage you on your birthday."

"I don't know why we're friends."

Allie stepped just out of the way of the subway entrance. "Love you too."

Emanuela frowned at the background noise on Allie's end of the call. "Are you going home? You won't make it back here in an hour."

"I forgot something, okay? Don't worry, I'll make it back. One hour, Em."

"Okay," Emanuela said, resigned. "See you soon."

Allie hung up and sent a quick text message, then disappeared down the subway steps.

****

Emanuela gave herself a final appraisal in her office mirror. She wore a blush colored cocktail dress that fit her like a sleeve and showed off her long legs. Turning, she admired the way the dress dipped to her waist and revealed the smooth, sinuous curve of her back. She tossed her hair a bit to give it some body after spending the day pinned up, slipped into her heels, and covered herself with the blazer she'd worn to work that morning.

"Goodnight, Miss Monroe," Lydia said as Emanuela approached her desk. "And happy birthday."

"Thanks Lids!" Emanuela smiled. She was actually feeling up to a night out now. Then she thought of something. "Do I have any meetings tomorrow?"

"No. You can indulge tonight," Lydia said with a knowing smile.

"I think I will. Go home. Nite, Lids!" She tapped a quick message to Finn and made her way to the elevators.

—Heading out now. Allie is determined to get me drunk. Fair warning.—

They video chatted early that morning so he could be the first to wish her a happy birthday. He knew not to send flowers since she could never manage to keep them alive longer than forty-eight hours. Instead, he had a card and truffles from Vosges Haute-Chocolates delivered to her office. She'd skipped lunch, shamelessly devouring all sixteen of the succulent sweets in flavors like sweet Indian curry and coconut, candied violet flower, and crunchy hazelnut praline.

Finn and Simon had their hands full lately, supervising the arrival and installation of the new lab equipment at SimLife Laboratories, and a million other details that needed their undivided attention. Finn promised to make it up to her next weekend when he came to visit.

She stepped from the elevator, smiling at his text response.

—Sorry to be missing that. You're a sexy drunk. Handsy.—

She expertly navigated through the lobby without needing to look up, tapping her reply.

—For your sake I hope not. ;)—

She narrowly missed colliding with someone on

her way through the sliding doors, and his response came a moment later.

—What? Watch where you're going.—

She stopped in her tracks and looked up, her heart pounding. *Oh my God.* She saw no sign of him among the annoyed passersby who had to go around her as she stood puzzled on the sidewalk. *Where are you?* Then the sidewalk cleared and her lips parted.

Finn's wide, satisfied grin spread across his face and out through his eyes. He was a few yards down the street, leaning against the shiny curves of a 1981 vintage marathon yellow checkered cab.

Emanuela gasped. "You didn't!"

"I couldn't get Morris, so I got the next best thing."

He looked so sexy in his thigh-hugging denim and black shirt, the curling waves of his hair smoothed back. His lips twitched and his arms remained folded, his eyes narrowing at her in amusement.

She grinned and stepped into his personal space, taking his arms and wrapping them around her. "I don't want to know how much this is costing you."

"Worth it."

He drank her in with his eyes, his fingers flexing against her hips. His voice was huskier when he spoke again. "You look too good to be going out without me. Allie's gonna be a no-show. I hope you aren't too disappointed."

"Not too," she said, against his lips. "Not at all."

They moaned at the soft, lingering touch of their lips, familiarizing themselves with touch and taste and smell again.

"Happy birthday, beautiful," he said, pulling away.

"Thank you. I can't believe you did this."

"We're just getting started, baby."

****

They sat on one of the plush, deep purple couches of Raines Law Room, partially hidden from the view of other patrons by semi-sheer purple curtains. The dimly lit cocktail lounge mimicked the speakeasies of the 1920s, with its exposed brick walls, luxurious antique furniture and vintage artwork.

The wallpaper design was of tiny black figures engaged in various positions of the Kama Sutra. "*Oh my God!*" she whispered. "This better not be a swinger's club, Finn."

He cracked up, leaning in to murmur in her ear. "Will you relax? I'm not sharing you with anyone, Emmi."

The waitress brought their drinks, and after instructing them to ring the tableside bell for anything else, they were left alone.

"Remind me to send Simon another thank you card," she said. "He keeps letting you ditch him for me."

"He'd do the same to me in a heartbeat if Jamie was the one who lived across the country. But I do still owe him for making him give the talk at MIT without me so I could satiate my horny girlfriend."

She gasped and pulled away. "*Excuse me?* You were giving me moony eyes and talking about marrying me the next day. How else was I supposed to respond?"

"I'm not complaining, Emmi," he said, pulling her back to him. "I like it when you get all worked up."

She was about to groan at his continued teasing, but something in his pocket pressed uncomfortably against her thigh. She decided to give him a dose of his own medicine, moving her hand deliberately over the small bulk at his hip. "Someone's happy to see me."

"I'm always happy to see you. Will you stop undressing me with your eyes? It makes me feel cheap."

"*Ugh*!" She elbowed his ribs. "You've been made. Hand it over, mister."

He laughed again and leaned away from her a bit, raising his hips slightly to remove a small gift box from his pocket. "I wanted to get you something meaningful. Hopefully it's the right size."

She leaned in to give him a peck on the lips and eagerly opened the box. She lifted a braided white gold watch from the box. There were tiny diamonds around the bezel and a shiny, mother-of-pearl face.

"Wow. Finn…it's beautiful!" Almost immediately, she frowned. "Wait…" She looked at the face again, bemused. "It's blank. How does it work?"

He took the dainty watch from her and undid the clasp, fastening it around her slender wrist. "It's a watch that doesn't tell time."

Her eyes widened in curiosity.

"There are no hands, no numbers, no calendar of any kind," he said. "It's essentially a bracelet that looks like a watch. I wanted you to have something to remind you that what we have isn't dependent on time. I don't count the weeks or months we've known each other to determine how I feel, or if we've been together long enough to trust in 'forever.' In my mind, we were a done deal before we ever met. We just needed to cross each other's paths so our souls would recognize each other."

Emanuela swallowed through a haze of tears—and

slight inebriation—before silencing him with a kiss. Her eyes were open, hungry for his features, but he was a blur. Her hands rose to hold his face. If she couldn't see him clearly, she at least wanted to touch him, to feel the muscles of his face move as he kissed her back. Her mind was quickly wandering away from her in that moment, and the last thoughts she remembered before she was swept up in him completely were that he tasted of scotch and mint, and that she didn't think it was possible to love anyone the way she loved him.

****

Emanuela sat next to Finn in the back of their rented cab, absentmindedly tracing the grooves of his abs beneath his shirt with her fingers. The cooler air of late September cleared her head from the cocktails she drank, and she realized they'd turned much too early. The street sign read "W. 46th St."

"Where are you taking me?" she asked.

He caught her roving hand in his and rubbed the back of it with his thumb. "You'll see."

A few minutes later, they arrived at The French Quarters, a boutique hotel that instantly reminded Emanuela of their time in New Orleans with its red brick façade, intricate wrought-iron balconies, and gas-lit street lamps on either side of the entrance. Finn smiled at her astonished expression before thanking the driver and taking her hand to guide her inside.

Their room was modest, but charmingly decorated with a modern take on the French style of historic New Orleans. There was an exposed brick wall behind the queen bed, the skirt and shams matching the white and navy floral curtains on the window. Two red-shaded lamps stood atop the buffet in front of the bed, reminding Emanuela of the lamps in their hotel room in New Orleans.

"Finn…"

"It's where I first realized I was in love with you," he said, drawing her into his arms. "I know it's not the same—"

"It's perfect," she said. "I don't even know how to tell you how much this means to me."

He held her a whisper away from him, his hands low on her hips, and looked into her eyes. "You just did."

They took their time, fabric against fabric as their bodies pressed together; skin against fabric as they undressed each other; and skin against skin as their hands trailed and stroked, kneaded and clasped.

"I love you, Finn," Emanuela said afterward. "I wanted to tell you first so I wouldn't be the one to say—"

"Ditto," he said, still recovering his breaths.

"Your nostrils are flaring."

Her grumbling stomach interrupted the response Finn had on his tongue.

"Animals, both of us." He rolled from her carefully to get cleaned up and order room service.

They shared crab cakes, crawfish cakes, and Cajun fries dipped in remoulade from the restaurant downstairs. Emanuela sat on the bed in one of Finn's T-shirts, and he sat in the only chair in the room, pulled up to one of the end tables, stuffing their faces and chatting contentedly.

"I can't believe you two pulled this off," she said. "I can usually tell when Allie is up to something— Well, she's always up to something, so maybe that's why I didn't think anything of it."

He looked at her in disbelief. "You're full of shit, you know that?"

She wrinkled her nose at him. "Fine. You're that good. But you know what you missed, Doctor Kane?"

"What's that?"

"I don't have a change of clothes, and I don't do walks of shame."

"Well, it's a good thing I gave Allie a room key earlier"—he stood to pull a garment bag from the closet—"or you'd never leave this room."

She wiped her hands and stood to open the bag. "*Oh my God!*" she shrieked, almost missing the card that fell to the floor in her excitement.

Finn looked concerned. "What's wrong?"

She removed the red Donna Karan wrap dress from the garment bag. "Nothing. I have a dress just like this in green because the red was sold out," she said, reading the card.

I still want the green one. It will look better on me. Happy birthday, Em.

Love,
Allie

Finn bent to kiss her nose. "There's one more thing," he said, pulling a familiar pale blue box from the shelf in the closet.

She grinned. "Canelés."

"Not quite."

She peeked inside and her eyes lit from the inside out. "Beignets."

Chapter Twenty-Five

Five Weeks Later

"Okay, I got one," Emanuela said. She lay on her side, peering at Finn on her screen through sleepy eyes.

"One more," he said. "Allie will kill me if you get run over by a taxi tomorrow because you can't see straight in the morning."

"Jamie would kill you first, and then ship your body off so Allie can tie weights to it and dump it in the Hudson."

His face went blank at the detail she'd come up with on the spot for his untimely demise. "That is decidedly morbid."

Her hand flew to her mouth to cover her burst of laughter. "Hey, you started it," she said when she could breathe again. "You wouldn't be at the bottom of the river right now if I hadn't been creamed by one of New York's finest."

His gaze roamed her face, his eyes narrowing. The only light in her room came from the bathroom, and the ever-present glow of the city through her window. He looked like he was someplace else for a moment, the thoughts running through his mind transforming his features from one expression, to the next, to the next...

"Finn? Where were you just now?"

He came to at the sound of her voice. "I'm sorry."

Emanuela propped her head up on her hand and waited.

"Do you remember what you felt last time?" he asked.

She nodded. They didn't have a name for whatever it was—the sudden onslaught of raw emotion that hit them every so often and ruined even the best of their days apart.

Some days felt normal—whatever *that* meant in their situation. They called each other to say "Good morning" and went to work, video chatting at night no matter how crappy the connection. The nights she went out with Allie, or Finn stayed late at Simon's, they texted each other, or at the risk of being corpses the next morning, video chatted anyway because they desperately needed to see each other's faces. Moments like this when their guards were down, when they shared moments other couples could have face-to-face, they felt tired with longing. There was no cure but to ride it out.

"I remember," she said, feeling traces of those feelings creeping back up at the memory. "You're feeling it now."

He nodded, offering a weak smile.

"Ugh, I'm so sick of this." She tore her comforter away and climbed out of bed. He called after her, but she'd already flicked on the light and come back to bed, this time sitting Indian style a foot away from her screen. She unceremoniously peeled her nightshirt up and over her head, leaving herself bare from the waist up. She grinned triumphantly at Finn's softly expelled curse.

"What are you doing?" he asked, stunned.

"Snapping you out of it. Now you… Chop, chop!" she said, snapping her fingers.

He shook his head and did what he was told.

"Good," Emanuela said, satisfied.

He reached out a hand, flexing his fingers, pretending to grope her.

"Knock it off!" she said with a giggle. "Now back to the question."

"You've got to be kidding."

"Dead serious."

"Emmi," he groaned. "Put your shirt back on. I'm okay now."

She preened a little, straightening her posture to push her breasts out even more. "You sure?"

Another wordless groan and she did as he asked, but took her time turning the shirt right-side-out and pulling it down once she had it over her head.

His face was stone. "Don't tease me, Emanuela. I've racked up quite a few flyer miles."

She swallowed. "Is it still my turn?"

He smiled, nodding once.

"Okay. Let's say we get into it while we're apart—something big that neither of us wanted to compromise on—What would you do?"

"If that was going to happen, I think it would have by now," he said. "We've discussed all the hard stuff, like faith and family."

"That's true… Let's say we have an argument that escalates and we say things that are hard to take back."

"Well, flowers are out."

"Mmm-hmm."

"And it's not clear who started it?"

"No, and I'm stubborn. But you're not," she said.

"So it's on you."

"Oh, I see," he said with a grin. He thought for a minute, and then his mouth widened into a brilliant smile. "I'd ask you to meet me halfway."

"But I just said we couldn't—"

"No," he said, shaking his head. "That's not what I meant. Hang on…"

She folded her arms across her chest and waited. He reached for his cell phone and tapped away at the screen. When he looked up again, she was waiting with amused curiosity. "Well?"

"Buffalo, North Dakota."

"*What?*"

"That's exactly halfway between Oak Harbor and New York City," he said. "Google it."

She picked up her phone and tapped the name of the city into the search engine. "Oh my God, Finn! This says Population 197! There are more *buffalo* than people!"

"I've always wanted to try a buffalo burger."

She snickered. "Stop! What the hell would we even *do* there?"

"Eat, sleep, have angry makeup sex."

"I can't believe you!" she said in disbelief. "You'd really do that?"

"I would. If I thought for a minute that we were falling apart, I'd book us a room at the…" He tapped something into his phone again and frowned. "Well, there isn't a hotel in Buffa—"

"*Oh my God!*" Emanuela lost it. "We're *doomed!*"

He ignored her, scrolling the small screen on his phone with one finger. "Fargo is very close by, several hotels. Can you live with three stars?"

She took a deep breath to halt her laughter, blowing slowly as she exhaled. "I can live with three stars. Only for you."

"I know."

"Fighting with you could get costly."

"Well, I've recently come into some money."

She snickered again. "Your turn."

Finn's expression sobered then. "What if I could help fix a broken friendship?"

"Finn—"

"I spoke to him, Emmi. We talked for at least twenty minutes."

"That's great," she said stiffly. "I'm happy for you."

"Emanuela—"

"It's not on you, Finn. Philip betrayed my trust. He has to come to me."

"I'm not denying that. I've lived long enough to know that even good people do shitty things sometimes. I know how much his friendship meant to you and how stressful it must be to work with him the way things are right now." He dragged his fingers through his hair. "I don't want you to resent me later."

Though his words were getting through to her, she wasn't ready to admit she wasn't completely indifferent to her fractured friendship with her boss. "Thank you," she said sincerely, but in her reserved tone. "I'm fine. The gala is just a couple of weeks away and then I can put this whole thing behind me."

****

"*Anata wa totemo shinsetsu desu*," Emanuela said courteously into her office phone. "*Oyasumi nasai*." The client on the other line graciously corrected her and her face heated. "Oh, I'm sorry," she said, switching back to English. "It's morning there. Of course! *Sayonara!*" She hung up with a sigh and rubbed her temples, scolding herself for her blunder.

"Your Japanese is still great," Philip said from her doorway.

"I—" She nearly jumped from her skin. "Thank you."

She eyed him for a moment, not sure she wanted to open up to him. He looked comfortable leaning against the doorframe, his hair tousled, his hands stuffed into his pockets. She narrowed her eyes. There was something different about him. His deep brown eyes were nearly clear of the circles that surrounded them for... *How many weeks has it been?* They'd been walking on eggshells around each other for so long— only speaking professionally and not daring to make prolonged eye contact—that she hadn't noticed his newly trimmed hair, his clean-shaven face and his noticeably less tense posture.

"Em." His gentle voice pierced through her thoughts, and she snapped out of it. She must have been staring a hole straight through him.

"I'm off my game," she said. "I was slower than usual. They spoke much faster than me."

"You're out of practice." He shrugged. "You missed Tokyo this year."

She looked away just in time to see Lydia quietly leaving for the day. "I know."

"Brian doesn't know a *lick* of Japanese. And he's not that nice to look at," he said with a grin. "I really had to have my wits about me this year without my partner around to keep me straight and charm our competitors."

"Philip…"

"I don't deserve it—I know I don't, Em. But if there's a chance that things don't have to end this way—" He looked at her more intently this time, pleading with his eyes. "Think about it, will you? Your forgiveness would mean the world to me."

He didn't stick around for her response, and she didn't have one anyway. She needed time to think about accepting the olive branch he'd extended.

****

"Don't call yourself a chef if you're gonna let a little tiny cake kick your ass, Jamie," Allie yelled across her kitchen, waving Emanuela over to a barstool.

Emanuela obediently sat down to observe the spirited exchange between her two friends and gorge herself on the smorgasbord of baked goodies resting on Allie's counter.

"Listen, okay? These are not *cakes,* babe. They're the vittles of little demon spawn. Even the pan looks evil." His exasperated complaint came loud and clear through the speakerphone.

Allie sighed and joined Emanuela at the counter. "Well, the little demon spawn is here in case you want to say hi."

His tone immediately brightened. "Hey, gorgeous!"

Emanuela grinned, quickly swallowing the macaron she'd stuffed into her mouth whole and barely chewed. "Hi, Jamie! What on earth are you doing?"

"I hate to break it to you, Em," he said in a deathly serious tone, "but the woman you thought was your friend all this time is actually a witch."

"Oh *come on!"* Allie said, planting her flour-covered palms against the counter.

"She is," Jamie said. "She's trying to force me to practice her black magic to keep you under her spell."

Allie rolled her eyes. "I'm *trying* to teach him how to make canelés and he's being such a wuss about it."

Emanuela gasped. "Yes!"

"Don't get too excited," he said, irritably. "I did something. Tell me what I did."

"I can't *see* you," Allie snapped. "Besides, it could be anything. You have to start over."

"*What*!" he yelled, and then something crashed to the floor. "No way. The damn batter sat in the fridge for *two days*. I am *not* starting over."

Allie threw up her hands.

"Okay," Emanuela said, mediating the quickly deteriorating situation. "Hang up and dial us back on video."

A few minutes later, Allie was watching Jamie on Emanuela's tablet, her face screwed up. "Put them back in."

"They've been in there for over an hour," he said. "They're going to burn."

"They're not gonna burn, okay? They're not even close to done."

"They're golden brown."

"They have to be deep brown," Allie said, patiently. "*Deep,* deep brown. They're gonna need another hour."

Jamie looked at Allie like she was certifiable but obeyed, placing the copper pan of precious little French cakes gently back on the oven rack and shutting the door.

Emanuela took the tablet from Allie and grinned at

Jamie. "You hate baking."

She got a snort in reply.

Jamie was put out, but Emanuela laid it on thick, opening her eyes wide and giving him a little pout. "You love me."

"Well, since you're obviously hopelessly addicted to these little demon cakes, and Allie *insists* they're only good for about five hours—"

"On the *outside,*" Allie said from her place at the sink.

Jamie wrinkled his nose. "Anything for you, gorgeous. You know that."

Emanuela mouthed a quick "Thank you" before Allie snatched the tablet away.

"Send me a photo when they're done. If they're ugly, we have to start over."

"Ugh, goodbye."

****

Allie and Emanuela walked arm-in-arm along Gramercy Park West. Autumn had finally arrived, the humidity of summer making way for the crisp, cooler air and shorter days of late October. The leaves of the tree-lined streets in the manicured neighborhood were a rainbow of reds, oranges and golds. They fluttered overhead, or drifted above people in chunky knits and wool-blend coats walking their pedigree dogs. Allie dragged Emanuela out for a walk beneath the old-fashioned street lamps to work off some of the dessert she'd devoured over the space of twenty minutes.

"Thanks for the dress, Em."

"Yeah, well, you weren't very subtle."

Allie nudged Emanuela playfully with her hip and navigated their path around the park's gated perimeter.

"Spill. I tried to stay out of your business until you were ready to tell me, but my patience has its limits! This is really happening, isn't it?"

Emanuela giggled nervously. "I guess it is."

"You *guess?*"

"I'm obviously moving," Emanuela said. "But I think we're both nervous about specifics."

They synchronized their turn onto North Gramercy, Allie shaking her head in amusement. "You two have been at it like rabbits since you met each other but you draw the line at shacking up?"

Emanuela laughed at that. Allie was right, of course. "I know it sounds ridiculous but it just feels different somehow. It's hard to explain…"

Allie glared at her. "I'm gonna need you to try, hon. My oven is still on."

"He wants me to move in with him. But I *know* him, Allie. We've been flirting with the word marriage a lot and it's— I know it's coming. I just don't know *when* he's gonna make his move."

"I knew it was coming too in an odd way," Allie said, slowing their pace. "I'm really happy for you, Em. I know I have a weird way of showing it—"

"The canelés."

Allie's smooth, pale skin blushed prettily. "Jamie and I thought you might get homesick—at least in the beginning. We wanted you to have something to make you feel better. And since I've never seen you use anything but a coffeemaker and a microwave…"

Emanuela gasped, stopping their steps abruptly. "Not true! I just don't have time to cook."

"Okay, hon," Allie said, giving Emanuela's hand a patronizing pat.

They were quiet for a moment, and it occurred to Emanuela that what they'd been referring to as "the future" was becoming a present reality.

"Oh my God," Allie breathed.

"I know."

"We have to pack! We have to list your apartment. We have to figure out what furniture you're taking—what clothes I get to keep—"

"Whoa," Emanuela said, her eyes wide. "Don't give me a heart attack, okay?"

Allie grinned. "Right. Sorry."

Emanuela took Allie's arm again and turned them back toward her apartment. "Okay, show me what you're wearing to the gala."

Chapter Twenty-Six

Two Weeks Later

Five hundred guests descended on the breathtaking colonnade of Grand Central Terminal. The women were stunning, every one of them an ethereal beauty in keeping with *The Midsummer Night's Dream* theme of the night. Gowns of every shade, intricately beaded or expertly ruched, swept their way across palatial pink marble floors. Travelers passing through the terminal en route to their trains stopped to stare and, if they were lucky, immortalize one of the beauties in a photograph as she paused to admire the painted heavenlies in the cylindrical ceiling far above their heads. The gentlemen were impressive in their tuxedos and polished shoes, captivating passersby with their confident mystique.

Ticketed guests were allowed entry into Vanderbilt Hall, its magnificent arch draped in twisting vines and braided branches illuminated by hundreds of tiny fairy lights. Once through, the effect was powerful—and immediate. The contrast between the busy terminal and what lay beyond that archway was debilitating, causing guests to gasp in awe and even clap in spontaneous appreciation. The elegant grandeur of the century-old great room was overtaken by a magical forest.

Burgeoning vines scaled the forty-eight-foot walls and stretched across the ceiling, the marble and stonework deliberately visible beneath living décor. Moss dripped from the ceiling in gorgeous shades of violet, maroon and pale green. Five large crystal chandeliers stretched from one end of the space to the other, shining dimly through the moss.

Hundreds of hanging glass terrariums of varying size holding tiny white tea lights dangled from the branches of each manzanita tree at the center of the round dinner tables, accompanied by antique candelabras. There were even custom crystal wine glasses for each guest to take home. Too many fairy lights to number wrapped around the branches of centerpieces, crept up walls and stretched across the ceiling, giving the enchanted space the appearance of a night lit by millions of stars.

Guests not participating in the silent auction enjoyed their cocktails, or snuck decadent desserts from the bars at either end of the room, waiting for the dinner portion of the program to commence. An eleven-piece orchestra, including a stunning golden harp and a vocalist reminiscent of Ella Fitzgerald's sweet, silvery tone, filled the space with entrancing sound.

Finn was *nervous*. He was scheduled to speak and the seat to his right was noticeably empty. Emanuela was busy rubbing elbows with sponsors and chatting up the silent auction tables. His wasn't the only admiring glance to follow her about the room, the sheer chiffon of her Watteau train trailing behind her. He shared a table toward the small stage up front with Simon, Jamie and four other esteemed guests and their dates.

The conversation was easy, since Finn was well-acquainted with everyone. He managed to convince four of the doctors from points abroad who'd received his printed prosthetics for their patients to attend the event. They, along with Finn, would be honored that evening, and being able to speak face-to-face for the first time was a treat for them all. He was enjoying their company, but he hadn't been able to greet Emanuela properly yet, and he was itching for a good look at her. She'd insisted they not see each other before the gala…

"We've never seen each other all dressed up before, Finn," she told him. *"I want us to be surprised."*

And surprised he was. *Stupefied*, more like it. She looked otherworldly, sheathed in royal blue chiffon that moved like air—or water. It was one with her body, fitted flawlessly from its one-shouldered strap, to her hip, where it fell like a curtain to the floor. She moved and his mouth went dry. The weightless fabric parted into a slit that reached mid-thigh, showing off a long, silken leg.

He noticed the gift he'd given her on her birthday gleaming from her wrist and smiled. He wasn't completely sure of his next observation, but he could swear her hair was longer, styled into forties waves like an old Hollywood star.

Fitting, he thought with open admiration. He couldn't find a coherent word the first time he spotted her that evening, and Jamie and Simon had shared a good laugh at his expense.

"Uh-uh." Jamie tugged Finn by his arm to locate their table.

Finn scoffed at the idea that the slighter man could stop him from going to Emanuela by strength alone. Jamie silently seemed to agree, trying another tactic altogether. "You aren't about to follow her around like a lovesick puppy."

Finn was unmoved by the insult and pushed along anyway.

"She'll be done schmoozing eventually!" Jamie said more insistently. "Have some dignity, okay? Come wait with us like a big boy."

"That's enough, Jamie," Simon said. "I think he gets the point."

Emanuela finally made her way to the table soon after, and Finn stood to greet her. He wisely opting to graze her cheek with a soft kiss, instead of enveloping her on the spot and ruining the alluring berry shade of her lips. He must have stared too long, because Jamie deliberately cleared his throat from his seat beside hers, and her cheeks flamed. She greeted everyone at the table, pecking air kisses to Jamie and Simon's cheeks before taking hold of Finn's arm.

"I'm just going to borrow him for a minute," she said with a brilliant smile.

"Please do," Jamie muttered with a pointed glance at Finn.

She mouthed, "Behave," and led Finn away.

Finn leaned toward her to whisper in her ear. "You slay me."

The elegant Emanuela Monroe missed a step, and his satisfied grin remained until they reached their destination. A man rose from his place at a table near the dessert bar to greet them and Finn recognized him immediately. "Morris!"

"Good to see ya 'gain, Doctor Kane," Morris said. "I want you to meet my wife, Alicia."

"Finn," he said with a smile, taking Morris's hand before kissing his petite wife's cheek. "I'm so glad you could make it."

"That was Miss Monroe's doin'."

Finn questioned her with a lifted brow and she winked.

"Morris entrusted me with a fifteen hundred-dollar donation during our stay in New Orleans," she said. "It got him and Alicia an entry in the raffle for a weekend getaway anywhere in the continental U.S."

Finn remembered the envelope Morris insisted Emanuela take at the airport before they left the Crescent City. "Thank you so much!" he said. "Your donation will pay for at least ten new prosthetic limbs. I can't thank you enough, Morris. Both of you."

The couple looked embarrassed at the attention.

"It's great what you're doin' Doc—Finn," Morris said humbly. "We're just glad t'help out a little, 'specially after how good you and Miss Monroe have been to us."

"It was the opposite!" Emanuela said warmly. "We really had a good time."

Morris nodded, not about to contradict a lady.

"I hope you win that raffle," Finn said. He took Morris's hand one last time, and turned with Emanuela to leave.

****

The first course was served promptly at eight. The music was sublime, conversation flowed, and guests mingled between tables. Emanuela spotted a copper-haired beauty in a beaded champagne gown and intricate high bun. "Allie! You look amazing!"

"I know," she said, pecking Emanuela's cheek. "Hi, love," she greeted Jamie, exchanging cheek kisses in turn. "Good Doctor," she said, nodding at Finn. She grinned before addressing the rest of the table. "*Other* good doctors."

After entertaining the table with her hilarious brand of small talk, Allie bent to Emanuela's ear. "Come find me when you're done working."

****

The orchestra took a break during the second course. A montage of photos, video footage and interview clips of the patients Finn and his colleagues abroad had helped with the printed prosthetics began to play, and he saw Emanuela's eyes prick when little Maddie and Simon Peter's faces graced the screen.

After a brief introduction from the paid hostess of the night, Finn's colleagues were honored with plaques for their charitable work under extraordinary conditions. Moments before Finn's turn, Emanuela squeezed his thigh beneath the table and he looked at her, absorbing every bit of warmth and encouragement from her eyes to ease his nerves. He'd given plenty of talks before, but they both appreciated how different this was. With a kiss to her hand, he rose to take the podium. The screen behind him flickered on, and the silhouette of a baobab tree, the symbol he'd chosen to represent his nonprofit, stood majestically in front of a setting sun.

"Thank you," he said, his deep, genuine tone blanketing the room. He examined the plaque he held, heavy crystal with his name etched in gold leaf. "Wow. You know, when I started this work a couple of years ago, I just wanted to use some part of my passion for good. It started out as an effort to help people who'd sustained severe injuries in communities that suffered recent tragedy. When someone is considered lucky to be alive, and food and water are the most urgent needs, it's easy to overlook the loss of a limb."

He straightened to his full height, looking out at the sea of well-dressed people with able bodies, and bank accounts that could afford the very best in medical care. His gaze took in the incredible doctors who shared his table, and finally rested on Emanuela. She was the reason he stood there just then, the reason he would be able to help so many more people for as long as he was able. At her subtle nod, he took a calming breath.

"Thanks to your generous donations, Budding Limb has grown from a grassroots effort that started in a two-car garage, maintained by the handful of doctors honored tonight, to a respected establishment that will help countless people across the globe. You aren't just providing a one-time service. You're giving child patients new limbs every four years. These prosthetic limbs will grow with the patients, ensuring old limbs aren't used past expiration, and improving overall quality of life. In addition, we are now able to print prosthetics in stronger materials, something we previously couldn't afford. This means injured men and women, out of work because they can't afford proper prosthetic limbs that can withstand the rigors of manual labor, will be able to care for their families again."

"Is there anything more important, more profound than that? To be afforded dignity? To be able to work to meet an end? To fulfill a dream? That's exactly what you've done tonight. You've helped to realize a dream that means more to me, even, than this amazing award. Thank you."

He said the last two words with a nod and, before he could step from the stage, the audience was on its feet, their applause and cheers going into the air and trickling out to curious travelers in the great terminal. Emanuela stood and clapped along with everyone else, her eyes brimming with pride and immeasurable joy.

When Finn returned to his seat, she didn't hesitate to reach for him and pull him into a long embrace. "I'm so proud of you," she said into his ear. "That was so moving. I love you so much."

"Ditto," he whispered back.

He was dying to peck her nose, her cheeks, her lips…but he knew the show of affection she allowed herself in the moment was a big step for her, and didn't want to ruin it by putting her on the spot in front of their table guests.

"*Ahem*!" Jamie said. "If you can't share with the class, save it for later!"

That brought another round of laughter to the table, and the orchestra returned to serenade the room. Those who hadn't gorged themselves made their way to the dessert bars. Volunteers for the event skillfully rearranged some of the tables to clear a dance floor in the center of the space, and the lighting was adjusted to turn the enchanted forest an enticing blue.

Jamie and Simon were already up and moving, along with countless other couples. Finn eyed Emanuela suggestively and she giggled. "Stop looking at me."

"I can't," he said, honestly. "You'd have to gouge my eyes out, and even then they'd roll in your direction from whatever sorry spot they landed."

"Oh my God." She wrinkled her nose.

He stood, lifting a brow at her in challenge as he extended his hand to her. "Dance with me."

He took her hand and she settled into his frame

comfortably, one hand on his shoulder, the other held gently in his. They moved, mere centimeters apart, and she looked up at him with pride in her eyes. "I don't know what I did to deserve you, but tell me so I can keep doing it."

Finn chuckled. "You tell me first."

"Well," she said, looking him over. "For starters, you're handsome."

He led them around their little circle. "Oh?"

"Pretty devastatingly so. You look so sexy in a tux. I've been trying not to bite you all evening."

Heat rushed to his ears. "Emmi," he groaned, gripping her waist tighter. "You're killing me."

She moved the hand at his shoulder and caressed his neck with the back of her fingers. "Right there."

Before he could respond with the dare on his tongue, Jamie discreetly caught Finn's attention with a meaningful nod, and Finn pulled Emanuela flush against him, forgetting himself for a moment. "Hold that thought. Jamie wanted to show me something. Will you be okay for a few minutes?"

She nodded, taking a nip at his jaw and moving from his embrace. "I'll find Allie. You go ahead."

****

Finn and Jamie left the great hall, and Emanuela turned on her heel, intending to look for Allie and nearly colliding with Philip. "Oh!"

She was perpetually startled by him, it seemed, and there was no sign of his date anywhere.

"Do you have room on your dance card for an old friend?" he asked.

The magnetic confidence Emanuela knew and loved had been restored, and she felt a smile tug at her lips. "I think I might have one left."

The song playing was slow, meant for an intimate embrace and softly spoken words, so it was awkward at first. They made the best of it though, opting for a conservative hold with space between them.

"You look beautiful, Em. You really did a remarkable job here. You didn't have much notice, I'm afraid."

"I didn't, but I'm not sure I believe in coincidences anymore." She smiled up at him, matching his steps easily. "Maybe *everything* doesn't happen for a reason, but I think this is a fitting conclusion for this chapter of our lives."

Philip nodded. "I know what you mean. It's bittersweet, isn't it?"

There was sadness behind his smile. He stopped their movement and released her with obvious reluctance, pulling an envelope from his tuxedo jacket. "For you—and him."

"What's this?"

"When I spoke with Finn a while back, I actually asked if he'd mind my speaking to you. Can you *believe* that?"

"No," she said, grinning.

"Well, it's true. He promised to break my legs if I tried anything."

Her face heated. "I *do* believe that."

He smiled and handed her the envelope. "I think you've earned this." He paused a moment so she could tuck it into her purse. "I saw you two together. He's a good guy, Em—*not* that it's any of my business," he said, quickly. "As a friend, I hope you'll be happy. That's the measure of true love, isn't it? To want what's best for someone?"

Her head jerked to the side. It seemed he'd done a bit of soul searching and the effects were obvious.

"I'll take that as a yes," he said, bending to kiss her cheek. "Goodnight, Emanuela."

After making a turn about the room, stopping to chat with a few guests along the way, Emanuela paused near the bar at the entrance. *Where* is *everyone?* Allie had been there earlier...and there was no sign of Finn, Simon or Jamie.

"Looking for someone?"

Emanuela grinned, turning around. It wasn't often her best friend was so chipper. "Oh, you're drunk again."

"Drunk is so pedestrian," Allie said. "I'm just a little tipsy, okay? Come on, we're late. Jamie is gonna kill me."

Emanuela frowned, but allowed Allie to tug her along. Some late commuters openly stared, and a few yelled catcalls at them as they crossed the expanse of pink marble to the elevators.

"Allie and Emanuela, I presume?" asked an older, scholarly man wearing horn-rimmed glasses.

"Yes," Allie said. "You must be Jamie's friend, Dan."

"I must be," he said with a warm smile. "Shall we?"

Emanuela looked at Allie with increasing curiosity.

"Come on," Allie said, still holding Emanuela's arm.

Dan allowed them to precede him onto the antiquated elevator and pushed a button for an unmarked floor. He entertained his passengers with little-known facts about the terminal, like the fact that the infamous golden clock that sat atop the information booth in the main concourse was worth twenty million dollars, due to its four large opal faces. They arrived at the mysterious level and disembarked to see Simon, Jamie, Finn, and a young man Emanuela didn't recognize waiting for them in the hall.

"You're late," Jamie said, but his happiness at having them all together at that moment betrayed him and he smiled.

Emanuela eyed them all with interest. "Where are we?"

Finn outstretched his hand to her, gently pulling her to stand beside him. "We are getting an extra special private tour."

"This floor isn't open to the public," Dan said. "The control room is housed here, as well as the Tiffany clock tower. My friend Brandon here can take a few of you to the control room, and the rest can come with me to see the tower."

"I'm afraid of heights," Allie said quickly, stepping closer to Jamie. "Looks like it's the control room for me."

"Sy and I will go with her," Jamie said helpfully.

"Splendid!" Dan said. "We'll meet back here at ten o'clock."

He glanced at his watch and then at Brandon. "I think twenty minutes should do it, don't you?"

"Twenty minutes is just enough time," Brandon said, turning to his small group. "Shall we?"

Dan took Finn and Emanuela through a door leading to a series of long, narrow metal ladders. Emanuela looked at the two men, perplexed.

"I'll be right behind you," Finn said. "You won't fall."

She glanced at his leg, opening her mouth to protest again, but Finn stopped her. "I'm officially a bionic man. I could climb with my eyes closed."

"Even so," Dan said, looking at Emanuela's long gown and heels, "please use extreme caution."

"Hang on a sec." Finn crouched at Emanuela's feet, gathering her dress at the hem and tying it into a secure knot at her knees.

"Careful!" she said. "This dress is couture. *Borrowed*. I can't mess it up."

"I think that's okay," he said, standing.

Dan seemed satisfied, and they slowly ascended the ladders. After reaching the top, they came to a tiny, dusty room that reminded Emanuela of an old attic. There were a few old oil cans in the corners, but their eyes were immediately drawn to the large bronze gears and thirteen-foot stained glass face of the storied Tiffany clock.

"Wow," she breathed. "This is incredible. It's so much bigger up close."

Dan smiled, standing back to allow them a good look at the world's largest Tiffany timepiece.

"It took twelve years to restore," he said. "Each piece of glass had to be removed, cleaned and repaired individually."

"Amazing," Finn said in awe.

"If I may?" Dan asked.

"Of course," Finn said, stepping aside to allow their tour guide access to the gold and blue glass of the clock's face.

Dan moved to the six o'clock position and, to

Emanuela's surprise, a portion of the stained glass window opened. "There's an impressive view of 42nd Street ahead, and a pretty clear view of Park Avenue South if you poke your head out to the right," he said with a smile.

He stepped aside, allowing Emanuela to look out of the window first. "Wow," she said again, looking out at the expanse of midnight blue.

The skyscrapers on either side looked so close. They were huge, the lights from their windows casting a blue glow over the yellow cabs that seemed to crawl along the street below. She looked out farther, seeing the gilded pyramidal roof of the New York Life building, brilliantly golden where it peeked out from behind the towering buildings to her right.

"Finn, you have to see this," she said, admiration deepening her tone. "Finn?"

She turned around when he didn't reply, a slight frown on her face when she saw that Dan was no longer in the room with them. "Where did Dan go?"

"He's waiting for us at the landing," he said. "We have a few minutes to ourselves." He moved to stand in front of her, taking her into his arms and turning his face into her hair. "I've wanted to do this all night. You're so beautiful, Emmi. I love your hair like this."

"Don't get too attached," she said. "I had some extensions put in for the occasion."

He pulled back a moment to look into her face. "I like you every way, Emmi, but you almost look too good to touch."

She frowned, not liking the sound of that, and put his arms around her waist again. She trailed her hands up his arms, reveling in the feel of his muscles beneath the smooth fabric of his tuxedo jacket. "I always want you to touch me," she said, and she touched her lips to his.

The magnitude of the evening was dizzying for them both, their many glasses of champagne, the view and each other's nearness blending to form a heady cocktail of their own, until Emanuela had to pull away and catch her breath.

"We should probably take advantage of this view," Finn said. "We may never get to see it again."

She nodded, but couldn't turn away from the adoration in his eyes. He smiled, seeming to understand her plight. He turned her around and lifted her gently at the waist, helping her to sit in the window and dangle her legs over the edge. His arms circled her waist and he stood behind her, silently taking in the view. Their contented sighs were amplified in the tiny space, their breaths swirling out in front of them.

"I'll never forget this, Finn," she said softly after a few minutes, enjoying Finn's nuzzle at her neck. "It's really special."

He stepped away and carefully helped her pull her legs back through the window, turning her around to face him where she sat. "Neither will I," he said, his voice gruff. He lifted her hand to his lips for a kiss, then brought it to rest at his heart above his jacket. "Crazy about you."

His body stiffened the moment she felt the tiny bulge in his pocket. It looked like he was mustering every ounce of self-control he possessed to not let the twitching corners of his mouth spread into a full grin.

"Finn?"

The grin won out. "Happy to see you."

She reached into the small pocket, her eyes never leaving his, and pulled out a black velvet box. Her heart seemed to pound directly in her ears, blocking out the sounds of the city behind her. The crinkles at the corners of his eyes appeared, and the grin he'd kept in check finally stretched fully across his face. Then he was on both knees in the dusty room before her, his empty right hand on her knee.

"Emmi," he whispered. The velvet box seemed so loud as it clicked open. "Emanuela," he spoke again, this time with sound that echoed in the small space and wracked her body with a shiver.

She couldn't even look into the box, so transfixed was she on his expression and tone.

"Although we've only known each other these short seven months, it seems like it's been much longer. Not because it's been hard to know you, but because it's been agony not being able to hold you at night and kiss you in the morning. I am not spending any more time away from you—not if I can help it. I love you, Emmi—more than I thought I had the capacity to love." He straightened a bit just then, like he was steeling himself. "Will you marry me?"

She was already nodding, his handsome face blurred by her tears.

"You have to say it, baby," he said with an elated grin.

"Yes," she whimpered when she was able.

He took her hand in his and slid the ring onto her finger. She looked down at it for the first time and gasped. It was simple and elegant, a single-carat, brilliant cut solitaire on a white gold band so thin the diamond seemed suspended above her finger. "It's perfect." She stood, tearing up again.

He stood and hoisted her up, his powerful arms holding her under her hips, and nuzzled his face into her tummy. He spun her around and she yelped, holding onto him for dear life.

"*Finn!*"

When he stopped, she pulled away, locking her fingers behind his head.

"You make me ridiculously…stupidly… incomparably happy," he said, pecking her neck between each word.

"Ditto," she said against his lips.

A throat cleared then, and Dan smiled awkwardly at the pair in the tiny room. "I think congratulations are in order?"

Finn lowered Emanuela to her feet and took her hand. "They are," he said.

Dan nodded. "You couldn't have chosen a better place to pop the question. Shall we rejoin your friends downstairs?"

At Emanuela's nod, they made their way back down the ladders.

****

Jamie was beside himself. "You're marrying us!" He snatched her up into a bear hug until she squealed for him to let her go.

"Jamie! My dress!"

Jamie kneeled to untie the knot at her knees and tsked at her in disapproval. "The dress is already a wrinkled mess, gorgeous. And there's enough dust on Finn's pants to write my name in it."

"Move!" Allie grabbed Emanuela into a fierce hug of her own. "Let me see it!" She reached for

Emanuela's hand, turning to Finn. "Nice job, Good Doctor. How'd you know not to go too flashy?"

Finn smirked. "I had a little help."

Emanuela looked at him, suspicious, and then she knew. "My *mother?* When did you..."

"I'm not telling."

****

The remaining guests prepared to leave Vanderbilt Hall, the orchestra playing its final song. The harpist plucked its strings, the pianist's fingers danced across the keys, and Mama Cass's "Dream A Little Dream of Me" beckoned Finn and Emanuela to the floor. They stalked each other in a circle, the intro floating into the air, and their friends looked on. Then they were in each other's arms, swaying side to side like seasoned partners. Her ring gleamed as bright as the lights strung about them, her head resting on his shoulder. There were other dancers on the floor, but for five people in particular, especially Emanuela and Finn, there was only the two of them.

Epilogue

Six Weeks, Three Days, Seventeen Hours and Ten Minutes Later

"Ten 'Til Sunset," read the invitations that were sent to the handful of family and friends gathered on the large deck of Finn and Emanuela's beach house in Penn Cove. They sat comfortably on plush, richly colored cushions tossed on the outdoor chairs and couch, watching Finn and Emanuela photographed on the beach. They sipped Prosecco and Manhattan cocktails, the fire pit and a few tall space heaters keeping them warm. The golden hour ended minutes before, and as the softer, redder hue of day's end signaled the coming twilight, Finn and Emanuela saw each other for the first time that evening...

So much transpired in that suspended moment. In the time it took her to walk the forgettable distance across the deck to his side, two sets of eyes remembered stolen glances, first kisses and fingers intertwined. They dashed, barefoot, under the arbor with its sheer white curtains billowing as they passed, and down the steps to the beach. The photographer's camera clicked away, blending with the sound of the waves behind them, and the ambient melody stretching out to them from the deck. They ran toward the water, turning to look back a few times so their happiness could be captured against a backdrop of blended blush and purple, mango and gold.

String lights hung overhead, coming alive the moment the sun dimmed and the shimmering mantle over the water turned midnight gray to blend with the sky. Garland of winter green and baby's breath wrapped around the deck's rails, pulling apart the gossamer curtains that hung from the wooden arbor. It was there, under the arbor, that Finn and Emanuela branded each other with eighteen carat gold.

****

Something played at Emanuela's subconscious mind, waking her in the middle of the night. She was afraid it was all a dream. Slowly, she became aware of Finn's presence. He pressed close to her back, heat radiating from his chest, his long limbs tangled in hers. His warm breath tickled her neck, and she nestled closer to him with a contented sigh. She closed her eyes, waiting for sleep to overtake her again, when she felt his fingers stroke her waist tenderly. She twisted around to face him, her body curling instinctively to his. He lifted her thigh and pulled it across his hip, his soft lips brushing her shoulder.

"Couldn't sleep," she whispered. "Had to make sure it was real."

"Me too. Hey, Wife."

She couldn't see his smile, but she knew it was there. "Hey, Husband."

Their kisses were unhurried, soft, probing in the darkness. He curled an arm beneath her, his other hand trailing gently down her spine to press her hips to his. They were wrapped up in each other, becoming one again and nothing else mattered but the two of them for several long, blissful moments.

****

The pilot's voice blared over the intercom, announcing their arrival at Phuket International Airport. Emanuela groaned. Finn's amused gaze skimmed her face, noting her sleepy eyes and the strands of hair that escaped her bun and stuck out in every direction.

"Morning, sunshine," he said.

"*Ugh*. Our first time ever traveling together and we get a thirty-hour itinerary. Good thing we didn't do this when we first started dating."

"Twenty-six hours." He twisted to pointedly remove an empty miniature wine bottle from between their seats. "Good thing I like you."

She pulled her neck pillow off and swatted him with it. Ignoring protocol, he turned on the camera and focused on her beautiful, travel-weary face.

"No, Finn—"

"Come on, Emmi. You know the drill."

She groaned, self-consciously tucking a few curls behind her ears. "Fine."

"Who are you with, baby?"

She shook her head with softened eyes. "My love."

"Mmmhmm, and where are we going?"

"Paradise."

A young Thai stewardess in her pristine royal purple uniform and pink scarf scolded Finn with a smile, and he powered off the camera to prepare for landing.

"Serves you right," Emanuela said, wrinkling her nose at him. "Ugh, I can't wait to take a nice, hot shower."

Finn looked her up and down.

"*Alone*." She smacked him again.

****

The speedboat ride from Phuket to the smaller, secluded island of Koh Yao Noi was an experience in itself. Stunning sheer limestone karsts towered over them on every side, jutting from the emerald waters of Phang Nga Bay. Finn documented everything he could on video, promising to dust off the footage in fifty years to remind Emanuela of how much she loved him when he was young and hot.

The boutique resort was built into a mountain, a hideaway on a remote part of the island overlooking the bay. Their open-air room was high on the magnificent hill, nestled among tropical trees with the most gorgeous view of the bay. Finn was sold on the room when Emanuela mentioned there was a Jacuzzi. And there it was, built into the private terrace with a direct view of one of the island's mighty limestone cliffs across the bay.

They dropped everything, clearing away the rose petals and "Happy Honeymoon" spelled out with twigs, and falling into the luxurious bed together. Comfortably shielded by mosquito netting, they drifted off to the distant call of the hornbill. They awakened many hours later after nightfall, recovered from the fatigue of a full day's travel—and *ravenous*. Finn arranged a romantic candlelit dinner on the beach, complete with soft torchlight and table service. They stuffed themselves on seafood salad, spicy Massaman curry, and fragrant Tom Yam Goong, finishing off with local fruit and plenty of champagne.

"I can't move," Emanuela moaned.

"That was amazing." Finn gazed at Emanuela, who

looked very much like a satisfied Cheshire cat.

"Have I told you how beautiful you look?"

"Not for an hour now," she said. "I almost thought you'd forgotten."

He chuckled, leaning back to take everything in. "We could move here. Build a house on one of these hills."

"We'd have to buy a hill first. I guess we can afford it now, with our additional ten percent stake in SimLife Laboratories…"

His heart thudded heavily in his chest. "Emmi?"

"I figured now was a good time to tell you." Her lips parted in an elated smile.

"Philip?"

"Mmhmm."

"Wow."

"I know, but it's not a consolation, Finn. We earned it. *You* earned it."

"I don't know what to say," he said, still reeling. "This is huge."

"It is, but you don't have to say anything right now." She stood and walked over to him then, sitting in his lap. "Finn?"

He rubbed her back softly, his questioning eyes lifting to hers.

"What did you say to my dad the night you two met?"

That night came to mind and he smiled, meeting her probing eyes with his.

"That he didn't need to worry about you," he said. "I told him I understood his fear, but I'm strong. You're strong. Whatever happens, we can handle it together, like him and your mom. I told him I admire them, the love they have and the strength they've shown in spite of everything. If I could be half the husband and father he is, then we'd be okay."

"You said all that?"

"And meant it."

Emanuela lowered her parted lips and moved them softly, slowly over his. She pulled away before they could get carried away, reaching for the camera atop the table. After fussing with it a bit and enduring his chuckles at her expense, she finally got the damn thing on and adjusted for darkness.

"Who are you with, baby?" she said in a singsong voice.

Finn's lips twitched. "My love."

"And where are we?"

"Paradise."

****

Finn lay on his side, naked but for his boxers, which hung low on his hips. His head was propped up on one hand to gaze out into the purple night sky and wait for Emanuela to join him. She went to the bathroom to freshen up a little in spite of his willingness to ravish her just the way she was. He wasn't waiting long before faintly familiar music began to play. Its distinctly seductive tone tingled his spine. She finally emerged, and he nearly choked. His eyes took their fill of her hair, which was fuller in the humid air, her sultry dark eyes, and the expanse of creamy brown skin in nothing but red sequined panties and extraordinary golden body ornaments. His mouth went dry at her wicked grin, and he spoke only one word. "Tassels."

A word about the author…

Lynn Turner is dedicated to writing stories that normalize diversity and celebrate what it means to be imperfectly human. She enjoys romance, historical fiction, science fiction, and anything with a healthy dose of travelogue and food. She and her husband share their home in California with their two extraordinary children, and a collection of books that has outgrown its shelves.

Thank you for purchasing
this publication of The Wild Rose Press, Inc.

If you enjoyed the story, we would appreciate your
letting others know by leaving a review.

For other wonderful stories,
please visit our on-line bookstore at
www.thewildrosepress.com.

For questions or more information
contact us at
info@thewildrosepress.com.

The Wild Rose Press, Inc.
www.thewildrosepress.com

Stay current with The Wild Rose Press, Inc.

Like us on Facebook

https://www.facebook.com/TheWildRosePress

And Follow us on Twitter
https://twitter.com/WildRosePress